PRAISE FOR KEVIN MACNEIL:

The Brilliant & Forever (Polygon, 2016)

'Ultimately, this is a book about how ev~~eryone has~~ a story worth telling, and one worth hearing too. Terrific stuff' – *The Independent on Sunday*

'By turns hilarious, mordant, heart-warming and heart-breaking, this is a true one-off that will leave an indelible impression' – *The Lady*

'This is a book that keeps the reader on hot coals, and my, but we caper the better for it. It is a joy to read such a charming, luminous novel' – *The Guardian*

'This is one hell of a book. It is a book that bounces effortlessly from one idea to the next with a compelling energy and a giddily addictive sense that anything can happen, and probably will. It's a wise, warm-hearted meditation on the human condition' – *The Scotsman*

'Lyrical, satirical, funny and utterly, utterly heartbreaking.★★★★★' – *Heat Magazine*

'A satire on egotism and a celebration of writing' – *The Herald*

'It is as rich a reading experience as you will discover this year. Great novelists do not tell us what to think and feel. They engage our interest and sympathies; they draw us into their world and thereby influence how we think and feel. At least half of [its title] accurately describes Kevin MacNeil's pitch-perfect third novel . . . brilliant' – *The West Highland Free Press*

'Funny, thought provoking, crazy and playful. *The Brilliant & Forever* is clever and intelligent and deserves to win prizes . . . It's a book that plays with language and doesn't stick to rules. It's a book that needs to be quoted from, talked about and read over and over again' – *Lovereading.co.uk*

A Method Actor's Guide to Jekyll and Hyde (Polygon, 2010)

'An artistic nugget, daring and burnished . . . from first to last an enticing read' – Tom Adair, *Scotsman*

'A phenomenally good novel. It is brilliant, touching, funny and clever' – Roger Hutchinson, *West Highland Free Press*

'A great book . . . intricate and powerful' – *Skinny*

'A funny, irreverent and moving 21st-century look at human nature' – Doug Johnstone, *Herald*

'A cleverly constructed and entertaining read' – *Daily Mail*

'A book riddled with meta-meaning and postmodern playfulness' – *List*

The Stornoway Way (Penguin, 2005)

'The best Scottish book since *Trainspotting*. I can't remember being so knocked out by a book. It's full of wisdom, jokes, poetic language and mind-burning imagery' – *Scotsman*

'A dark tale of life beyond the Minch, illuminated by a fierce humour and a poet's love of language' – Michael Palin

'Originality, verve, audacity and power, doing something quite new in the context of the Scottish novel. It blew me away' – *Herald*

'Maniacally amusing. An entropic tale of energies sparked to life and quenched by landscape, language and culture. A novel of consistently hilarious verbal invention' – *Independent*

'True 70-proof writing . . . This is a funny, touching and authentic slice of life on a Hebridean island' – Ian Rankin

'Impressive . . . A triumph of vibrant storytelling, a coruscating, rattling story which is hilarious one moment, heartbreaking the next' – *List*

'Does for the Western Isles what Rankin and Welsh did for Edinburgh. An alcohol-fuelled roller-coaster ride to the heights and depths of human emotion' – *The Times*

'A novel with real spirit, whose honest bleakness is outdone by its sheer good humour and energy' – Ali Smith

'Captures the spirit (and indeed the spirits) of life on Lewis and is bleak and funny in equal measures. It is written with a poet's heart' – *Herald*, Books of the Year

'MacNeil writes with real affection for his native isle in a book which will both amuse and chill . . . the language sparkles' – *Scotland on Sunday*

'Highly lyrical, very funny. More than just a cautionary tale littered with great anecdotes, it's a novel steeped in the contradictory, difficult beauty of Lewis itself [which] counters the romanticised perception of island living' – *Metro*

'This highly original take on island life is a novel to make you laugh, cry, think and, above all, care' – Anne Donovan

'If Kevin MacNeil gets any more talented I'm going to kill him and eat him to steal his juju' – Denise Mina

'Absolutely bursting with energy, radiant in its rage, its love and its passion. There are also moments of hilarious comedy and truly heart-rending sadness mixed in to a tale which brings into sharp focus the bleakness and beauty of life. *The Stornoway Way* should see MacNeil established right at the heart of the best new Scottish writing' – *Big Issue*

Be Wise, Be Otherwise: Ideas and Advice for Your Kind of Person
(Canongate, 2001)

'I don't know if it's his living in the Outer Hebrides that does it,
but Kevin MacNeil's work gives me that good bracing feeling you
get from exposure to the elements. It has a freshness that sharpens
and invigorates. he can be crisp and cool, and funny and warm, but
he always hits the spot' - Michael Palin

'Not only talented and dedicated he is also original' - Andrew
Greig

Love and Zen in the Outer Hebrides (Canongate, 1998)

'At the heart of this bold, serious, playful poetry lies a lyricism
brave enough to be defiantly tender as it staggers, pained and
joyous, through our times. It's a joy, and promises more to come'
- Andrew Greig

'Here's a live mind who's been out for language, movement, light,
and has found a good deal of it all, laughing a new laugh in the
process. If you fancy a mixture of dancing logic, loving grace and
cosmopoetic jazz, this guy's got it. And he scatters it about in stories
from the bothy of the heart written in fast, humorous prose, as well
as in poems fresh from the bottom of the heart' - Kenneth White

'To meet one so in tune with his language(s) and with his subject-
matter, so young, is a rare and special experience. At the beginning
of his poetic career, Kevin MacNeil is already in the uplands of
achievement' - Aonghas MacNeacail

The Brilliant & Forever

Kevin MacNeil

First published in Great Britain in 2016 by Polygon Books,
an imprint of Birlinn Ltd. Reprinted in 2016 by Polygon Books.

West Newington House
10 Newington Road
Edinburgh
EH9 1QS

www.polygonbooks.co.uk

A CIP catalogue reference for this book is available from
the British Library.

ISBN 978 1 84697 337 6
eISBN 978 0 85790 892 6

Typeset in Goudy by 3btype.com
Printed by Grafica Veneta, Italy

For Charlotte

'He thought back on what had happened like a reporter. He started to answer, shook his head when he found he was wrong, and then started out again. "All there is to thinking," he said, "is seeing something noticeable which makes you see something you weren't noticing which makes you see something that isn't even visible."'

Norman Maclean, *A River Runs Through It*

'One should be light like a bird and not like a feather.'

Italo Calvino, *Six Memos for the Next Millennium*

'Goodness, like murder, will out.'

R. H. Blyth

Contents

If on a Summer's Night
an Alpaca

On our island, everyone – human and alpaca alike – wants to be a writer. The standard greeting is not 'How are you?' but 'What are you working on?'

On our island, everyone knows everyone. If you sneeze, ten people offer you a tissue, one prays for your soul, six laugh as though they've never sneezed in their lives, five secretly hope it's the sign of a serious, perhaps fatal, ailment and thirteen people know it's a cold and who you caught it from. A small island is a sad, safe, familiar, nurturing place. I grew up wanting to murder everyone with loving-kindness.

On our island, the air always tastes of salt, as though a person, you, has just stopped crying. The wind hurls rain showers around and it hasn't snowed here for years.

You can't survive life on a small island if you don't have friends. Mine are Macy and Archie.

Macy Starfield works alongside me, scrubbing scummy plates and charcoaled pans in a rancid hotel kitchen.

Archie is an alpaca.

One night we were in the Lucky Golden Eel ('Don't go to other restaurants to be poisoned or cheated come HERE'), eating MSG with some food stuck to it. The Lucky Golden Ee, as we call it for short, is the third best of the island's three

Chinese restaurants, but we're tired of the others, or they're tired of us, who can remember.

Archie swallowed some crispy calamari with grass sauce, made a face. 'Ugh. I wish they'd just serve grass with a grass sauce like I asked for. Why'd they need to fancy it up?' He's the greatest author alpacahood has ever had, which is a big deal for someone from such an oppressed species.

With a fluid hawking and a liquidy bulleting, he gob-shot a thick mess of phlegm into his private spittoon, parked semi-discreetly beside the pilau rice dish, which in turn sat beside Archie's stetson. (He calls the spittoon his 'cuspidor' and is fond of pointing out that James Joyce, 'who knew a thing or two about language', considered cuspidor the most beautiful word in the English language. There's a group of young upstart alpacas in the south of the island who've got a punk band called Archie's Cuspidor. Archie's already a cult figure among alpacas.)

Archie wiped his mouth with a grass-stained napkin and smiled, though in fact through a quirk of jaw genetics he always looks like he's smiling. 'This week I'm going to start a new catchphrase. Get it trending.'

'Impossible,' said Macy, ripping a naan bread to pieces. 'Hey, this piece looks like the Arctic,' she said, 'and this piece looks like the Antarctic.' She handed me the former.

'Arctic naan,' I said, enjoying speaking two words that don't normally go together.

Alpacas are regarded as second-class citizens by many humans on the island. The only thing they've ever got trending was the anti-alpaca demonstrations of '88, before trending was even a thing, but when fist-to-hoof combat was very much a thing.

'Possible,' said Archie. 'There was a guy who invented the phrase "the cat's pyjamas". And another guy who decided that "like" could be used like "said", instead of like "like". Another guy changed the meaning of "gay" to "gay".'

'Yeah,' said Macy, chewing Antarctic naan, 'the original meaning of lesbian was "straight".' We paused, testing this information in our brain, but only because Macy is a lesbian and only for the splittest of seconds, then we laughed along with her. Macy knew suffering, and had an occasional edge, but hers was an upbeat soul really. She was a kind and thoughtful person who read widely and deeply and often. In literary circles there was a quiet conviction that her best work was ahead of her. She read everything with a pen in her hand and her bright black eyes moving at just the right speed. Macy meant it when she smiled and she smiled often; you felt safe in her company.

'How,' I said, 'do you make it popular – the catchphrase, I mean?' but at the same time as I asked that, Macy said, still chewing, 'What's the catchphrase?' and I'm one of those people in life who is always overridden in simultaneous conversation so Archie cleared his throat and said, 'It's like a jazz thing you don't get.'

Macy and I exchanged looks. 'That'll never catch on,' said Macy.

Archie shook his head and offered Macy some rice. 'You're wrong. It's got the cool jazz thing – jazz itself has two Zs, the grooviest letter in the alphabet. And plus it's versatile. Listen.' He started acting out scenarios while Macy and I chowed down on some juicy prince prawns and pilau rice. '"Hey, I read *Ulysses*. It's so boring I gave up." "No, man. *Ulysses* is genius – it's just a jazz thing you don't get." "Dude, I'm totally going to marry a supermodel." "Nuh-uh. A supermodel's a jazz thing you don't get." "I watched a *Family Guy* episode and didn't laugh once." "Only cos it's a jazz thing you don't get."'

'Ain't gonna work,' I said, and took a huge drink of iced water because my mouth tasted like the seafloor but not in a good way.

Archie's eyes looked sad though his mouth was grinning and there's nothing like a crestfallen alpaca so I added, 'But, hey, good on you. Give it a red-hot go. It's a dodo egg's age since I heard a new catchphrase. I'll drop it into conversation this week, if, y'know, I have any conversations.'

'I appreciate that, man,' said Archie. We fist/hoof bumped.

'Even though I do get jazz,' I added. It was the wrong thing to say because it gloomed out Archie again and because it isn't true. I like jazz – Dave Brubeck, Lady Day, Gary Burton – but I don't *get* it. Jazz sends vivid colours streaming through my ears, is all, and that's enough.

Macy and I felt sorry for Archie. Alpacas get lonesome and frustrated, and Archie was still distantly wounded from a divorce some years ago. There are two flocks of alpacas on the island, one in the north end of the island, the other in the south; his wife had been a northern alpaca. The flocks do not get on well with each other. Such, alas, is so often the way with minorities. Their animosity developed years ago, growing, as feuds frequently do, out of a minor disagreement over a John Wayne movie.

Archie didn't have it easy, being a southern alpaca, with accent to match, living in a town in the north. (For example, if, say, someone is up to a shenanigan, they pronounce shenanigan as shenanigan in the north, but in the south they pronounce shenanigan shenanigan).

What began as a pity-and-tolerance friendship with Archie grew into genuine affection and whenever anyone made a slur like 'camelface' to him I was the first to defend him, with fists and, if necessary, witticisms. Well, okay, not fists. Or much in the way of witticisms. The intention was there, though.

We always tarried at the Lucky Golden Ee because although it was even less renowned for its desserts than its main courses and even though they liberally sprinkled MSG on their (bought-in) desserts, they served ice cream in these cute little hollow plastic robots.

Tan the Ageist brought us our ice-cream-and-MSG filled robots. We liked him; against house rules, he always let us keep the robots, though the professional dishwasher in me appreciated that repeatedly shoving a dish scrubber into every crevice of a robot's innards must be a grind. And any kind of grind that adds to life's general grind is suspect.

'Hey, Tan the Ageist,' Macy said. 'What you working on?' Here, as I say, literature is as important as a beating heart (my passport describes me as Professional Dishwasher and Author), and literature itself, or its interpretation, can stop hearts.

'Ah,' said Tan. 'Some terrible haiku.' He shook his head. 'Terrible. Vanilla ice-cream robot?'

'Terrible vanilla ice-cream robot,' said Macy. 'That really is a bad haiku. Joking. Looks . . . nice and roboty, thanks.'

'Who's your money on for the Brilliant & Forever?' asked Archie.

Everyone bristled at the mention. We all loved each other – hugs, support, doing things you don't like doing for the sake of your friends' happiness – but we were all undeniably involved, implicated, in the Brilliant & Forever.

The B&F is an annual literary competition by which reputations are made and writers unmade. It takes place on the Castle Green, a gentle verdant slope in front of the island's castle, and is the cultural highlight of the year.

Tan placed ice-cream-filled robots in front of Archie and me, sucked air through his teeth. 'Ahhh . . .' He cast his towards-the-mystical-horizon gaze at a dead light bulb opposite. 'Ahhh . . .'

Still, it was hard to look at him. Tan's skill, or curse, is to see, when he gazes upon someone, exactly what they will look like when they are old and/or verging on death. He's twenty-five. But when he looks at you or me for more than a moment he sees us as we will be when we are an instant away from death.

We suppose Tan just sees older versions of us, like masks, over our actual-age faces. It's a weird and beautiful tragedy. Tan has tried going out with girls, but will, he acknowledges, be a single man for a very long time. If he goes out with a girl and leans in to kiss her, he is suddenly confronted with a granny. He gets creeped and scarpers the hell out of there. Once, he dated a girl whose face aged negligibly; she died in a dreadful incident (champagne, chainsaw) three months into their relationship.

He has sworn not to go out with anyone until he himself is old. Hence the island has deemed him Tan the Ageist and, though the nickname is cruel, there is nothing he can do about it. Like ageing itself, some say.

'My money . . .' Tan paused. 'My money is on . . .'

'Yes?' said Archie.

'My money is not worth the paper it's printed on.' He sighed. 'But I'd maybe put it on Summer Kelly. Leave me a good tip, will you?'

'Sure, Tan, a good tip deserves a good tip,' said Macy. Tan nodded and moved away to a table of semi-raucous businessmen.

'This week,' I said, 'I'm hoping the gold I bought on eBay super cheap arrives and—'

'Wait, what?' spluttered Archie, looking every inch the flummoxed alpaca. 'How much gold – the postage alone – and it'll be fake—'

I nodded. 'Most likely. I ordered a bunch of gold ingots and I'm going to plant them in peat banks around the island.'

'Plant them,' said Macy, 'like they're going to grow?'

'Bury them, I mean. So people will find them randomly when cutting the peats. If, you know, randomly has meaning, which I don't think it does.'

Macy jammed her tongue inside her little plastic robot's chest cavity and licked hard. Looked strange, like she was a giant.

Archie said, 'After the first chunk of gold is found, everyone's going to go digging for gold. The island will have a gold rush.'

'Thus,' I said, 'boosting the economy. Hey, so maybe it is like planting gold.'

'You want to boost the economy?' said Archie.

'No. Yeah. I don't know. How does the economy even work?'

'It's a numbers racket,' said Archie. 'A lowdown dirty three-legged numbers racket.'

Macy stopped licking what was now non-existent ice cream from inside her robot and thumped the plastic toy down on the table like a declaration. 'I want to ride a fishing boat out of the harbour and into dusk. Into dawn. Into rich fishing grounds. I'm going to become a fisherman. Woman. No more dishwashing for me.'

'You can't become a fishermanwoman,' said Archie, 'least not according to island tradition. Women have always been considered bad luck on fishing boats. You know that. Mother of God, even saying "woman" on a boat, they used to believe, and some still do, could attract danger.'

'So what did fishermen call women?'

'I don't know. They called ministers "upstanders". Ministers were bad luck, too.'

'Our ancestors clearly had OCD,' I said. 'Hey, Archie, you're not sexist?'

'No, no. Hell no. If anything I see Macy as a trailblazer. But you know how people will talk when they hear of a woman with a fishing boat.'

Macy shrugged, swatted the potential gossips away. 'Meh. Let them eat fishcake.'

'Where you gonna get a boat?' said Archie.

'Yeah, I'm gonna need serious moolah. Like a mil, mil five. I'll get a grant or a loan.'

'I'm impressed,' I said, thinking about it. I read a business manual once, until it depressed me. 'Try and get a grant instead of a loan.' I pictured how things could be. 'Hey, can we come ride on your fishing boat?'

'Sure you can,' said Macy. 'You can even help me think up new seafaring superstitions.'

'Being at sea's not right. We count on the world to stay beneath our feet,' said Archie. He spat into his cuspidor.

'The sea is part of the world,' I said. I changed tack. 'Superstitions. Right, it's going to be bad luck to bring a glockenspiel onboard. And if anyone ever mentions Dan Brown, they have to spin round three times on one leg, grab an anchor and jump overboard.'

'Yeah,' said Macy, 'and you can't say the word "horse". You have to refer to it as a "meat bicycle".'

Tan reappeared, looked at us, or one of us, or each of us, with a kind of sad misgiving, and placed on the table a saucer with three misfortune cookies.

'Thanks,' said Archie. I gritted my teeth. Tan vanished.

Macy breathed in audibly. 'You guys choose.'

'Believing in this stuff,' said Archie, reaching out for a cookie, 'is no more sensible than believing in the superstitious crap about women not being allowed on boats.'

Macy grabbed and cracked open her misfortune cookie. 'It says, "Quit professional dishwashing, though carry on doing your dishes at home, and keep on writing, of course, but you must purchase a fishing boat. Go forth and fish. Slay those naysayers, if you're woman enough."'

I opened my misfortune cookie. 'Mine says, "Achieve what you aim for."' I lied, since I thought Macy was lying. Mine actually read, 'Do not Google yourself. Intention never truly hits the mark.'

'What about yours?' said Macy to Archie.

Alpacas smile a lot – like I said, some, like Archie, smile even when they're not smiling. And it was an inscrutable smile that lit up or darkened Archie's face when he said, 'Mine says I will be torn to pieces in a painful, gory manner.'

'Nonsense,' I said, grabbing his misfortune cookie. 'It doesn't say that–' I scanned the biscuit-gestated printout. 'Okay,' I said. 'Okay. It does say that . . . But it also says that after the howling shrieking pain you will become still and solid and . . .'

'And that's all it says,' said Archie, slumping down on the table.

'There's another word,' I said, 'but it's in Pali.' I squinted. 'Is it? The word keeps changing. My eyes aren't right.'

'Torn to pieces,' said Archie, glum once more.

I pulled at my collar, made a mental note to protect Archie from limb-wrenchers and decapitators.

Macy shifted in her seat. 'All we really know is this; we're going to go fishing. And slay those naysayers.'

I trembled with fear and excitement and too much MSG and a kind of simmering anticipation, like the kind you get when you reach the end of the first chapter in a book that feels much like your real-life future: uncertain; teasingly alive with potential (which could go either way); and peopled with diverse characters you feel you know, though we never truly know anyone because they, like us, are continually changing. Come to think of it, you're not even sure that the book has a place in your future, but you are pretty sure that you have a future and that your future could be filled with wonderfully unpredictable things, including, though not necessarily, the book held for the moment in your living hands. Squeeze it and you feel your own pulse.

Born Surreal, Think Like a Boat

Under a vast sky of glittering stars, under a bright scratchy moon, we lurched, against the odds, against the irregular waves, on a mad mission, on an old black fishing boat. The air was the high blood pressure kind, thick with salt and a fretting restless anxiety. Macy had secured a loan from the bank and bought a fishing boat via a local 'buy-and-sell' page on the internet. She christened this boat the *Born Surreal, Think Like a Boat*, but hadn't told us why. Frantic gusts of wind scurried, howling, through gaps in the rotten wood, sounding like a great keening. It'd be nice, I thought, if the wind were mourning all the sailors it had drowned. But really it just seemed like it was trying to drown *us*.

It was a primal, oddly satisfying thing, being out here in the elements, but Archie's face was already green and puke-flecked.

Going fishing was like being on a weird fairground ride, one that was infinite with possibility. A school of fish over yonder? Grab 'em, gut 'em, freeze 'em. A swordfish spotted off the starboard side? Net it, weigh it, sell it, spend the cash on books. A whale's blowhole erupting? Chase it epically and reduce it to soap and scrimshaw or elevate it to a literary icon.

So far we'd caught nothing.

A full moon – poor man's torch – lit the way and the mad

swell of the sea had a boisterous lilt that was calming and hypnotic once you gave yourself in to it. Resistance, work of the ego, is a major unrecognised problem in this world. And the moon is not the blackhouser's torch. That's a saying of the rich, the whitehousers. The moon is the most inspiring sight there is, and it's freely available to those who look. More people should indulge in moongazing. It's the same moon we wondered at in childhood, except it's not; just like we're the person we were, but not.

Macy looked happy, grinning beneath the hood of her glossy lemon-coloured sou'wester.

'Gonna tell me now, then?' I shouted over the wind.

'When a human first wanted to conquer the seas,' Macy yelled, 'she could've just imitated the fish or remembered she herself began in the sea. Instead, she invented the boat, which does not look like a fish or like some ancestral pre-human ocean goer. Proof positive, once again, that humans are born surrealists. Our ancestors' triumph was not to think like a fish, but to think like a boat – which had not yet been invented and which in any case has no thoughts. Hence, *Born Surreal, Think Like a Boat.*' She grinned as the wind lashed her face.

We shouted for a while about how the sea is both masculine and feminine in our native language, and how a boat is masculine on land and feminine on sea.

On our island we speak more than one language – we have our indigenous language and we have English. It is said that when the world was young, the very birds spoke our language. Our indigenous language has a singsong cadence that is often likened to the rise and fall of the sea. Its vowels are either long or v-e-r-y l-o-n-g. Like the sea, our language makes some people sick.

Words in our ancient, surviving, far-from-thriving language, when spoken or heard or even looked at, give off pheromones that trigger hostile reactions in certain types of person; a sudden anger, confusion or resentment will seize hold of them, exposing their bigotry and causing them to lash out against the language – either literally, by kicking and punching road signs, or metaphorically by trying to make it illegal again for us to speak it.

And yet scientists are discovering that our very DNA is composed of letters, words and books – and some of these books are written in our own language. It gives me comfort to think that a percentage of the books in everyone's blood is encoded there in our oppressed language. Allowing a language to die is thus not only unethical, it is impossible. The language lives within us, always will. It continues, too, in the birds. When we feel a pang of bliss or nostalgia or sweet sadness at a bird's singing, it is because our innermost DNA recognises something in the song that the birds have superficially lost and which we might lose, too.

Only English-language writings are permitted in the Brilliant & Forever.

'No,' Captain Macy was saying to no one/everyone, 'the sea's definitely female. See how she keeps bitchslapping the *Born Surreal*. Yeehaw!'

She had learned to operate the boat and its equipment by doing an evening class last Thursday for night fishing, then she learned how to do day fishing by asking her neighbour, Captain Moby, to take her out for a spin in his boat, the *Graceful Bucket*, on Saturday afternoon. She's a quick learner. Captain Moby smoked a pipe and drank rum and Captain Macy, as she insisted we call her, had taken a pipe and rum bottle onboard but Archie and I had banned her from using them in our company.

A heavy slab of water thudded the side of the boat, and the

Born Surreal shuddered, like taking an elbowing to the ribs, and the wallop sent Macy and me off-balance, while Archie's hooves made a wild clattering as he went skittering across the deck.

'Careful, Archie,' I yelled.

'Mammy,' he screamed. There was an endearing panic in his voice.

Just as he was about to go overboard – 'Macy,' I shouted, 'what colour flare do we use for "alpaca overboard"?' – the boat tilted the other way and Archie came reeling past us again, greener than ever. We had, of course, earlier tied a huge inflatable ring around his middle and attached it by rope to each of us, so he was not at risk at all and if anything it made us feel more secure than ever, made our friendship bonds actual.

The boat pitched-plunged-soared-fell-shoogled through the night. The moon sent stolen-and-silvered sunlight bouncing off the waves. It was fine – weirdly beautiful – to be in and part of Nature, even though a greenish alpaca went skidding past every few moments leaving a near-visible comet-tail stench of sour puke trailing after him.

'Where are we going to shoot the net?' I asked.

Macy gazed into the distance, a look that suits a captain well. 'When we find the sweet spot. I know a place where we're practically promised a boatload of fish.'

It all felt very right to be going on a journey tonight, even if we'd end up back where we started. That was the point of sea journeys: it was *us* who changed. This reminded me not to mention the *Odyssey*, which usually sparked a debate (argument). Macy loves Homer. I prefer Virgil. What did Homer do, except persuade the world he may not have existed? Virgil's a badass. He took Dante through the rings of Hell. So Macy's hero was Homer, whereas I was a Virgil man. (This gave me an idea for an awesomely terrible sitcom.)

The main reason why whales and birds and such migrate is that the Earth is off-kilter. The planet's rotational axis is not at ninety degrees to the sun, so everything has to move to keep up. Therefore the seasons change. The Earth plays a game, tilting here and there – from a god's perspective, a tedious pinball. But hence migration. The Earth's journey, too, is one of return – not just chasing its horizon like a bleary kitten snapping at its own tail, but the annual journey around the sun, ending where it began, changed, ready for the next, same, unsame orbit.

Is our life journey a pointless repeating circle, or a spiral of progress? Do we 'earth' our way through life, or do we do better? Think about where you were before you were born.

Now I had a mild epiphany as I shifted in my wellies to compensate for the boat's spontaneous lurches: *The human heart is just like an alpaca skating back and forth on an amateurishly captained fishing boat tumbling around at the mercy of a sea it cannot fathom.*

'Whatcha thinking about?' asked Macy, pulling her hood down.

'The Queen of England building a sixty-foot falafel out of fibreglass.'

'No, really.'

'Ah you wouldn't get it, it's a jazz thing.'

'It's "It's like a jazz thing you don't get".'

'Ironic, I can't even get the phrase. But hey, jazz phrasing is notoriously diffic–'

'What were you really thinking?'

'The world,' I heard myself saying, 'is not actually off-kilter, else we'd fly off into space and die.'

Down there, waves sloshed, twined and licked and consumed each other like young lovers. I pictured the bony ghosts of the drowned rising above the sea, I saw colossal skeletons sighing for their eyeballs – one eyeball which nondescript fish fought over and burst and crunched and swallowed, and the other eyeball which fell sightlessly down into the depths like a slow ping-pong ball dropped from a satellite back down to Earth, down to absolute nothingness. When would those eyes reconvene, reconfigure their vision? Would voyagers murdered by wreckers ever get their revenge? It occurred to me that skeletons, like Archie, are doomed to be forever smiling.

The sea unfurls forever, just like time is one eternal unfolding moment, one huge story that never comes to an end. What gives the universal story its meaning? Maybe all is unified sentience. Yes. I'll go with that. All is unified sentience. How, then, to prove it? And can an omnipotent God make another being omnipotent?

I squeezed my living eyeballs, shook my head, came back to the moment. I watched Macy untie herself from the rope connecting her to Archie and me and stride into the wheelhouse to plot our course, or her next story, or both. The boat plunged onwards, creaming the waves away from her sides. The wind had eased and now went through Archie's coat with firm, friendly hands, but he looked too reflective to enjoy it. I put my arm around his neck and pulled him close. Lovely and warm, if wet. I was wearing an alpaca jumper underneath my oilskins, one that Archie had given me for my birthday. When an alpaca gives you a sweater made from his own wool, that's love. It's not just about the money he could have made from the wool; a present like that makes tangible a very special bond. He gets a kick out of my wearing something he formerly wore. Guess I pulled that cosy brown jumper on as often as I could.

His heat felt good close up, and I stroked his head and he nuzzled against me and said something about how grand it was to be alive for the time being.

I knew him well. 'You're thinking about the Brilliant & Forever.'

Reading Archie's expression is sometimes hard, but I detected something flitting over his eyes like a bird winging momentarily across the moon.

'You're worried, feeling the pressure?'

It shocked me now to see a tear well up in his eye and drown that non-existent moonbird. He exhaled a quivering sigh. 'I . . . I want Macy to do well. And you.'

'Oh yes, I'm going to win,' I said, sarcastically. 'Archie, my friend, if any of us wins it, that'll be amazing, as good as if you won it yourself. That's what friendship is.'

Archie nodded unconvincingly.

'What? You love Macy and me, we love you. We're a team.'

'I know. And I appreciate and love you guys, for treating me the way you do. But . . . if an alpaca won this, it could mean the start of a new way of humans treating alpacas with better dignity and equality and . . . It's almost like I'm doing this for all alpacahood.'

I hesitated.

What if what he was saying was true?

What he was saying *was* true.

'You're a great writer,' I said. 'The best alpaca writer of all time. Seriously.'

'I feel the whole weight of alpacahood pressing down on me, the north flock *and* the south flock. Can you imagine?'

Alpaca writers of merit were rare. Archie was easily the best author they had; he was the only alpaca competing in the Brilliant & Forever. Privately I wondered if an alpaca could seriously win the B&F in our times. But wasn't that all the more reason for him to go all out for the win?

'Have you spoken to Macy about this?'

Archie shook his head. 'Hardly. I mean, she wants to win this as much as I do. It's just that our reasons are different.'

I smiled. 'So you'll turn down the cash prize and the book deal, and just make a speech about alpaca rights?'

'I'd take the money as happily as you or Macy would.'

I nodded. 'It's gonna be interesting. I'm rooting for both of you. Alpacas deserve – well, you know.'

We leaned on the gunwale and watched the moon splash and bounce in the waves.

At length I spoke. 'Cyril Connolly, I think it was, said that not having the ambition or ability to fulfil our potential is one of the great negatives of the human – uh, or alpaca – condition. Remorse at not having fulfilled our potential. Anxiety at not being able to fulfil it. That really speaks to me. I always feel like a failure – I'm being honest, not self-pitying or anything like that. Hell, I'd probably still feel like a failure if I won the B&F.'

Archie kept his attention on the waves. 'I think I've achieved the best story I've ever done.'

I smiled. 'What's yours about?' I was teasing him. It's a written but more persuasively an unwritten rule that you never show anyone, not even your closest friends, the story you are going to perform at the B&F.

'A doofus on a boat who gets hit on the arm by an alpaca.' He whacked me on the arm. 'How about some food? My stomach's unaccountably empty.'

'I should just throw you overboard right now.' I untied the safety rope that tethered us. 'C'mon.'

We started making our way across deck. 'You're not gonna be sick again?' I asked.

'Dunno. Haven't tasted dinner yet.'

I'd stripped out of my oilskins down to my jeans and alpaca sweater in the kitchen, and was busy rustling up a meal for the crew. It felt good to be here, in our little gang, bobbing around together, out at sea, a world unto ourselves. If I'm ever with any beings other than Macy and Archie I always feel one third alone.

They were sitting at the table, yarning about this and that, playing with their cutlery. Macy had put the boat on automatic captain and was sloshing a half-empty glass of rum.

'It's refreshing,' I said, 'and healthy to escape a small island from time to time.'

'You're telling me,' said Macy, grimacing. Macy doesn't live the linear life, never did. She had an unconventional upbringing, used to hang with a rough crowd. Her parents died when she was fourteen (mother: after years of using a pencil to give her face a beauty spot, died of psychosomatic melanoma; father: Christmas jumper turned noose).

Macy doesn't seem romantic but sometimes, I know, she pictures her parents when they were in love rather than engaged, before they were married, before they loved each other rather than being in love, before they chose to tolerate each other instead of wishing each other dead, before they were in fact dead (at which point their feelings on the matter are unrecorded). They were buried twenty feet apart and Macy is one day going to build a subterranean tunnel joining the two grave sites, if she can avoid other graves as she goes. When I start writing poetry again, I'll turn this into a ballad.

I was designated chef or more accurately haiku-k (pronounced hi-cook) due to my experience gained that glorious summer I worked at a short-lived Japanese restaurant in town and was rapidly promoted from dishwasher to commis haiku-k. Haiku-kery (from haiku cookery) is a discipline based on ancient poeto-cuisinary principles:

One must freshly prepare three, and only three, meals per day.

The first meal is composed of five, and only five, ingredients.

The second meal is composed of seven, and only seven, ingredients.

The third meal is composed of five, and only five, ingredients.

The ingredients must include at least one item of seasonal produce.

The meal shall ideally bring about an 'mmmmtasty' moment in the diner(s).

The chef's ego is not allowed to intrude.

No garnish is permitted.

There are five methods: boiling, grilling, frying, steaming and serving raw.

There are five colours: yellow, green, white, black and red.

There are five tastes: sweet, salty, vinegary, spicy and shoyu.

Remember: 'In this plate of food, I see the entire universe supporting my existence.'

Cooking is often compared to chemistry in the scientific sense, but it is also chemistry in the sense of rapport. The more attentively and caringly a haiku-k haiku-ks, the more love will be tangible in the sensual marriage of flavours and tongue. One day I'll write a haiku-kery book, if I'm spared.

Tonight I was making salmon with a cheesy crunch crust, using salmon fillets (1), butter (2), flaked almonds (3), chopped fresh parsley (4) and grated Emmental (5) and, for Archie, I was rustling up a quintet of grasses, incorporating marram grass (1), wheat grass (2), buffalo grass (3), perennial ryegrass (4) and Kentucky bluegrass (5). I specially order some of these online. Whenever I haiku-k for Archie, the menu is always a quintet of grasses.

'But, really, Macy,' I asked, 'how d'you come up with the stories you do?'

Macy brushed my praise away with a shooing hand. 'Meh.'

'You've been practising – performing as well as writing?' Archie's question sounded more like a statement.

Macy sipped at her rum. 'You guys are coming to the launch party, I take it?'

'For what it's worth,' said Archie.

Macy's eyes narrowed. 'You're not worried about the B&F? You've got as much chance as anyone, and more talent than most.'

'Talent, maybe. Chance, no.'

'Ah, c'mon.'

'You don't know what it's like, always to be treated like a third-class citizen. Humans don't know how lucky they are.'

'I feel kinda grateful,' I said, truthfully. 'To be alive, to have what I have. It's not much materially, but I got food, warmth, a measure of knowledge, a moral compass that only sometimes lets me down. And we live in the part of the world where literature is most highly esteemed.'

'That's something,' said Macy. 'It really is. Ever wonder why it's like this?'

'Because,' I said, 'in other places their culture centres around money or science or doctrine.'

'Sure. But as you pointed out earlier, there's a financial impetus to win the B&F,' said Archie.

I shook a pan, releasing a rich aroma of salmon. 'It's really about the publishing deal, though, and the kudos. The money will disappear in time, but the fact that you won it – the prestige and fame and everything – will be around as long as the island exists.'

'Exactly,' said Archie. 'But for me it's about more than that. I want to win it for the sake of alpacas. If I won it . . .' His voice trailed off and he looked momentarily drugged. 'Imagine.'

Macy nodded. 'See, this is it. The value lies in putting literature at the central place in our lives. If we begin with literature and work out from there, we come to know who and what we are. Literature has the same relationship to life that life has to death.'

Archie scowled. 'How so?'

'One thing is missing from a book – it's pointing towards something, not the thing itself. That's what words do. One thing is missing from life – it's leading towards death, which we don't know or have. But we can grasp at it. Without it, life would be impossible. The same imaginative impulse that helps us understand life through literature can help us come to terms with, and even appreciate, death.'

'Wow,' said Archie. 'Yeah, maybe. I mean, the world is bigger than you, in the same way that death is bigger than a graveyard. So, too, a story is bigger than a book.'

Macy tilted her head to one side, concentrating. 'And it's also related to how memory, in retelling a story, changes the details slightly, so that ultimately the story is so different to the original, only its essence remains.'

I nodded, smiling, mixed some grasses together in a bowl. 'But see, there *is* an essence. That's the crux.'

'I think that's right. There's a serious relationship between – wait, what is it? Yeah. D'you reckon . . .' Archie trailed off. Then came back to us. 'I don't know if you do, or even can, fully appreciate what it means to be human. No, hear me out. We have this inferiority complex, this chip-on-the-shoulder thing in alpacahood.'

Macy and I swapped an embarrassed look. Maybe it should have been an honour, not an awkwardness, that Archie was talking about the never-mentioned. 'We feel servile to humans, or at least inferior. Deep down, we've bought into that. Long since. And we believe that story about a human birth – we take it literally. "Imagine a blind turtle roaming around the Earth's great oceans. Somewhere out on the waves a ring-shaped piece of wood is bobbing around. Once every hundred years this turtle comes to the surface and raises its head into the air. To be born a human being is more rare than for that turtle's head to go through the wooden ring when it surfaces."'

I finished mixing the grasses. We were silent with our thoughts for a moment.

'Is it that bad being an alpaca?'

'No,' said Archie, shaking his head. 'No. It really isn't. It's just more difficult. You're born into privilege, we're not. Yes, even blackhousers are privileged. I guess it's all relative. But if I could win the B&F – I know the odds are dead set against me, they're against all of us – but if I could . . . Well, who knows, but don't you think it's possible that if you lived a good life, at least the best one you could, and you did good things, like emancipated alpacas and resolved differences on a worthwhile scale, just maybe, you'd find that rebirth is actually a thing, and you'd come back as a human?'

'My god, Archie, I never realised you felt this way,' said Macy, her shining dark eyes stunned wide.

'I kind of almost feel like withdrawing from the B&F to give you a better chance,' I heard myself saying.

'Me, too,' said Macy vigorously.

'Nope. No way. I appreciate it – love you guys for even suggesting it, but it's got to be a clean and open competition.' Archie cocked his head and gave us a look and we moved instinctively together and group hugged. 'If I am going to win this, I gotta win it properly. But I wish us all luck.'

As I pulled away, Archie bent over and bit some Kentucky bluegrass out of my hand.

'I'd be the same. About the competition, not the grass theft,' I said, waving more grass under his mouth and snatching it back.

Macy said, 'And I mean, I'm not naive about it. I know my chances are – well, they're not great. They're not even good. But I'm gonna give it a red-hot go.'

'I can't wait to hear your piece,' I said.

'Yeah, me too. Everyone's piece,' Archie said.

'Maybe even being born in a place where literature is a life-or-death matter is like the turtle and the wooden ring. And maybe you will be born human in the future,' I said.

'Right.'

'And those anti-alpaca bigots will be Twilight Zoned into being reborn as alpacas.'

Archie grinned.

'Anyway,' I said. 'Food's ready.'

Macy made a face.

'What's wrong?'

Macy smacked her forehead. 'Damnit, I forgot: I wanted the first meal we had on the *Born Surreal* to be fish we caught ourselves. Shop-bought salmon? We took shop-bought fish to sea in a fishing boat?'

We laughed nervously at the salmon.

While we dined, the wind died away altogether and we decided to ride the boat home via a scenic route, passing by the south of the island, what with it being a moonlit night and all. We stood on the deck of the boat breathing in the fresh night air and enjoying the moonlight. One of the south end's most distinguishing features is a hill, the highest point on the island, though actually it's not that high. The local authority wanted to twin it with Mount Fuji. The audacity! They even wrote to

24

the government of Japan to ask permission to call it Mount Fuji II. The Japanese authorities, to their credit, emailed a response in their own language which, once our authorities ran it through an online translator, read as follows:

'Honourable islander people on other side of world! We are thinking you joke. Our joke back: David and Goliath not twins. Laughter laughter laughter. Thank you and do not trouble us again.'

The island authorities, whitehousers to a man, and indeed all of them men to a man, were red faced. Until one of them put the rest out of their humiliation. 'Hang on. Didn't David *beat* Goliath?' A Bible was consulted, a subcommittee formed, and it was concluded by the subcommittee, subsequent to lengthy consultation and a pricey report, that David did indeed triumph over Goliath. The councillors were now red faced merely with lifestyle issues. 'In any case,' someone said, 'it's not a mountain, so it's not as if we *really* wanted to call it Mount Fuji II.' It was suggested that the hill be known henceforth as Hill Fuji, a blatant and disrespectful snub to the Japanese. (Incidentally, the Fuji furore resulted in the Japanese restaurateur for whom I haiku-ked being passive-aggressively driven out of town, sending me back to the less glamorous world of dishwashing.)

Hill Fuji is a good example of how our culture is always desperate to be associated with others, even by tenuous, self-imposed or non-existent links, all stemming from an innate and inane cultural insecurity. The end result is that we always assume our endeavours – and we ourselves – must be second rate and unoriginal, even if they and we are not. It's part of the reason I am the way I am. Still, most of life is imaginary.

The boat rocked gently, chugging its way north on automatic captain.

'Most of life is imaginary,' I announced. 'Mark Twain said something like "I've been through terrible experiences in life, some of which actually happened."'

'Sure,' said Macy. 'And aren't those the ones that count.'

The islander/Japanophile/haiku-k in me savoured the view of Hill Fuji's reasonably but none too high peak standing resplendent, but not overly so, in the cool glow of the bright, but soon to wane again, moon.

'Isn't that something,' I said, breathing in the fresh salt air and grinning at the fine, naturally qualified, beauty of the scene.

'Meh,' said Macy. 'Everything's something.'

I knew she was saying it to annoy me. 'You can't get a rise out of me any more than you did with the fish.'

'Listen, what about God and such?'

I frowned.

Macy said, 'If God's omnipotent, he can make someone who can keep secrets, but if he's omniscient he can't. So an all-powerful, all-knowing god is impossible.'

'Who knows what's possible. I was thinking about omni-potence conundrums myself earlier. If you're omnipotent you can do anything. We could've caught a whale tonight. Then I got thinking about the lack of fish. Did anyone bring a glockenspiel onboard?'

'Hell no,' said Archie.

'Or even like in the form of a song on your iPod with some glockenspiel on it?'

'Wasn't it bad luck to say the word glockenspiel?' said Archie.

'No,' I said, 'that was Dan Brown.'

'Oh.'

'Thanks for that,' said Macy. 'You said Dan Brown. Now we gotta throw you overboard.'

'What the hell?' I said, pointing to where they didn't look.

'Nice try,' said Macy, grabbing hold of me and unhooking the rope that tied me to her and Archie. 'Just got to attach you to an anchor—'

'No, really. That's completely insane. LOOK!'

I pointed again, louder, and they followed my arm to the top of Hill Fuji. 'That triangle,' I said. They released their grip on me.

There was a triangle of some sort on top of the hill.

'That's never been there before. In fact, it wasn't even there a few minutes ago.'

'Wasn't it?'

'I don't think so. What is it?'

'Wait,' said Archie. 'Are trig points real? Like you see on a map? Do they correspond to actual triangles in the real world? They do, don't they?'

Macy and I squirmed and grunted non-committal answers to suggest 'everyone knows the answer to that' or 'don't ask stupid questions', but really meaning 'I don't know and I feel silly for not knowing'.

'Maybe it's a sentinel,' I said. 'Like, you know, the one from 2001: A Space Odyssey.'

'The year 2001 happened,' said Archie. 'Hey, if any of us ever writes about this, we need to set it really far in the future, not like 1984 or 2001 any of those—'

'If we wrote about this,' I said, 'why would we set it in the future when it's happening in the present?'

Archie said, 'Alright, smartass. If you're so clever then what is the trig point triangle thing?'

I wasn't ready to let it go. A phrase was repeating in my

head, so I said it aloud. 'If I do set it in the future, my first line to you is going to be, "What's an alpaca like you doing in an indifferent era like this?"'

'I worry about you. You,' he stepped closer and tried to make his face comically solemn, 'have an alpaca worried about you. How's that feel?'

'I don't know. Weird. In a good way. And so does that triangle thing. So there's synergy. It's not very tall. A few feet high? Definitely wasn't there earlier. No sign of any people around, on or above Hill Fuji. Weird.'

We looked at the triangle.

'It's an enigma,' said Macy suddenly in the voice of Tabitha Tessington, a pretentious, self-mythologising author we all knew. 'I feel a great affinity with it. I feel drawn towards it, like I did when I created [and here she named one of Tabitha's characters]. I feel that same magic.'

'Maybe it's her divine typewriter.' I put on my version of Tabitha's voice. 'I don't write my books, the characters come to me and dictate as if from the very heavens. I am visited by muses constantly.'

We laughed hard because imitation doesn't need to be accurate to be funny, it just needs to be plausible in a more hyperbolic world, and then we grew silent and stared again at the triangle.

'Could be an Egyptian pyramid that fell through a portal in time,' Archie said.

'Could be a massive block of Toblerone,' I said. 'In which case I'm going up there tomorrow before it rains.'

Coffee at the Nightingale with Toothache

I walked home at dawn. The sky stretched vast and changeable above me, the road felt solid under my shoes, though it swayed slightly, aftermath of a night at sea. I had changed back into my civilian clothes. Catching no fish whatsoever was fine by me, though Macy said she couldn't call herself a fishermanwoman until she'd landed a good haul and I said we'd go out again soon.

People sometimes assume islanders are naturally pulled towards the sea the way the sea is drawn to the moon. We – humans and alpacas – all have our lovely strange gravities. But most people I knew when I was growing up couldn't swim any more than they could walk into outer space. What was the point? The coldness of the sea this far north would kill you within fifteen minutes.

I smiled as I approached my home. The village, a dozen miles away from the island's main town of Balmore, was composed of bleating sheep and crofts meandering with a gentle slope towards the erratic U-shape of a sea loch which widened into the forty-mile, infinite stretch of water that divided and connected our island and the mainland. On any day except Sunday, hens clucked and strutted outside. As in the island's other lazy-going villages, most of us lived in blackhouses: long, low simple dwellings powered by peat-fired generators.

Whitehouses are for the urbane; they're built mainly in Balmore. The whitehousers seem to have (I almost wrote 'enjoy') greater comfort. Their toasters accommodate cinnamon-flavoured bagels. They have a boy to help them untangle their earphones. They use words like 'bespoke' and 'artisanal'.

The judges for the Brilliant & Forever are usually from whitehouses.

Whitehousers have problems, though. They're lonely, but they do not much like other people. Isn't that sad? And they seek counsellors to treat them for the guilt they feel at having a poor work ethic. They need counsellors because sometimes they endure traumas, such as when they drop their MacBook on their other MacBook. Yes, some people are so impoverished all they have is money.

People in whitehouses want to live like they're in an advertisement and their tragedy is that they never realise they're paying actual money to maintain an illusion, one that increases their dissatisfaction in life.

Instead of heading to my blackhouse, I decided to go down to the shore to see if an idea would come to me. Beachcombing, but for stories. This was a habit of mine.

The sea was where it was usually to be found, chipping away at our island as if trying to reclaim it. I like the sea. Sometimes it's a reflective moonlit mirror, sometimes a chuffed and glittering splasher of surfers, sometimes a tetchy, grumbling bruise-coloured soup. It's human and non-human, like the imagination.

I watched the sun rise over the water, pouring cool pink light around the village. My heart beat in harmony with the waves and it was like watching your watch's hand sweep in unity with the ticking mantelpiece and I felt implicated in life like a real person who really exists, like every drop of every wave was exactly where it had to be and that's why it was where it was.

Shorelines cure the blues – they should be available on prescription.

As a kid I'd try to outstare the waves' systole and diastole and wonder why I couldn't be perfect. My parents often raised their voices at me and as I became better acquainted with life and language, so I grew more and more convinced that I was a failure. Worst of all was when they lowered their voices and whispered acidly or gurned and hissed at me in staring, measured tones, as if to prove these weren't angry criticisms in the heat of the moment but deliberate observations.

I decided as flawed a thing as me could not naturally be theirs. I asked my father where I came from. He pointed to a far corner of the croft. 'We found you floating in a ditch over there.'

A ditch. Cold, filthy, ugly.

Inevitably, I learned of a world in which I was successful and even heroic: the world of stories, of books, infinite, birthed not by a ditch, but the imagination, big enough to have seeded, or to have seeded itself in, beginningless time. All you had to do was hide yourself somewhere and open up a book. I could throw away my own 'I' and assume, easily, the role of adventurer, astronaut, ghost-hunter, detective, cowboy. I started writing stories of my own. One of my teachers encouraged me.

When I wanted to write something about the sea, she asked me not to describe the waves as I thought I saw them, nor to let great seagoing stories influence me. 'Leave your pencil and paper at home,' she said, 'and take yourself down to the shoreline. Sit there. Sit there and forget yourself until you are absorbed in the sea.'

I did this day after day that summer. Provided I completed

my morning and evening chores, my parents were happy not to have me around the house. I learned to sit very still and to let any thoughts that arose in me drift away like the clouds overhead. I was not quite the same person from one day to the next, and neither was the sea the same sea, quite. This seemed to me very profound.

I changed. One day towards the end of summer, I became the sea.

And, being the sea, I now knew the sea well enough to write about it. I wrote a story about a man who goes fishing with a straight hook.

My teacher frowned and bit her lip as she read the story. When she finished it, she gazed at the page for a long time, then looked up at me, her eyes shining.

She just nodded, smiling as a couple of tears spilled over. She didn't need to say anything. I walked out of her room, beaming, and burst into a sprint and flew all the way home.

I knew that I could become a writer. If I could make stories of value, stories that moved people to laughter or tears, some of that value might reflect back on me and help forgive the failure I somehow was.

I picked up a stone and asked whether it and I had indeed begun our lives in exploding stars and if the stone had been sitting by the shore for centuries, waiting for me to pick it up – because frankly I knew I wasn't going to do anything exciting with it – and also was it true the air molecules I was breathing were the same ones inhaled and exhaled by Alexander the Great and Julius Caesar and Dante and Beatrice and Dan Brown. The stone did not respond or at least I don't think it did, but I imagined it answering quietly, telling me that my left hand and my right hand are made up of atoms from different stars and I looked this up in a library book later and discovered that theoretical physics did indeed affirm the awesomeness.

I gazed at the whitening clouds meandering overhead, teasing images slowly ricocheting into infinity, and I tried hard not to doubt myself.

I lobbed the stone away into the sky.

If we're stardust, who rekindled us?

Splash.

Later that afternoon, I met Archie for coffee. As I'd approached the Nightingale with Toothache café, a woman had said (to me for holding the door open while she exited the coffee shop with a pram), 'Thank you so much,' and in the same breath, to an impoverished alpaca begging outside near the door, 'Get lost.'

There are no franchise cafés and restaurants on the island. That's one of the things that makes it hard to leave here on any sort of permanent basis. Also, they're introducing a law next year to dissuade smoking. From next June, if you see someone smoking in a public place, you are permitted to spray carcinogenic water all over them and they're not allowed to retaliate. Special supplies of carcinogenic water are being packaged into litre-sized containers that look like little transparent fire extinguishers.

The café, like my cup, was half full and, also like my cup, smelled of coffee. I had paid the equivalent of four hours of dishwashing for two watery coffees plus, in an aspirational mood, a couple of slices of millionaire's shortbread, so sweetly sick I couldn't quite stomach them. When I was a kid, food at home was either deadly bland microwoven chicken korma that tasted of melted plastic, or sweets to rot the greediest heart.

The millionaire's shortbread depressed me. But the Nightingale with Toothache was one of the only cafés in Balmore that was alpaca friendly.

A solitary woman seated underneath the Hopper print 'Automat' looked as if she were trying to stave off loneliness by force-reading a book but it had a sexy vampire on the cover and she kept grimacing so it seemed to me the book made her more lonely still. My heart gave a dull pang.

Archie was distracted, checking emails on his phone. 'Cool,' he said. 'Robert Louis Stevenson just endorsed me for fiction and editing.'

'Sweet,' I said. 'Chekhov didn't even respond to my friend request. Kinda hurts.'

'Hey, remember when that Creative Writing lecturer we met at last year's B&F kept accidentally referring to him as Checkout? "Remember what Checkout has to say about the gun in the first act."'

I laughed. 'Oh yeah. And wasn't his argument that because human beings all die, "in-con-tro-vert-ible fact", and given that death is "life's most in-ev-ita-ble feature", any living human beings you have in the first act must, "all else being equal", be dead by the end of the third.'

'Dead by the third? What date is it today?'

'Don't you think "all else being equal" is the world's lamest get-out clause? "In a universe of infinite typing monkeys, all else being equal, one of them would improve on Shakespeare, and his name would be Ben Jonson".'

'Heresy!'

'Heresy.'

'All else being equal,' said Archie, 'I hereby declare that the phrase "all else being equal" be known henceforth, all else being equal, as "all else being non sequitur."'

'Agreed. Backdateable. So reality needs to find the equivalent of a word processing "find-and-replace" function.'

Archie grew serious. 'And is all else equal? Alpacas wouldn't agree. "Alpacas, all else being equal, are held in equal esteem in society as humans."'

'Think it'll ever happen? In our lifetime, I mean?'

'I hope so, for my sake and all the alpacas'. But it's like that time I said to Ray Genovese over by the counter there, "Why'd you always look so unhappy?" and he said, "Believe it or not, I used to be a people person," and I said "What happened?" and he said, "People."'

'Wow. Ray was, like, sociable?' My mouth hung open.

'Yeah.'

'Mind you, sociable's kinda how I am right now,' I said. 'Almost. I mean, I feel like I'm experiencing life. I was thinking back to childhood when I was down by the shore this morning. I feel pretty good.' I looked around. 'Some of the people in this café do not strike me as people who feel good at this moment. I could go over to that woman there and recommend a book that would likely change her life for the better. Literally.'

Archie became animated. 'Do it. Do it do it do it! Harper Lee said something like, "The book to read is not the one that thinks for you but the one which makes you think." When you recommend whatever book it is, tell her that quote as well. Creative reading – active, not passive. This could be the start of some amazing reading adventures for her! Make a date with her for the B&F.'

'She's reading that book because she can't bear to see her own loneliness reflected back in her coffee'. I winced. 'But I can't. Damnit. Somehow I just can't bring myself to do it. Shyness? Fear of rejection?'

'Excessive humility is a form of egotism,' Archie said, raising his tumbler of grassuccino and licking it clean.

'Ain't that the truth. But I know I'm not going to do it, which is kind of a shame. Also I'm afraid she'll just think I'm trying to chat her up.'

'And you wouldn't be?'

'It's sad there's so little room for altruism, so little trust . . . and that most of all I'm too much myself to do something one-sidedly good.'

'Don't we all have a massive fear of rejection?'

I sucked air through my teeth. 'When it comes to the B&F, we do.'

'Elephant in the room.'

I whirled round. 'Where?'

We both giggled but the mention of the B&F made us thoughtful, little possible movies of the B&F flicking through our minds, then I shrugged and Archie smiled and we glanced around the café. On our island this often results in seeing someone you know. Not always – sometimes there are locals whom you've somehow never seen before. The local is the universal but some locals are more universal than others.

And today felt different. There were many unfamiliar, self-important faces – a sign that the B&F was approaching. Agents, publishers, fans.

Archie said, 'It would be cool if an elephant really did walk into the room.'

We instinctively looked around again, both of us thinking, 'I know there's no elephant here.'

'We'd have probly heard it,' I said.

'Anyway,' said Archie, 'we live in an age of narcissism and entitlement. That's the point. It's those who are content to be nothing special who are noble.'

'Winning the B&F would be special.'

'I'm doing that for alpacahood.'

'You know what, Archie? You never really talk much about your childhood.'

'You never talk to me about lepidoptery. Or the conference of Regensburg. Or armoured vehicles. Hell, there are more things you don't talk to me about than I don't talk to you about.'

Even though I could think of a dozen responses to that, it kind of silenced me.

We sat in comfortable reticence for a moment.

A strange arrogant-looking man caught our attention. Mid-forties, with greasy curly hair, he had an invisible zeitgeisty sleaze oozing out of him; yep, two parts entitlement, three parts narcissism – the personality of our times.

He was sitting on his own, frequently scanning the room, with an attitude that exuded 'don't-you-know-who-I-think-I-am'-ness, as if he expected film cameras to be swirling about him. As he panned around, he looked through us without seeing us. Archie and I were neither beautiful nor ugly, just normal, a guy and an alpaca hanging out in a café.

'Check him out,' said Archie wonderingly.

'No, that's what he wants us to do.'

'No, he wants us to check him out to admire him. We want to check him out to understand what particular kind of douchebag he is.'

'I-love-me-who-do-you-love douchebags like that creep me the hell out.'

'Ssh.'

We listened. At a table between ours and the stranger's, a couple of hipsters, twenty-something women, were chatting over their lattes. One of them had a portable ornamental typewriter set artfully to the side of her drink. The other wore a sundial for a wristwatch. We tuned in to their conversation, mainly because it was obvious Douchebag was eavesdropping.

Typewriter Hipster: 'So he says, "I like my coffee like I like my women."'

Sundial Hipster: 'Shut *up*. He's meant to be, like, a talent so original there's no word for him in English yet. What a jerk.'

Typewriter Hipster: 'I just cut him off with, "I like my coffee like I like my hot caffeinated beverages." He's not a jerk, exactly. I mean – he's not vain. He's, like, slightly vain. He's an author.'

Sundial Hipster: 'You should've said, "I like my men like I like my coffee – ground up tiny and shoved in the fridge."'

Typewriter Hipster: 'Lol.'

Sundial Hipster: 'Hey, so I arranged a screening in Paris for some sales agents. But they were so mainstream-biased I just wanted to slit my wrists. Ultimately, it's just so cutthroat.'

Douchebag's ears pricked up, he turned in his seat and said in loud blank awe: 'Ma'am! Did you say you cut someone's throat?'

Sundial Hipster: 'No. Ew! No. I said something about my industry being cutthroat, and . . .'

Douchebag: 'And what? Don't hate the players, hate the game?'

Sundial Hipster: 'Yeah, exactly, I guess.'

Douchebag: 'Well, that's the shaving industry for you, very cutthroat.'

Sundial Hipster: 'What? No, I'm a successful international agent, thank you very much.'

Typewriter Hipster (placing her paperless typewriter into a leather typewriter case, and speaking with venomous politeness): 'Sir, this was a private conversation.'

Douchebag: 'Well, ma'am, I just had to intervene as a result of my own vocational interests. Being a murderer and all. Slashing up throats, shooting to death and such.'

Typewriter Hipster and Sundial Hipster gathered their belongings and cast a powerful disgusted look in Douchebag's direction.

Exeunt Sundial Hipster and Typewriter Hipster.

Archie and I stared for a moment.

'Well!'

'I know,' said Archie. 'He kinda intrigues me.'

'Maybe he's a sort of human troll, a living spambot, winding everyone up?'

'You ever see him before? He doesn't look like the usual tourist.'

On a semi-regular basis, a ferry arrived at our island and the tourists who came to sample insular life swapped places with the ones who were just leaving, as though all tourists were part of a huge, neverending tag team. Sometimes a tourist would clamber off the ferry, amble onto a bus and open up a guidebook or a newspaper and, instead of looking out the window at a characterful, rainbow-splendoured islandscape, would outstare a crossword puzzle or read about a trite, meaningless version of the island created by an impersonal travel writer.

The island the tourists came with and the island the guidebooks came with and the island the tourists left with were never the same.

'He's no tourist,' I said. 'Is he here for the B&F?'

'Hmm. Wonder if he's a writer, publisher or agent.'

It was permitted for outsiders to participate in the Brilliant & Forever, but very few seemed to do so because they, unlike locals, had to pay an exorbitant 'administrative fee' for taking part, on top of travel and accommodation expenses. Still, the odd optimistic author felt it worth the expense and some writers doubled up

39

their participation with a holiday, believing it was a win-win situation, but a non-local author had never won the B&F.

A shadow fell on the table, startling us both. I grinned up at Ray Genovese, tenacious but embittered middle-aged writer and waiter. His face was crosshatched with old acne scars. I always smile when I see Ray – I make a point of this – to show him that there is hope and there need not be bitterness. Unlike others, I never call him by his sarcastic nickname, 'Ray of Sunshine'. People are cruel.

'Hi Ray,' I said. 'What you working on?'

'Yeah, just stuff,' he said in his weary way. He held up a jug of filter coffee. 'So?'

'You doing bottomless cup now?' I asked.

'Nope, owner's watching and charging anyone who accepts.'

'Stealth charge,' said Archie. 'Capitalist fiend.'

'I think we'll make like Archie's cycling proficiency test and somehow pass,' I said. 'Ray, seriously, what are you working on at the moment?'

He shrugged. 'I was working on my autobiography. But I had to give up due to an inherent failure of the form.'

'Huh?'

Ray let out a small sigh. 'See, a book about the self has no meaning in this life wherein the self has no fixed form, no lasting identity. The self being an illusion, autobiography is innately fiction. In any case, it would be tedious to just have one self all the time.'

There was a silence. Quite a long one.

After which, Archie said, 'I actually agree with that.'

'So do I', I said. 'Totally.'

'And yet,' Archie said, 'autobiography sells.'

'So does burned coffee,' Ray mumbled and he sloped off to another table.

'But people and alpacas are fascinating, see?' said Archie. 'Burned coffee, not so much.'

Archie and I were about to swap opinions on good autobiography versus bad coffee when we realised we'd been missing some action over at the table vacated by the hipsters. Now two bored guys in their teens were drawling out a conversation, slouched territorially over their soft drinks. Their anti-uniform uniform was made up of whimsical T-shirts and skinny jeans. They kept primping the feathery dyed-black hair visible from underneath their lurid baseball caps.

Baseball Cap One: 'I knew it was time to go to bed last night when the Scrabble board started talking to me.'

Baseball Cap Two: 'God, you were drunk. That wasn't Scrabble, that was a ouija board.'

Baseball Cap One: 'Weird if, when you die, you become so useless the only thing you can do is slide a glass around a ouija board . . . The conversation in this café is kinda dead too.'

Baseball Cap Two: 'And yet it's happening right now.'

Baseball Cap One: 'What can you do.'

Baseball Cap Two: 'What can you do.'

Baseball Cap One: 'I can say something interesting.'

Baseball Cap Two: 'Go on then.'

Baseball Cap One: 'Hot roast beef!'

Baseball Cap Two: 'That's not interesting, that's just random.'

Douchebag swivelled round and said to Baseball Cap Two, 'You're right. He is just *tedious*. Would you like me to shoot him for you? No charge. It's what I do. Seriously.'

Baseball Cap One: 'Fuck you.'

Baseball Cap Two: 'Yeah, fuck you.'

Baseball Cap One: 'Fucking paedo.'

Baseball Cap Two: 'Let's find a cop and say he touched you.'

Baseball Cap One: 'He'd be more likely to touch you.'

Baseball Cap Two: 'Yeah, cos I'm the good looking one.'

Baseball Cap One: 'Fuck you. I'm outta here. This place is full of dicks.'

Douchebag (beaming): 'S'alright. You can't touch me. I'm above the law.'

Baseball Caps One and Two picked up their drinks and left, offering Douchebag a manual gesture you didn't need to be street-wise to understand. Douchebag redoubled his shit-eating grin.

Archie and I were pretty much smiling and frowning at the same time.

'Just – *what?*' said Archie. 'Double-you tee fucking eff?'

'I know.'

Douchebag got up to go to the toilet – he moved with a pimp-swagger – and when he reappeared, instead of going back to his table, to our disappointment he walked out of the café. As he was leaving, he took some keys out of his jacket, causing a piece of paper to flutter out of the pocket. Archie and I waited an agonising few seconds for him to get out of eyeshot then we leapt at it. I got there first, snatched it. We sat back at our table. I opened the paper out. On it was written, in a surprisingly suave hand:

'All plots tend to move deathward. This is the nature of plots.'
– Don DeLillo

And, beneath that, but in green ink this time:

Self-referential. Self-reverential. Whatever.

And, below that, again in green:

Some They'll Think I Did, But Which I Didn't

On a street corner, an off-duty cop, male, white, thirties, shot in the back.

White middle-aged male, dressed in chicken outfit, generally if incompletely decapitated.

Japanese male, twenties, car park, bound, hanging upside down by ankles, 'YOUR' and 'NEXT' tattooed on knuckles.

Bland-looking bald middle-aged man – garrotted – in beige suit with suitcase handcuffed to his left wrist. The suitcase contains a near-empty bottle of twelve-year-old malt and a manuscript about the Illuminati.

'None of this makes sense,' I said. 'Does it?'

'I kinda hope not, because the only sense I can make of it isn't pretty,' said Archie. 'We need to keep an eye on that guy. And this paper could be evidence.'

'Of what?'

'Who knows. Nothing good.'

'Out of everyone I know, you're the one least likely to lose a piece of paper,' I said and Archie looked proud as he tucked it away in his tote bag. Then he looked prouder still. 'Oh shit, I nearly forgot! I sold a work of short fiction to *Enervating Resonance* magazine.' (Alpacas enjoy sending work out for publication; editors can't distinguish between human and alpaca submissions.)

'Cool. How much d'you get?'

'Nah. Freebie,' he said. 'Man, I need some more grassuccino.'

'Then you can't say you sold it.'

Archie frowned. 'By that logic I can't say magazine either, because it's an online thing, not an actual publication. A website, I guess.'

'Sold it!' I smacked my forehead with an open palm. 'For nothing.'

'I non-sold a work of short fiction to a non-magazine.'

'How many words?'

'About 18,000.'

'What? So it was hardly short.'

'It needed to be that long, because I had to tell how it really happened. But it wrote itself. It was stenography. Easy. You know, it was about that day I saw the drunk guy punching the southern alpaca, distant cousin of mine, and what happened after.'

I sighed. 'The world's not right.'

'Damn straight,' said Archie. He shook his head, marvelling at how things are, not in a good way. 'I non-sold a non-short non-work of non-fiction to a non-magazine.' When he raised his head to look at me he was shaking slightly and I'm not sure but I thought he was being serious when he said in a whisper, 'Tell me this, who will save us writers?'

'Why can't we save ourselves?' I sighed again, more heavily this time. 'The world's just not right.'

'I know what'll make it right,' said Archie, getting up. 'Vanilla latte for you, wheatgrassuccino for me.'

Over our drinks I told Archie about how I learned injustice as a ten year old, watching an Indiana Jones movie. I loved going to the cinema, munching on popcorn as the films faded me in to another world, another self. If you've watched the film you'll maybe remember the scene. In an outdoor market, Indiana Jones faces a bad guy who wields, with formidable skill, a large sword. Jones observes him for a moment, then pulls a gun and shoots him dead. That is when I lost my innocence, disillusioned that a hero could be such a cheat and a coward.

'You need to get over that,' said Archie. 'I don't know about Indiana Jones. In real life, heroism's about doing your best, no matter what.'

'I feel like I could use some redemption. The B&F will be our saviour,' I said. 'Like, if I win I'm splitting the money with you and Macy.'

Archie gave me a look. 'Serious?' I realised he had not thought about splitting the money with us at all and it might now seem as though I was hinting in a generouser-than-thou manner that if that's what I would do that's what he should do too, and a weird, awkward pressure passed between us, like a small invisible jet plane through a tunnel, between two trains.

'No,' I lied. 'I'm just kidding.'

(But I will split the money (if I win (which I won't (unless I get very lucky indeed (I realise I'm conceding I do have an actual, real-life chance of winning (the thought excites and terrifies me (I need some kind of a hug (any kind at all)))))))).)

In the Future It Will Be Hard to Be Real

I went home and lay on the bed with my laptop open. I typed up the beginning of a short story, but deleted it without saving. I found a photograph of Archie and I spent twenty minutes manipulating it, giving it a humorous speech bubble and unnaturally bright colours, then I deleted it, too. I switched the laptop off. Switched the TV on, flashing schizophrenic machine of the low IQ. Watched five minutes of an unreal reality programme which was soon interrupted by a too-loud advert urging me to watch the programme I had already been watching. Changed channel, heard a weather reporter say it was going to be partly sunny. Partly sunny, I thought, that's like saying the chicken soup's partly vegetarian. And why the hell don't we ever get snow anymore? I channel hopped, looking for a cartoon, couldn't find one. Found instead a programme showing a botoxed man whose ridiculous hair should have been grey but was jet black, and he was sitting transfixed, eating artificial food as he played a computer game. In the future, I realised, it's going to be a challenge for people to be real. I turned the TV off. Found my notebook and thought up some new haiku-kery recipes. Cried for an hour. Decided to make some food. Went into the kitchen. I tried to open a packet of rice but couldn't. Found my phone and attempted to tweet:

I rename this resealable tab unopenable tab. #tabs #tweets #tweetsabouttabs #hashtags #statusupdates #tropes #inconsequentialstuff #sequitursthatarenotnon

But it was too long a tweet and I deleted it without posting.

Then I attempted, again, more determinedly, to open the bag of rice and the bag of rice exploded, shooting rice all over the room and I felt sad for the waste and the fact I was to blame more than the rice bag manufacturers, probably, plus it put me in mind of various friends' weddings, via rice confetti, and I remembered I will likely never get married and I sat down and cried a little more, which cheered me up, and by the time I'd swept the room with wholehearted penance and concentrated physical effort, I felt refreshed and it stunned me to think I had converted food waste to mental, physical and emotional advantage and so I was revivified with a true belief in actual hope. In happiness. In the future.

Am I happy on the island, I thought, or should I go someplace else?

If I were not here right now I would probably choose to be in Galveston, a place I have never visited, but whose name I like. I'd fly and then hop freight trains to get there. I'd be a hobo in the Seasick Steve mould (person who moves around looking for work), rather than a tramp (moves around, no interest in work) or a bum (doesn't move around, doesn't care for work). I picture Galveston as a glittering, edgy kind of city at night, as the train rolls in and I leap off it, nimble as a cat. The motel I'm crashing in for the night is the wrong side of clean, but it's all I can afford and I have a feeling if I slept under the stars I'd wake up dead. The motel staff are weird and surly and make a resident feel as though they're in the *Twilight Zone* or *Twin Peaks*.

The next day I get up and walk about in bright sunlight and I spend my last few dollars on eggs, pancakes and black coffee in a diner that is dazzlingly efficient in food prep and small talk.

'Sup?' says the waitress, pouring me another coffee.

I shrug, cool as I can, meaning 'Nothing special'. But inside I'm fizzing with excitement, now that I've reached Galveston.

'Going anywhere exciting?'

'Hope so,' I say and smile. I wish I had money to tip her properly.

In the heat of the midday sun, I wander through the city towards the docks, where life is real and dockworkers are sweating as they haul ropes and boxes, the sun flashing off forklifts and containers, shadows peeling off from bigger shadows and becoming people-shaped.

Beyond this is the blue sea, alive in the sunlight, sparkling, infinite with possibility – except, that is, the possibility that I am far away across the ocean, sitting on a chair in my living room in this old blackhouse, feeling the early poundings of what I used to think was called a 'mind-graine', induced by the painful frustration of being unable to escape myself/my circumstances, or perhaps brought on by the bright flashing lights of the sun bouncing off the waves in the Galveston harbour of my mind.

I shook my head, then convinced myself the mind-graine was imaginary and in any case the thing to cure it was a bike ride. Plus I'd already promised myself I'd investigate that triangle thing. Who cared that it was already getting dark outside.

Single-speed bikes play a vital role in my life. Bikes, meditation and writing saved my life.

I used to look at my dad's racing bike and dream of the day

I would have one of my own. At six years of age I went missing for the first time. I was found hours later, nine miles away. I'd gone cycling off on my bike, with the stabilisers still on. I'd pedalled all the way, happy in the little bubble cycling had created for me – and still does.

I need my fixie fix five days a week. It's the global cooling machine, the mobile device that charges me. Those who use multi-geared bikes haven't yet realised; limitation is a means towards liberation. We don't choose the limits of reality (gravity, a nose that's too big, lottery odds that are against us and forty squintillionbillion other things) but we can choose how we respond to them and that's how we realise who we are. 'We are happy,' said Yeats, 'when for everything inside us there is a corresponding something outside us.' I don't know if Yeats rode fixies; maybe.

I dictated a note into my phone: 'Idea. Write a play about cycling. In which Yeats and Basho are competitors in a six-day track race at Madison Gardens during the era when it was regularly turned into a temporary velodrome. The Swedish Academy is in charge of betting. Make it a lyrical, atmospheric, graceful drama – lots of tension and cycling action. The actors ride their bikes on rollers or turbo trainers, and wear cycling helmets and masks. Rob Schneider, someone from Creative Scotland and Lance Pharmstrong are the referees.'

Fixies and single-speeds were in fashion for a while, but like all fads it faded so the folk who still ride mono-geared bikes are those who do so for interior, not superficial, reasons. Everything eventually settles.

The only other thing I'd like to do is be the first person to cycle on the moon. Sometimes I lie in bed at night picturing myself up there in a light and flexible spacesuit, pedalling a fixed-gear bike, easy and fast, my legs orbiting, describing circles in the vacuum, the tyres leaving prints in the dust. I'll pull a wheelie or two, for the hell of it. Moonwheelies! Could life be more exciting than to pull moonwheelies, with the universe twinkling above and around you?

I stepped outside with my bike. The chill in the night air was invigorating. I looked up. So many stars! Mirroring the heavens, my mind shimmered and stretched . . . Dizzying, to think that those countless tiny sparks riddling the darkness are colossal floating furnaces, some of which attract and touchlessly hold on to their own planets. Solar systems' relationships are always platonic, which is inspiring and sad.

I sighed with a six-point-four-out-of-ten feeling of happiness, the mind-graine already receding, then went back inside to collect my peat iron, my 'gold' ingots from the internet, backpack and rain cape. The rain cape was a sardonic present from Macy. You wore it around your neck and it splayed out like a tent, covering you and much of the bike. Macy thought it hilarious to buy me the least cool cycling gift she could think of. But I used it to puncture her sarcasm and to top it with a better joke. Macy had an unoriginal saying that I was 'Third Policemanning into my bicycle', which she shortened to 'TP-ing into your bike' and which I then changed to 'tepeeing into my bike' when I used the rain cape because I basically became a tent on wheels.

Cycling with all these things, especially the peat iron, was a bit awkward, but I have a refined sense of balance and I relished the challenge of it. Witness the fitness, I thought, as I cycled along the quiet narrow roads. The swish of the sea in the distance blended nicely with the swoosh my legs made as they pumped up and down. Outside the village, there were no streetlights and the pool of white that my front light provided gave me that safe, cocooned feeling.

My legs hammered harder on the pedals and I sliced through the night quickly, despite my peat iron, 'gold'-filled bag, and non-aerodynamic cape. Ahead, the road unspooled. Soon I was throwing the bike and myself into bends, leaning in, my legs pedalling themselves into a blur. I plunged along the invisible line my mind instinctively plotted before me. The verges swiftly smudged past.

After thirty or forty miles of happy cycling, the peat iron, designed for digging into the turf, was digging instead into my back so I halted and dismounted and laid the bike down gently by the side of the rough track road. I'd taken a right-hand turn onto a disused old road I knew. It was in a remote part of the island and there was no one around at this time (the wee small hours), though admittedly the moorland here was seldom graced (or besmirched) by human company even in the big enormous hours.

I walked a few yards onto the moor and stopped at the first peat bank. I crouched with the peat iron and used it to dig a letter-box shape into the thick sludge of oozy black in the side of the bank. I scooped enough squelchy peat out to make enough room, say, for a large hardback book, then took the first ingot of 'gold' out of my backpack and buried it in the space I'd created. Taking handfuls of the slimy peat I plastered it around the gold bar and smoothed off the face of the bank so it looked untouched.

Pleased with my work, I set off towards another peat bank, then hesitated. I should really bury them in peat banks as far apart from each other as I could manage. It was going to be a long night.

It was a long night. But by six in the morning I had buried all of the 'gold' and felt that I had done some worthwhile labour.

At least the backpack was light now, so the ride home would be easier. I felt like a poet whose work would lie undiscovered until long after his death, but would then be regarded as an unexpected marvel; however the analogy itself made me queasy so I cursed myself for thinking it.

I stood up straight and stretched my arms and legs, bone-weary from the night's exertions. As I did so, I realised I was near the top of Hill Fuji. I'd forgotten to check out the triangle and I was too tired to go up to the top of the hill now, though it wasn't far off. Instead, if I headed south then west, cycling the fast descent down Fuji was going to be my little reward.

Curiosity made me look up towards the top of the hill. The triangle was still there. I squinted. Was that . . .

Surely not.

'Weird,' I said out loud.

Changing my mind, I got on my bike and cycled further uphill. The road only took you so far, skirting the top of the hill, and I was too fatigued to walk the boggy moorland to get to the triangle at the very top, so I stopped and dismounted to see if my eyes had deceived me.

Now I was closer, I could confirm it.

The triangle was not a triangle but a statue of a person sitting in a meditation posture.

Still, serene.

Who the hell put that statue there?

I would like that kind of serenity, I thought.

The B&F was just over a week away.

I shrugged. I didn't want to think about statues, I didn't want to think about the Brilliant & Forever. I didn't want to think about anything.

I climbed into the saddle, adjusted the peat iron, backpack and rain cape, took a deep breath, and pushed down hard on the pedals. The lights of Starburt village below glimmered and sparked like a constellation and in the headlong rush of cycling downhill, gravity seized hold of me with a heavy thrust and suddenly the pedalling took no effort and my limbs scissored up and down and the slight burning in my thigh and calf muscles melted away to nothing and I was lifted and there was a silence in the huge night, a silence that was celestial and I felt as though I was falling upwards into space, pulled high towards a glittering constellation, with a vast familiar force drawing me upwards.

It wasn't quite cycling on the moon, but the harder I pedalled the more I felt as though the Earth had released me.

When I reached the bottom of Hill Fuji, I stopped pedalling and braked hard. The village of Starburt lay ahead, sleeping. Elated, I dismounted by the roadside and grinned like a safely re-Earthed spaceman, looking back at the steep length of road I had just flown down to sea level. What I saw killed my thrill.

I jumped back onto my bike and pedalled towards home, fearful.

I had just seen the statue get up and walk away.

The Great and Good of the Brilliant & Forever

The annual Brilliant & Forever launch party had arrived. The evening sky was a deepening bruise; the very air over the island seemed to crackle. I could hear it. Normally the sky doesn't talk. Yet a palpable static of anticipation and apprehension fizzed and sparked at my ears, hissing words like 'failure' and 'disappointment' as I cycled around, trying to keep my mind in the moment, rather than projecting into worrisome futures. Maybe the sky was echoing my own inner voice? Maybe that's outrageous arrogance.

The streets bristled with adrenalised people dashing in and out of houses, cars, shops, shouting platitudes about clothes and haircuts and drinks. Alpacas bounded along in jittery, alert packs. They weren't allowed to attend the party, but some of them showed support by bearing homemade flags with painted 'Archie for the B&F' or 'Alpacas are Brilliant & Forever' messages fluttering. Some flags had an image of Archie in his stetson, grasping his spittoon, grinning cheesily.

Back home, I had a long hot soak in the bath and read chapter eighteen of *Life and Fate* to remind myself to be grateful for the countless opportunities I had and the immeasurable terrors I didn't.

Macy and Archie came round to my blackhouse at eight.

Macy wore a strapless dress; its top half was green, then it fell in black silken pleats from her waist to just above the knees. She'd gathered her hair into an Ecclefechan plait, complete with diamond hair clips. She looked sensational.

'You look sensational, Macy,' I said.

'And you look shit,' she said, presenting me with a quick hug and a solid good-natured slap across the shoulder. 'My face is like an early hagiography, or the world's greatest novel.'

'What?'

'Not yet made up.' She smiled, pleased with herself.

'You never wear make-up.'

'I know, just practising some lines for a story.'

'Very good,' I said. 'Hey Archie, you smell like vanilla shower gel. I'm going to eat you.' I made a play of grabbing him and attempting to bite into his neck. He thrust me away, beating at me with his rhinestone stetson.

Archie is one of those alpacas who showers regularly as a concession to humans, an act some hard-line alpacas shun and politicise, and today he had brushed his coat, too.

He put on and adjusted his stetson, which I knew, and he knew I knew, was his favourite one. 'Gotta make an effort.'

Maybe I did look shit. I had dressed in a yellow tartan kilt and purple shirt.

'I don't know,' I said. 'Parties aren't real. They make me uneasy.'

'Your dress sense makes me uneasy,' said Archie, trying to lift up my kilt.

'Oi! Quit it. Let's just stay in and watch a film instead,' I said. 'Who needs parties. The B&F itself is what it's about, the party's a superficial event for whitehousers and posers. I want to stay in and watch a film. Yeah, I'm gonna fight for my right not to party.'

'Is there a John Wayne on?' said Archie, suddenly alert.

'No, but there's a Jeff Bridges. It's called *True Grit*. From 2010. Jeff Bridges and his actor pals make a good effort at repeating just about every single quotation from *True Grit*, in order.'

'Like a film would have more drama than the B&F launch party! You just have social anxiety, and face it,' said Macy, who was perfecting her hair in front of and inside a wall mirror 'you'd be crazy if this society *didn't* make you anxious. Ergo, you're worried because you're intelligent.' Macy had a theory that intelligence caused people to be unhappy. I had a theory that any intelligence ascribed to me was exaggerated.

I opened my sporran to see if I'd remembered my eye drops, cash, pen, inhaler and blank page. 'I just feel it's weird. Eight o' clock, Saturday, you are granted permission – no, you are obliged – to be happy. Let's synchronise watches.' (Archie didn't use one, Macy in lieu of a watch had a tattoo of a watch on her wrist; the watch's face read 'Now'.) 'Impossible,' I said, 'or is it easy, to synchronise your watch with itself.' I suddenly panged, wanted to be a watch in sync with itself, just as quickly shook the thought away. 'But parties – how can people even do that? Just start being happy because someone decrees this is the time to be ecstatic? People don't get together every Wednesday morning at eleven fifteen to share a few hours of poignant behaviour. We don't congregate every second Thursday at midday to express our communal outrage.'

'Maybe we should,' said Archie.

I paused. 'Maybe we should,' I conceded. 'Maybe there's a revolution on the horizon.'

'You're nervous and havering,' said Macy. 'Don't make me slap you in the face.'

'I,' Archie announced, 'am going to get rip-roaring drunk and persuade everyone to get nekkid and dance the fandango with me. They'll see how much fun an alpaca can be. I'll show them Bohemian living, fandangoing alpaca fashion. How's the fandango go? Such a great word.'

'I know nothing about it,' I said. 'Nothing. So you can't call me intelligent.'

'I don't know the fandango either,' said Macy, 'and I'm supersmart. It's no indicator. Straighten your sporran, mister.'

'Parties aren't real,' I said again.

'You'd pass up the chance to watch an alpaca do the fandango?'

I sighed. 'Well, when you put it like that.'

'Here's a taster.' Archie started shaking his hindquarters and scatting random syllables – 'doo-wa-doo-woo-a-shoobee-doo-shoobee-doo-way-a-bom-ba-shoo-a-weeeee eee-wee-ba-ba-boo' – and in this fashion he shook and shimmied and sang his way around the room, his rump occasionally crashing a book or a mug to the floor. Macy and I grinned. Archie was as excitable as a kangaroo. It was wonderful to see him in exuberant mood.

At last he stopped and struck an exaggerated, disgruntled pose. He pouted and made his face look as hurt as he could, which didn't work too well with his perma-smile. 'The hell you pair laughing at? You got no class. It's just a jazz thing you don't get.'

We laughed at our brilliant mad alpaca pal. No humour as endearing as unselfconscious self-deprecation. And no question, I supposed, but that we were going to this party. I tried to don the mental equivalent of a yellow kilt.

Macy sped us to the castle in her battered Datsun, cornering at screeching right angles. The landscape streaked by like we were on a train. Boyracers hurtled past in the other direction, millimetres away, sound systems blaring repetitive beats.

'She's going to kill us,' Archie shrieked as Macy's latest handbrake turn sent him shunting across the back seat into my side. 'We were safer on the bloody boat.'

'It's fine,' I shouted back, resting my hand on Archie's arm to comfort him. But I wondered if I believed it myself, because now that my social anxiety had lifted, I realised there was a deeper, more inscrutable worry lodged somewhere deep inside me. I couldn't give it a name. It knew me, though. All I could say was that it was bigger than me, the same way our planet's ongoing graveyard houses billions of dead beings, but death itself is always bigger.

We reached the castle about six times quicker than we should have, but intact. The castle itself – two hundred years old but renovated in the godawful 1970s – was grand without being ostentatious. Macy skidded the blue Datsun to a halt with squealing precision, slap bang in a parking space between a people carrier and an alpaca carrier.

'We made it. I'll walk home. Hey, surely,' said Archie, frowning as he noticed the vehicle on our right, 'there won't be any other alpacas here?'

'Scared of being upstaged?' I said.

'Likely just a family of alpacas going for a walk in the castle grounds,' said Macy, unclipping her seatbelt. 'C'mon.'

On the way in, I nodded to my favourite gargoyle, the one carved, an asymmetric afterthought perhaps, under the north-east turret, and which always looks like it is smiling benignly at a private joke. It nodded back, but only because of the way the light and shadows shifted as I walked past the burly security guards, who specifically did not return my nod.

The party, being about half an hour old, was at the politely thrumming stage, yet was already, you sensed, bordering on the disinhibited stage, as if someone had made punch that tasted of fruit juice but was absinthe based. I say this because I know such a drink fuelled one of the B&F parties a few years previously, the time the partygoers went en masse to a local roundabout, set up a makeshift bar there, and put up chalkboards that read, 'You honk, we drink'. Seventeen people ended up in hospital.

The great and good of the Brilliant & Forever were here, milling under the ornate golden chandelier of the plush crimson room. The judges, recognisable in their cravats (men) and extravagant hats (women), mingled primarily with each other. They didn't seem to be chitter-chattering; they were conducting serious conversations about Literature. Maybe. They all looked superior. Did they really believe they were better than the rest of us? My neighbour Senga always says of them, 'They're awfy guid tae themselves, so they are.' The judging committee had the reputation of being as crooked as the devil's tail, of having the scruples of a Trojan cavalry.

Still, some of the judges were nice enough to have spoken to me in the past and one of them even seemed friendly and outwardly encouraging, though he had never helped me with my career in any way, far less intimated he expected me to do well at the B&F.

Many of those present were whitehousers, part of the social stratum of 'middle-class unemployed' and as such were inordinately concerned with appearances and with having an important and distinctive – that is, loud – voice. Being here was already giving me a mind-graine.

I stood on the fringes, leaning against the wall.

I heard a hunched figure saying to someone I recognised as a local journalist, 'The term "cult author" sits fine with me. I'm cool with it. Just as well, too, since what could I or anyone else do about it? It's alright by me because I don't crave the blandness of mass acceptance. There's still a place for integrity in literature. Even nowadays. Especially nowadays. Author of four, father of none, husband of one, friend of 882.'

To some writers, other people are not people, they are threats – especially when something like the B&F is imminent. I looked about the room, trying to read the people there. You could see the fakery in the false smiles and defensive body language.

Macy berated me. 'Stand up straight. Isn't that Ray Genovese? Go and talk to him.'

'I'm not in a sociable mood. I told you, I can't do parties. I never learned how.'

'It's a party, for crying out loud. There are emphatically no rules! Archie's making a go of it – look, he's away mingling already.'

'He's helping himself to drinks, is what he's doing. Listen, Mace – you and Archie both have a real shot at winning this,' I said. 'The stakes are higher – you should both be networking, glad-handing, that sort of thing. Me, I have nothing to offer, not like that anyway.'

'Yo, Ray G! Ray! C'mon over and give us some love.' Macy flung her arms wide and a morose Ray sauntered into them and more or less accepted a hug.

'Jeez, Ray, stand next to him,' said Macy, indicating me. 'It's like when I used to hang around with the plain girls at school to make me seem prettier – you two are making me look a party animal. Get into the spirit!'

'I'm not one for parties,' said Ray. 'For me it's about the writing.'

I patted him on the shoulder. 'Well said, Ray.'

'Then why are you here?' asked Macy.

Ray sighed. 'Either integrity towards literature because I'll endure this if it helps me by a single percent to move nearer to getting my book published. Or it's no integrity at all, because

I don't want to be here, and being around these people makes me a stinking low-life manwhore hypocrite.'

'Steady on, Ray,' I said.

'You're not "these people". They are.' He jabbed a finger in the direction of the judges.

From the steadily increasing crowd a ruddy-faced Meredith Mondrian appeared. Squat, frizzled, garrulous, she was always jumpy and nervous, which made her seem like a fit and healthy person, though she was morbidly overweight. She brushed some short, dyed-black hair away from her penny rounder glasses and launched into a monologue.

'Hey, you guys. How's it going? Did you hear? About Death? No? The goddamn motherhugging Grim Reaper? You didn't? Death was seen the other night. Death! Where have you been? You've heard of the triangle at Hill Fuji, at least? Well, one night last week the triangle vanished. Just disappeared.'

I kept quiet.

'And that ain't even it. We all knew that. But this morning Old Johnny Gold emerged from hibernation to say that the same night the triangle disappeared, he saw the Grim Reaper flying down Hill Fuji – flying! His feet were just above the ground, he had a cape on and he even had the scythe, which you know everyone always thought was just a fanciful image. Death has a scythe, after all! Johnny swears he wasn't drinking. He did a polygraph test at the police station. They're saying it's a sign. You know, "these are the end days" sort of thing.'

I stifled a laugh with a cough.

'Death,' said Macy uncertainly.

'Death,' I said evenly, inwardly smirking at the thought that I was mistaken for death when I felt at my most alive. I cheered up. Gratitude, gratitude.

'Everyone's saying it's a sign. What if it's a sign of – wait, isn't that your friend Archie trying to do, what, the fandango with one of the judges? What was I . . . Oh yes, whatever it's a sign of, it's nothing good. Nothing good can come of it and nothing gold can stay. Amirite? That *is* Archie, isn't it? My eyesight's getting lousier by the minute. The other day I misread "extreme unction" as "extreme unicorn"'. Goddamnit and no offence, but he's just giving alpacas a bad name.'

I started to say, 'He's a good mover, he's the origin of the phrase "party animal",' but we seemed to be looking to Ray for a contribution instead so I clammed up. Ray's melancholy eyes appeared to take the news as an affirmation of doom, which tempted me to speak up and enlighten them about 'Death'. But I couldn't. At last Ray said, 'They used to see death on the island all the time, glimpse funerals before they happened, witness strange lights hovering in the graveyard. So there might be something to it.'

'What about you?' Meredith said to Macy.

'I had this dream last night,' she replied, 'in which Gandhi goes up to a parking meter but he has no coins to feed it. So he closes his eyes, concentrates and says, "Be the change you want to see in your pocket."'

'What the hell does that mean? Is that even funny?' asked Meredith, confused. 'Oh, here's Seth, you gotta meet Seth. Seth!'

She pulled a familiar figure towards her and airkissed him on both aircheeks. It was the douchebag Archie and I had seen in the café. Taller than I remembered. Just as sleazy. I tried to get Archie's attention, I didn't want him to miss out on this, but he was flapping and boogying and thrusting his way around the floor, lost in a world of his own – well, his own and Johnny Walker's. Archie was the only one in the room dancing, but he didn't care.

The douchebag, meanwhile, suave in a tailored cherry-red

suit, his mouth wreathed into a sly charismatic smile, nodded at each of us in turn. He showed no recognition.

'Folks, this is Seth Macnamara, a guest of our island. But he's no tourist. He is actually in the B&F. Isn't that something?'

'It sure is,' I said, neutral as I could. We all named ourselves and then I asked Seth, 'What brought you here?'

'Why, of course it has always been my ambition to compete at the B&F,' he said, smiling a smarmy smile.

'Isn't he an absolute darling?' said Meredith, angling her head so it momentarily rested on the side of his upper arm.

'Oh Meredith, you're stealing my heart,' said Seth. 'But that's alright. I have three others in the freezer at home.'

Some of us laughed. Some of us - me - didn't.

'How d'you fancy your chances?' asked Macy. I realised I hadn't told Macy about this guy.

'Yeah,' he said, nodding. 'Confident.'

'No kidding,' I said. 'What are you working on at the moment?'

'A memoir and, do you know, I find this island so inspiring I've come up with an idea for a new book. I mean, this whole island feels like a film set. Today I went up to three separate strangers and asked them to repeat what they'd just said because I thought they'd fluffed their lines. And I mean, some of you people wear sundials for wristwatches? Adorable.'

'Isn't he wonderful,' said Meredith, simpering gleefully; she clapped a hand to her chest with vigour and, with her other hand, jolted her glass and spilled prosecco on herself.

Macy said, 'Hey, d'you all wanna hear my joke?'

'Do we have any choice?' Meredith said.

Macy punched her affectionately on the arm. 'Listen. So an Irishman, an Englishman and a Scotsman walk into a bar. Over a couple of drinks they discuss some problems their respective countries have faced historically due to their interactions with each other. They go home, a little wiser in the ways of being a good neighbour.'

No one laughed, though a few – me – smiled. Macy didn't take it personally because her motives were bigger than that. She's brave in that way – she can live with an implied rejection.

'Yes,' said Seth in a dismissive tone, rocking on his heels with self-importance. 'My new book. It's going to be a touching romantic narrative about a zombie who tries to kill, then runs away from, but now falls in love with, a raging necrophile.'

Meredith spluttered her drink, spraying it all down her front and onto my brogues.

'Serious?' I said.

'What's death but sleeping, only you're doing it properly for the first time.' Seth grinned, ambiguous as a cat. '"There's nothing like death," said Arthur Miller. But how did he know? He was still alive. What we can say is death is necessary, otherwise there'd be no end to the pointlessness.'

I held his gaze for a moment, then wavered and looked instead for Archie. I felt confused. I needed Archie's opinion, even his tipsy perspective would be worthwhile.

'God, I love death,' Seth was now saying. 'Why would our creator have invented death and predestined every single one of us towards it if it wasn't something very, very special indeed?'

I wondered if Seth was here for the People's Decision. Archie was doing wobbly pirouettes across the floor, occasionally bumping into people – people who were unimpressed with this ungainly alpaca's dance moves.

'You almost sound, Seth,' I heard myself saying, 'like a man who's tired of life.'

'Only when dullards like you are in it.'

I bristled. Dullards like me? He slapped a large hand on my

shoulder and grinned. 'Only kidding, my friend. I thought to myself, there's a fellow who can take a joke. Take it lightly.'

'I am,' I said, trying to smile. I turned away, blushed self-hatingly, and tried to think of a clever thing to say but all I could think was 'That man's a psychopath' and my attention fell unswervingly on Archie's dancing antics. He was about to get himself into trouble. His moves were angular, haphazard. He could hit someone.

'This could be dangerous,' I said to Macy. 'How much has he had to drink already?'

'Hell's cowbells,' said Macy, wincing. 'Quite a lot. You did realise he was drinking before we got to your house?'

'Of course,' I lied. 'But damnit, he ain't winning himself any friends here.'

People were glowering at Archie and clearly badmouthing him (and likely 'his kind'). I worried that he was indeed doing alpacahood a disservice – the very last thing he wanted to do.

'Goddamn alcohol,' I said.

'He's just been so nervous about it all, deep down,' said Macy.

'Haven't we all,' I replied. 'We gotta save him from himself, c'mon.'

I started making my way across the floor and was almost there when I realised that Meredith and Seth had followed, too.

Archie was doing some slurred scatting and his dance moves were now a mixture of body popping, pseudo-ballet, mild seizures and the Lindy Hop. I couldn't believe *this* was the fandango.

I watched for a brief moment, clicked my tongue, deciding what to do.

Okay.

'Slow down there, maestro,' I called and, reaching out, tried to put my arm round Archie to slow him down and lead him confidingly aside. But at that moment he executed a flamboyant unfurling movement and somehow managed to hit me in the face. In half an instant I'd jerked bodily away from him – cycling gives you quick reaction times – but he had clobbered me all the same. It was no biggie, though, I think I even smiled at the future memory.

Before a sozzled Archie had time to apologise, Seth yelled 'That's enough!' and hurled himself on Archie, grasping him in a violent bear hug or, I guess, alpaca hug. His voice was deafening, his actions over the top, and everyone in the hall fell quiet and stared.

'Goddamn alpaca, ruining the party!' yelled Seth, wrestling poor bewildered Archie into a headlock, sending his stetson flying.

'No,' I said. 'He's our friend – leave him – he's our pal.'

'Ow-ow-ow!' said Archie.

'Enough, man – enough!' I cried. I reached out to grab Seth but at that moment my own arms were seized. I yelped.

And as I half turned I caught a glimpse of one of the B&F's notorious security personnel looming. Hands with fingers as thick as my wrists had already twisted my arms high up behind my back.

'No, it's that guy,' I said, jerking my head in Seth's direction. 'You should be restraining him. He just attacked Archie for no reas– OUCH.'

'Sir,' said Seth, looking up at the security guard and tightening his own grip on Archie. 'This alpaca is very drunk and causing a public nuisance. Not the first time you've heard that, I'm sure. He's a danger to himself.' There was a small round of applause and a murmur of 'hear-hear's.

Archie looked as though he was struggling to breathe. His face was scrunched and lopsided, his eyes registered distress. His perma-smile was pitiful.

'Don't worry, Archie—'

'I respectfully suggest,' said Seth, 'that we remove the camelface from the premises.'

One of the security guys lashed a foot out at Archie's hind knees, kicking him so hard the poor alpaca's rear half collapsed to the floor. Archie cried out in pain.

'Leave him alone,' I said, struggling to wrench free from the grip that was now causing my shoulder blades and wrists to sizzle with pain. 'That's too tight. Let Archie—'

I heard Macy crying out but her voice was killed by the sound of Archie screaming. Seth was kicking at Archie's front legs now, forcing them to buckle so he crashed fully to the floor. Seth booted him in the chest so hard I thought he must have broken some bones and the security guard grabbed Archie's rear legs and dragged him across the floor. I burned with pain and rage but before I could say or do anything else I was lifted off the ground as if by a mechanical device and carried to the door. I felt everyone's gossiping eyes on me.

They threw Archie first; Seth and the guard had two legs each and they swung him back and forth like a sack of peats – one – two – three – before hurling him into the air. The momentum carried him a dozen feet or so then he fell with an almighty crash onto the path, the breath knocked clean out of him.

Now they did the same with me, someone holding me by the wrists, another thug clenching me by the ankles – one – two – three – they launched me into the air and, deliberately, I think, flung me through such a trajectory that I fell down straight onto Archie, wounding him further. He gasped in pain and groaned. I think he was crying softly beneath the moans.

I rolled off his warm body. 'Sorry, Archie,' I said when I'd caught my breath. 'Those hooligans. Are you – how are you?'

Archie shook his head a few millimetres, very slowly. He lay still on the ground.

'Hurts to move, old pal?' I said. I put my hand on his neck and stroked him and we lay there.

'We . . . got . . . get . . . up?' he croaked.

I turned slightly, looked over to the door. The guards were laughing: seemed they were finished with us.

'No,' I said. 'Let's just lie here for a while, Arch. Under the stars.'

The path was tarmacked smooth and did not feel too uncomfortable for now. The air was cold. I inched closer to Archie for warmth and stroked him again and again on the head and neck. The dark sky glittered with silver stars and we lay there in silence, each of us absorbed in our own thoughts yet completely aware of the other's presence.

'You'll be alright, brother,' I said. 'We'll show them. We'll show them yet.'

He didn't answer. His body shuddered. He inhaled and exhaled ragged breaths.

'If things get any better,' said Archie, 'I may have to hire someone to help me enjoy them.' He coughed. 'Ignore me. I actually feel like I can learn from all this.' He paused. 'Small egos thrive on grand gestures. The bigger, nobler thing to do is nothing.' He looked down at his plate of grasses. 'Least I'm still breathing both ways.'

Macy frowned, thinking.

I swallowed another couple of painkillers and reached for my favourite Japanese coffee mug. 'In a just society,' I said, quietly because my own voice vibrated painfully through my head, 'we wouldn't need to do anything, the authorities would—'

'Here, the authorities *hire* the thugs,' said Macy. 'And what the hell's that Seth guy about?'

'Yeah, we saw him before, Archie and I. He's a wrong 'un. Reckon he's a psychopath. Serial killer, maybe.'

Macy gave me a look. 'Your head feeling better yet?'

'Feels like someone planed the top of my head off. Or tried to and botched the attempt a few times.'

Macy and Ray Genovese had, with the help of the group of alpacas whose vehicle was parked beside Macy's, managed to drag Archie and me into the blue Datsun. Macy drove us to my blackhouse and Ray had helped patch Archie up while Macy worked on me. Ray left in the middle of the night to do some writing back home, while I fell into a sleep that was mostly unconsciousness, I think.

Today, just twelve hours after the B&F party, I felt pains in my arms, shoulders and head that respectively pierced, throbbed and pounded. Archie looked as though he had crossed the pain threshold into sheer numbness. My kitchen had a subdued atmosphere it had likely never experienced before.

'At least there'll be people who were caning the booze last night and probably feel worse than you two combined,' said Macy.

For a while no one spoke.

In the distance, church bells rang, far enough away that they didn't clang in my head; they pulled at an innermost piece of me. I've always thought of church bells as being equal parts poignant, beautiful, grounding, ethereal. A golden oblong of sunlight swooned through the window and fell on my old red-and-white chequered tablecloth. We all looked at it and without saying so, felt a little soothed.

'Hey,' I said quietly. 'Nice moment. Despite everything.'

We sat in slow silence again, thinking, drinking, eating.

'Hatred for someone is a way of taking an interest in them,' said Archie at length. 'It shows you're curious about them.'

I gave a small nod. 'They hate alpacas because deep down they secretly want to be one.'

Macy gave me a look. 'Thank you, professor. No. But it *is* a messed-up society. The other day,' she said, 'I was talking to someone – was it yourself? – who said we live in an age of narcissism and entitlement. Yet it's also the age of knowledge. How can we reconcile these contradictions?'

'Because knowledge is not wisdom,' I said. 'We devalue literature even as we commodify–'

Archie held up a hoof to quieten me (nicely, like a true friend can without seeming rude). 'The other day I bought a book on Zen and somebody had already written my annotations in it. Imagine! The margins were filled with handwritten notes, the exact thoughts I *would've* had, except in someone else's handwriting. I hope people don't confuse my apparent criticisms of Tibetan with Zen, which I – ouch. My brain's in splinters. No, see, the story I was going to read at the B&F was actually about–'

'Whoa, whoa, whoa,' said Macy. 'Hold your horses there, Laureate of the Alpacas. There are at least two things wrong with that sentence. First of all, you know you can't tell anyone anything about your story.'

'Unless you want to tell me,' I said, somewhat joking.

'And secondly, you are *so* going to read at the B&F. "I was going to read" does not compute. Hell, you are going to read at the B&F more than ever!'

'That I agree with,' I said. 'All the alpacas I saw yesterday had flags and badges and posters supporting you. You're a folk hero.'

'I'm kinda physically broken, which is fine. I feel mentally washed out, though, and that's a thousand times worse.' He sighed. 'I just can't do it, the B&F. You don't know what this is like.'

'You can. You must. You will,' said Macy, bringing her fist down on the table with each pronouncement.

I winced. 'No fist-gavelling, Macy – my head. But yeah, Archie. The alpacas are counting on you, and a good many humans, too.'

'My kind aren't welcome. My kind wouldn't win.'

'You wouldn't be in the B&F if you weren't welcome and talented. And if "your kind" wouldn't win then all the more reason, isn't it, to go ahead and win,' I said.

'We believe in you, Archie. And so do the alpacas, north and south. This could be massive,' said Macy. 'We love you. You maybe don't realise this, but you're a beautiful alpaca, you're an intelligent, energetic, amazing alpaca who improves the day-to-day lives of people and alpacas. Everything about you exudes friendliness and wit. What I mean is – you're very special.'

'Sactly,' I said. 'You can't let those idiots beat you.'

'They beat me good and proper last night.'

'Yes, physically. But not in other ways, the important ways.'

'That's kind of what my story's—'

'Save it,' Macy and I said together.

'Let's agree,' I said, 'that we all compete and all three of us do our best. And if one of us wins we make a speech in support of alpaca rights.'

'That's a great idea,' said Macy.

We gently chinked coffee mugs.

Macy laughed. 'Now all we gotta do is win!'

Archie's expression changed. He nodded slowly, looked at Macy then at me. His eyes teared up.

Macy slammed her hand down on the table. I flinched and laid my hand on hers and Archie placed his hoof on top of both.

'For alpacahood,' said Archie.

'For alpacahood.'

'For alpacahood.'

The B&F

Midsummer's Day. The morning of the Brilliant & Forever. After an island night so pure and thick with stars you couldn't put a finger's breadth between them, a crisp morning arose and the stars faded and the sky shone a bluish silver, the streets and trees and tombstones glistening with dew. My mind was wide open, glittering with remembered starlight.

Now at ten a.m. the day was medium sunny and blue skied, promising warmth rather than heat, which was ideal. The crowds were assembling in front of the castle, on the green velvety grass that might be churned into mud by the end of the day.

The stage was set up with a B&F sponsorship banner, central microphone, a long table to the rear at which the seven judges would sit, and large screens on either side of the stage, broadcasting live so that the 20,000 people and alpacas could see the authors' expressions as they read.

The front rows were reserved for B&F dignitaries and sponsors and their relatives and friends, then there were some rows of seats for wealthy whitehousers, and everyone else stood, in generally well-behaved, if ill defined, lines. Those at the very back of the audience, the least well off of the blackhousers and all the alpacas, were actually standing on slabs of rock on the shoreline.

The competition always took many hours, but there was

never very much restlessness in the crowd, a fact that surprised visitors and was a matter of deep pride to locals. Because I regularly did long bike rides (100 miles plus, ie five or six hours in the saddle), I found the stamina required none too demanding, but when I was a kid the B&F experience was gruelling – until, of course, the Decisions.

People can have grave misconceptions about literary readings. They believe, for example, that readings are more fulfilling for the writer than the audience. They think being a member of an audience at a literary reading is an act of altruism. They suppose their face and everyone's face must eventually slowdroop into the silent anguish of tedium – glazed eyes, toothachey smiles, pleading frowns. But the B&F is nothing like that.

By ten fifteen everyone had gathered into groups of family, friends and neighbours, and they stood around gossiping. Most folk had a similar routine: a large breakfast at home, a visit to the toilet (B&F comfort breaks were anything but comfortable), a close read of the event programme and some money invested/squandered via QuickQuidSid, the local bookmaker who had a monopoly on the betting, being a judge's cousin.

I stood with my arm hanging around Archie's neck. He was studying the programme for the umpteenth time. I'd naturally invited him to spend the night at my house – it's a tradition we've eased into – and I fed him an exquisite (if you like that sort of thing) five grass breakfast, which he had vomited over my kitchen floor, so rattled were his nerves, though he blamed it on me. I hadn't prepared the grasses badly – to prove it, I'd even eaten some of the marram grass myself. You have to be very dedicated to your alpaca friend before you can confront a taste like that. The earthy green dewy flavour awakens some innermost part of you, a primitive, animal-like portion of you that is as ancient as the very drive to live. It is like eating the past, or the ground itself, perfumed with mud and urine and river water, a taste that acknowledges the earth we shall one day lie under.

Yet it hadn't made me sick. Archie offered to clean his vomit up, but I liked the work of mopping as it took my own mind off the B&F. Archie had shuffled about, silently mouthing words to himself, practising his story or rehearsing possible answers for his interview. He had hailed a taxi to the Castle Green and I'd cycled. Took me a while to learn it, but this was the best way to conquer nerves: hard physical exercise. The symptoms of stage fright – accelerated heart rate, sweating, blood thudding in the ears – are pretty much those of intense cycling. Even though my reading wasn't for quite a while, I felt better for the bike ride and knew its effects would carry through and help keep me centred for my reading.

Here we were, standing in the gathering crowd, feeling the near tangible excitement and apprehension of the Brilliant & Forever.

'I can't believe Macy's up first,' said Archie, for the dozenth time today.

'Like I said, she's fine with it. She wants to get it over with.'

'There's that,' Archie conceded. 'But,' he lowered his voice to an anxious whisper, 'no one who read first has ever won it.'

'Neither has an alpaca, for that matter.' Even as I spoke I couldn't believe I said that.

'Oh god,' said Archie and distress flared in his eyes.

'No, no – sorry. No.' I patted his shoulder. 'I just mean, don't be defeatist.'

A tall blond man in front turned his head fractionally and said, loud enough for us to hear, 'There's the fandango-dancing alpaca that's reading, if anyone wants a laugh later.' And quite a few people did laugh at his comment.

I stared at the back of the man's head, sensed Archie looking at me from the side. 'Your own work not good enough for the B&F?' I asked, with a firm, even edge to my voice.

Blondie whirled round and sneered at me. 'My writing's more than skilled enough to beat an alpaca.' He as good as spat the last word out; some of his saliva flew into my face like rain spatters.

I smiled at him with sweet malevolence. 'Obviously not, since you're not in the competition. By the way, would you like to borrow Archie's spittoon?'

This earned a deal of laughter. 'He's got you there,' one of his friends said. Blondie turned away, muttering.

I wiped my face with a sleeve. 'Right,' I said, to distract and refocus Archie, 'let's see that programme again.'

I flicked past the author bio pages – they'd used an old, almost comically ugly photograph of me – and we looked at the running order:

Singing of the Anthem
Macy Starfield
Ray Genovese
Summer Kelly
J-M-Boy
Peter Projector-Head
Tabitha Tessington
Lunch
Me
Myrtle Budd
Archie the Alpaca
Tan the Ageist
Calvin O Blythe
Seth Macnamara

Stella
The Judges' Decision
The People's Decision

At ten thirty sharp, the wordy, long-since 'anonymously commissioned' anthem, *Island of Mine, You're a Beautiful Story for All Time*, was bleated out on trumpets and bagpipes and hurdy-gurdies and those who knew the words droned along. This was nearly everyone (first verse and chorus), the righteous few (second verse) and the B&F organisers (third verse).

While the song was trundling along – you could feel its desultory rumble vibrating through the ground, shaking your feet – I sensed Archie looking around and I guessed he was scoping out how many alpacas were here (a good turn out), how many were northern alpacas (about three fifths, discernible by the mustard stetsons they favoured) and how many southern (black stetsons, two fifths, standing recognisably apart from the northerners).

As the anthem fell away to a kind of silence in which coughs and foot-and-hoof shufflings were almost embarrassingly audible, a slim man with a red handlebar moustache approached the microphone. John XYZ Johnstone was a wilfully eccentric writer and relentless self-publicist who, via his 'vital and terrific' or 'pointless and terrible' novel *Plate on a Table*, had either earned or bought a major literary award which I can't bring myself to talk about here.

'Ladies and gentlemen,' he said.

'And alpacas,' Archie said under his breath.

'It gives me great—' His next few words were destroyed by a shriek of feedback. '—here today. This is partly because the rest of the world could learn a tremendous amount from your passion for literature. And partly because I was in a bookshop one evening recently after a long day's novel writing. I remember that night well, for believe it or not the evening was spread out against the sky exactly like T. S. Eliot etherised upon a table. Not to mention a cloud up there floated darkly and looked like it wrote confessional poetry, smoked heavily and had converted to Anglo-Catholicism. Now, isn't that remarkable?'

Apparently it was, since the judges and B&F front-rowers were in an uproar of laughter.

John XYZ Johnstone smiled indulgently at his own 'wit' and continued. 'I walked into this bookshop and I was confronted by an extraordinary shelf, which I spent a great deal of time perusing. And let me tell you I was never more proud of the island's literature. Because here, on this particular shelf, were the significant books of my time. And, get this – they were laid out on the shelf, spine to spine, in the very order in which I had read them. Amazing!

'There was Roderick MacGyver's book *The Sweet Antelope Ate a Bitter Cantaloupe*, which first inspired me to try my hand at poetry. That hand was later to shake MacGyver's own hand as he handed me the Banker and Cupcake Bookwriting Award.'

Some applause smattered.

John XYZ Johnstone resumed. 'Then there was a book by Sandy Beaches, whom I met at college. And beside it, a book by Gregory Kaftan, the first published author whom I called a friend. Then a book by the first poet I punched outside a pub. Well, come on, ladies and gentlemen – it has to be done. Then a book by Madelina Argentina, the first author, if you'll permit me the indiscretion, the first famous author with whom I, as it were, slept. Then one by one, books by authors whom I met at various book festivals, all these books shelved in the order in which I had met their respective authors. At the end of the shelf stood my own two books, those which have been called classics of their type, works of unique brilliance, stories of genius and other' – he swept a bony hand in the direction of fake modesty – 'embarrassingly fulsome praise of that nature. And beside my own humble bestsellers, and here I get to the point of my little speech, were the notebooks. Yearning, I say to you, *yearning* to be filled. Thank you very much.'

His cadaverous figure gave a bow. And again. And again.

Archie and I exchanged looks while John XYZ Johnstone basked in his average-level applause.

Dalston Moomintroll bounded heavily across the stage and clapped him on the back.

'Isn't he marvellous? John XYZ Johnstone. There he goes.'

As John XYZ Johnstone retreated from the stage, walking backwards, bowing, Dalston Moomintroll gurgled a few obsequious laughs. Dalston Moomintroll was a round red-faced man whose head was bald at the front, though a grey ponytail hung down ingloriously at the back. He wore a tailored black suit and his trademark bowler hat, tilted back in a way that made his forehead look grotesquely large. 'John XYZ Johnstone. Whose books are also available on non-magically-autobiographically-organised bookshelves, and nowhere more so than our bookshop stall, conveniently situated between the famous castle and the, shall we say, equally infamous portaloos.

'Well, I'm sure you all know who I am – Dalston Moomintroll. And that it's my privilege to compere the Brilliant & Forever, introducing the authors and indeed sharing a brief discussion with them after they've read.

'You are, I know, familiar with the format. After all of our authors have presented their work, we shall have the Judges' Decision and then the People's Decision. Remember, we are judging the authors on their writing primarily, not their actual performance per se.

'Well, without any further ado, it behoves me to introduce the first author of this year's Brilliant & Forever. She – for it is a she – has many strings to her bow. She recently gave up her dishwashing job and took up the captaining of a fishing boat.' He chuckled. 'They'll be giving them the vote next.'

Dalston Moomintroll's patronising words evoked a general murmuring of disapproval in the audience. I seethed. 'She's got more talent in a single toenail clipping than that prick will ever have in his life,' I said to Archie.

'He'll get his.'

'No he won't, he's been doing this for years. I reckon there's an underlying homophobia, too.'

'God help him if he pisses Macy off. She can look after herself.'

What Archie said was true. Macy's face appeared on the screen; she gave Dalston Moomintroll a wry smile, one eyebrow raised, as if to say, 'That's all you got? I won't waste my time'.

And here she was, approaching the mic in miniature life-size on the reality of the stage and in simultaneous massive close-up on the twenty-foot screens either side.

Macy faced down the audience with a winning confidence. There were some gestures of disgruntled body language from the more conservative elements in the audience: sighs, rolled eyes, shrugs. Perhaps going first would work against Macy, after all. People were geared up for something, someone, they could immediately and assuredly love, to generate a happy, bonded feeling among their gathered thousands. Macy was a divisive kind of person, being neither the average islander nor the person the average islander aspired to be.

She had her supporters, though. Many in the crowd, human and alpaca, of varying ages and genders, admired her for being a strong woman and a talented writer. QuickQuidSid had given her respectful odds on being outright winner. Earlier, I'd put seven days' dishwashing wages on her winning. And the same amount on Archie winning. QuickQuidSid had wiped his boozer's nose; he couldn't hide his smirk so well that I didn't glimpse it. Another dim-minded one who looked down on alpacas. 'Good luck,' he'd said, in a tone that could almost have seemed earnest but was really, I thought, sarcastic.

'Yeah,' I said. 'Hey, who d'you think's going to win?'

He swiped a finger across his nose again. 'I'm sure I couldn't say. Maybe the girl that was in America, Summer, whatsit, Summer Kelly. Maybe her.'

'Nope,' I said. 'You. You're the one who always wins here. You and the judges, who pay themselves handsomely to do the little they do.'

He gave some approximation of a pained smile. 'Now, now. Don't be a sore loser – er, that is if you do lose, which I'm sure you won't.'

'I'm sure you're sure I will.' I frowned. 'Hey, what odds you got me at, anyway?'

He blushed and vaguely gestured towards the chalkboard. I expected relatively poor odds, but the 100–1 stung me senseless.

'Oh,' I said. 'Um. Oh.'

QuickQuidSid leaned in towards me, reeking of garlic and vodka and Blue Stratos. 'Here. Word of advice. Put a bundle on yourself. Then if – when – you do win, you're quids in.' He chuckled wheezily as though he were doing me a favour.

I had turned and walked away.

So now Macy, potential outright winner and my best human friend, stood, one foot planted either side of the microphone, and said, 'Thank you,' in a clear, strong voice. Her confidence made me grin. 'My piece is called 'Homer and the Cèilidh'. For those of you unfamiliar with the word, a cèilidh is an informal gathering in which neighbours come together to share songs, stories, poems.' She looked around. 'Kinda not unlike this, but non-competitive.'

It was a brave or foolhardy choice to use a word in our indigenous language, which caused nausea immediately in a number of people in the audience, and near apoplexy in some of the judges. One of them turned purply-red and moved flailingly around, in distress, as if seeking something to vomit into. If Macy used any more non-English words, some people, I knew, would be physically sick and/or become aggressive. Surely Macy hadn't planned to sabotage this by reading an entire piece in our language?

'Come on, Macy,' I mouthed. I realised I had crossed my fingers, something I hadn't done since I was a child.

In that steady, powerful voice, Macy read:

Homer and the Cèilidh

Everyone took their turn at the cèilidh except Homer. Donald sang his song about the Jacobite rebellion, his voice quivering through age and whisky. Michiko told a sober and therefore terrifying story about how the insects we kill in this life come back to nibble at the flesh of our buried selves and how we, too, are brought back to life, temporarily, just to feel the needling agony of the insects' gnawing.

That put a cold tingling through us and we moved a little closer to the fire and Marin took out his guitar and fingerpicked a fizzing, summery sort of melody that restored us to good humour. And when Carson followed that up with a risqué joke at Gabriel's expense, we bellowed with laughter.

All of us, that is, except Homer. He sat back, a small thin shape a half-tone lighter than the shadows. We didn't know much about him, other than the obvious. He was a quiet, unobtrusive man with plain, regular features. We barely noticed him when he turned up, so placidly did he saunter into the village one day. We did, of course, welcome him wholeheartedly. We're known for our warmth here. He received our greetings with a shy mumble – you could hardly hear what he was saying – and we quickly understood he was one of those people who doesn't like drawing attention to himself.

Homer's manner was so subtle as to be almost characterless.

His presence was a kind of absence. Karin, being a poet, described him once as being 'like the smell of fresh water – essential and essentially non-existent'.

In the early days I invited him to stay at my house, intuitively emphasising how he would have absolute freedom to come and go as he pleased. I pictured him being like a shadowy cat that goes about its private concerns without flourish – observant, silent, self-contained. Homer's reply was too soft to hear, but I recognised it as a polite, bland, well-practised rejection of my offer.

No one knew where he slept. In a barn? We looked out for indentations in the hay, a stashed-away jacket, a surreptitious bag containing . . . what? Homer left no more trace than a bird leaves in the sky.

Every kind of rumour went scuttling round the village. He'd had a mental breakdown. (But he seemed as sane as any of us.) He'd had his heart broken. (I never met a less passionate person.) He had a wet brain. (Again, he was compos mentis; plus, we're the last community that should be accusing anyone of that.) He was secretly composing an epic story about us. (Don't make me laugh. Nothing happens here. I'd like to know whose ego thought up a rumour of such colossal vanity.)

We had many a cèilidh that year and Homer was a regular guest. But never a participant. Perhaps he didn't appreciate that it was considered rude not to take one's turn. Perhaps he didn't care.

Of one thing we were certain; the man was renowned everywhere as a storyteller of genius. Did he simply wish to avoid embarrassing the rest of us? Because that, to my mind, was the kind of humility that full-circles into deep arrogance. And yet he didn't seem the conceited kind of man. He didn't seem the anything kind of man.

84

Winter came and it was a severe one and this affected our general temperament. On the night of that final cèilidh, I had taken a drink – most of us had – but my memory of it is very clear. The air in the house was icy, as if the large fire weren't blazing away there, licking brightly against the tasteless dead bone of night. We were a bit restless to start with, like animals possessed by an eerie uneasiness. I had a sudden insight that the fire in its hearth was a lifeless and meaningless thing, with no more vitality or heat or sparkle than the stars up in the sky, pointless distances away. I saw that time was a sick, humourless joke, grinding us down into the grave, itself a ditch of nothingness without even the novelty of insect-touch. There wasn't a song or story or poem or tune that could save us. I found myself turning to Homer and snarling, 'Tonight, everyone's taking their turn – sharing a story, song, anything – and that includes you, Homer.' The room went quiet and everyone turned to look at the far corner where Homer was slouched in the darkness and he didn't move but with a deliberate unspoken effort we all just kept looking at him, willing him to say or do something and minutes passed and still he didn't move and after a while time spasmed and Homer started weeping but still he didn't move and then we realised that the shadow in the corner was just that, a shadow, and Homer was long gone and the crying, in fact, came from one of us and to be truthful it has never really stopped.

There was a pause. Everyone, myself included, had expected her piece to be longer, given that she was a real contender, and it was often the longer pieces of writing that won, but there was no doubting the power of her short story. She received a very strong round of applause and some 'yeah!'s and a few outright whoops. It seemed the kind of story you immediately wanted to read again, to get its nuances, and as a live audience we didn't have that option. Still, it left a good impression.

Just . . . not an overwhelming impression. I thought it was a story I could grow to love, with a couple more readings. I was a little worried for her.

Dalston Moomintroll said, 'Thank you, Macy Starfield. "Homer and the . . ."' He paused, stricken. '"Homer and the . . ."' He couldn't say the word. He despised our language, a language his own ancestors and some of his living relatives spoke. 'Homer and the other classicists are a big influence, then?'

I could have laughed at his 'save' but I was too tense.

'I love Homer,' Macy said. 'He taught me the power of storytelling. And he taught me personal growth is possible even, or especially, in adversity.'

Dalston Moomintroll mugged at the audience. 'So you think he existed?'

Macy's withering look was all the answer he needed.

'It was certainly a very . . . thought-provoking story. Very fine.'

I brightened inside. Dalston Moomintroll tended not to give compliments like that to writers unless he believed they were in the running to win. And if he thought so, the judges likely did, too. This endorsement had a knock-on effect on the audience – gamblers and non-gamblers alike.

Yes. Macy was a real contender. The judges wrote notes in leather-bound books, impassive.

Macy walked off stage with, I thought, a kind of subdued confidence. I knew her well enough to read the subtext of her body language. The slight sashay in her hips was usually a sign that she was consciously trying to make herself look more assured than she really felt.

Dalston Moomintroll took to the microphone again. 'Well now what an opening to this year's B&F. And we have plenty more surprises in store, I'm sure. I want to quickly remind everyone that one of our sponsors has a stall set up beside the food tepees; the well-known photographer Ahab Klintoff is taking portraits of you, your family, perhaps even you with some of the judges or other literary celebrities, right there for very reasonable prices. "Ahab Klintoff, Portrait Photographer, Shooting People Successfully Since 1998."

'And next up, patrons of the Nightingale with Toothache café will be no stranger to overpriced coffee – just a joke, just my little joke, folks. Jeez. And nor will they be a stranger to this next gentleman, who always reminds me of a cowboy, with his cool demeanour and his muddy coffee. Joke, I said!

'In the interests of fairness, I should say it is equally likely he composes a mean gingerbread latte. I don't know. I've never tried one at the Nightingale with Toothache. Do they sell gingerbread lattes? Perhaps he can tell us. Ladies and gentlemen and not forgetting alpacas, please welcome Ray Genovese.'

Ray Genovese walked slowly with a slight swagger over to the microphone, an expression between blankness and solemnity etched on his face. As he moved towards us, the audience, he looked like he was approaching a grim boxing match with a huge cash prize, and he knew the fight was rigged, but he was going to win the fight or die trying anyhow.

He seized the mic and sized us up. His lips curled into a half-smile. 'Alright,' he said, in his deep Johnny Cash bass-baritone, a voice as measured and defensive as his walk. 'I don't know what you were expecting. But this is called "Late".'

He paused for a moment.

And said: 'Don't look so forlorn.'

Many people burst out laughing. It was so unexpected, so

self-effacing in context that he immediately won over those indifferent to or intimidated by his demeanour. Ray shrugged and smiled.

'Classy,' I heard someone say. 'You gotta like someone who can make fun of himself.'

The screen showed a close-up of Ray's eyes, now twinkling. It zoomed out to show his figure standing confident and strong. He nodded. 'Still, don't expect any great witticisms or slapstick, either.'

There was low laughter and very many smiles. Ray had thought this through. Though he had yet to start reading, I mentally added him to my 'possible winners' list, and, further back in my mind, my 'give-more-respect-to' list. What I knew of his writing was like the little I knew of the man himself: enigmatic with a touch of melancholy and an overall likeability.

He read in a rich, calm voice that resonated well:

Late

The girl at the bus stop grinned hard, tilted her head, slipped her tingling hand into mine and softly tugged me onto the number 33. It was late. I felt like she needed to tell me something. As Rome's sparkling lights glided past, we sat close together on the leather seats and there were these terrific frissons and we talked about the shows we'd seen, where our weird accents were from, how gorgeously the full August moon glowed, how equally stunning her face looked (I said this, and she didn't disagree, but carried on smiling madly as though a kitten were kissing at her toes) and then, when leaning in, whisper-exclaiming something about the moon, her lips almost touched my ear and I quivered with full-body goosebumps.

The bus pulled up alongside a hotel – my hotel, I realised with a happy frown. The journey had been so fast and smooth I felt limousined there, and on alighting I thanked the driver, and checked my hand when it reached into my pocket searching for a tip.

Inside the hotel, there was no one at reception.

'What's our room number?' she said as we climbed the lavish staircase. My arm had found its home in hers.

I fished in my pocket again, this time producing a key-card, and I handed it over. She beamed and guided me to the door. I felt like she still needed to tell me something but maybe she had temporarily changed her mind. The room was large, gently lit. We sank down, smiling, into exhausted sleep with such a synchronising of breath I half imagined we would share the same dream, maybe something about twins swimming in tandem, streaming breaststroke through the night sky like a whole new emotion.

Morning opened like a Japanese novel and I wanted to tell her so, using words like understated, askew, natural, perfect. But she was gone from the bed.

'Morning,' she said, startling me. I turned. She stood sober, collected, already dressed, handing me a glass. 'Got you some tomato juice.'

I sipped, tasted blood. 'What's wrong?'

She laughed. 'Drink it all down.'

I did. 'Wait – you're leaving?'

'I gotta be somewhere.'

'You are somewhere.'

'It's nine fifteen. I'm already late.'

'You can't leave. I'm going to kidnap you.' The way I said it just didn't sound right.

She glanced at a wall, looked at her watch, analysed briefly a fingernail. Her black hair swayed heavy where it was still damp. She wore no make-up. Somewhere a clock ticked, moving us forward.

'You are every bit as beautiful without make-up.'

She brightened for a moment as though seeing herself in my mind the way I saw her. I pulled her close, pressed a hot slow meaningful kiss onto the back of her hand.

'Silly,' she said. 'I gotta go. I'm so late. I'm going.' I felt like there was something she couldn't tell me.

'Call me?' I said. She let me give her my number. I traced the words 'Tell me' onto her thigh with my finger, a secret gesture.

What I wanted was to have her undress, slide back into bed with me, let me hug her and kiss her and praise her and listen to her for the rest of the day.

I was to spend two decades composing poems about her smiling beauty, only to burn all of them, inadequate.

I know myself, know that if someone, something, offered to give me the rest of that day with her in exchange for, say, cutting my life short by ten or fifteen years, I would sign my blood away and thank him, it.

The power to make someone feel complete or empty is terrible. Anyway, she left.

I lay there, brimful with a kind of ongoing mental hunger, a craving, an emptiness that hurts even though it's as empty as what you can't remember from before you were born.

That emptiness subsides, but don't kid yourself. Ten, fifteen years later, when it chooses to, the emptiness will rise up and crush you. Rome is half a world away and she . . . she is altogether further away than that. I am no longer me. Time grows slowly, reveals itself to be made of bone. The moon is an inhospitable chunk of rock. In real life no one smiles as hard as a skull does, that should tell us all something.

I heard quite a few 'wow's from the crowd at the end of Ray's reading. I believe he moved up in the whole island's estimation that day. The audience loved him. I think it's fair to say many women were looking at this dour guy from the café in a new, wounded, romantic light.

He gave a slow, informal, and very cool salute to the audience and sauntered off stage, shaking his head at Dalston Moomintroll, who was asking him to stay to answer a few questions. Put Ray in a leather jacket – hell, put Ray on a book jacket – the guy was just very, very cool.

'One way or another, that guy's on to a winner tonight,' said Archie.

Maybe, I thought, the power to make someone feel complete or empty is inherent in literature, too. 'He was really good,' I said. 'Look! Here she is!'

Macy was threading her way through the crowd to us. Some people were staring at her, looking at her with fresh eyes, now that they had seen something of her mind.

I opened my arms wide. 'Hey Macy-Mace, that was fantastic. You were so great. Really confident, and that piece, oh my god – I need to read that in print.'

She pressed into me, warm with need. 'You really liked it?' Her hair smelled of coconut.

'Loved it,' I said. 'I'm so proud of you. Email me a copy today. I was yearning to reread it right away. Well done.' I kissed her head.

Macy unpeeled herself and embraced Archie.

'Macy,' said Archie, 'it was terrific. You were terrific. Just the right amount of darkness and I, you know, I just didn't know where it was going. And then BAM. It took you to the place it just had to go.'

'It did,' I said. 'It really opened up something in me.'

Macy stood between us as we faced the stage. 'Aw, thank you both. I'm so nervous. I love you guys.' She gave my hand and Archie's neck a gentle squeeze.

'Ssh,' said a prickly voice from somewhere. 'We listened to you.'

We shushed. As a general rule it was rude to talk when a writer was reading, though not when Dalston Moomintroll was introducing one, and we'd missed his intro for Summer Kelly, who now breezed across the stage carrying a beer in one hand and, all around her, a fake-it-till-you-make-it confidence which I think most of the audience saw through and found endearing. She was young – twenty-two – but youth could be an advantage in the B&F. An agent might sign you up as the next big thing, a sexy commodity. A young writer could be outrageous, precocious, immature, drunk; these, in youth, are eccentricities, or can be spun that way.

Summer was not sober, but not drunk either. She was pretty in a quirky way bookish folk might find appealing.

'Summer's hot,' I said.

'Death and Summer have such fine breasts,' said Macy.

I gave the admiring grin-and-nod of the conquered in smartassedness.

Yet. My fear for Summer was that her inner self and the versions she projected seemed at odds with themselves. I knew all about that. I could imagine her 'needing' the artificial courage of society's favourite poison at every reading she did. And in time either her confidence would increase or her alcohol dependency would. If she were to win the B&F, it could immortalise *and* destroy her.

'She's real competition,' said Macy and when I didn't respond she poked me in the ribs and added, 'Isn't she?'

I watched Summer take a hefty swig from the beer bottle. 'I know her a bit,' I said. 'And like her a lot. Almost feel like I want to protect her from all this. She gives off this air of bravado, but you can tell she's totally vulnerable.'

'You think she'll win?'

'I hope not. For her sake. And yours.' I sighed. 'Long as she doesn't get the People's.'

Someone shushed us again. We quietened, focused on the stage.

'Hey,' said Summer, tilting the microphone towards her lips. 'So, here's the thing. This story's kinda long, but, y'know,

I kinda like it. I like think it's the best thing I've done? And plus there's humour in it, so like, maybe you'll enjoy it, right?'

Many people called back, 'Right!'

Another one popular with the crowd.

'It's not supposed to be taken literary – oops, I mean literally.'

The crowd laughed indulgently, encouragingly, at her minuscule faux pas and as Summer used the opportunity to drink some more, I noticed the tinge of embarrassment that coloured her face.

'Anyway, yeah, it's not meant to be taken too literally when – well, you'll see what I mean. And, um, yeah. So this comes from the time I spent in America and, uh, it's really meant to be read in an American accent, which I can't do even though I spent all those months over there. Can you like pretend it's in an American accent and then, uh . . .'

Perhaps it's cruel to say that an older, less kooky writer would have possibly lost the audience at this point, but Summer's inexperience was coming across as charm. I think, as with Ray, some members of the audience were falling in love with Summer. Not Macy, though. 'I'm kind of finding this girl irritating and superficial,' she said. 'I like my "kooky" chocolate chip.'

At any rate, I felt anxiety for Summer again. Could very, very well be she deserved success by virtue of her loveliness as a human being, but I could see success ruining her.

'So like maybe I should just read the story.'

Maybe.

She drew a long swig from her bottle, motioned for someone at the side of the stage to bring her another, and began to read:

I'm Your Inner Goddess, Dumbass

'Seek thine inner goddess,' the book said. What it neglected to mention was that my inner goddess is a four-foot tall, three-eyed, crow-faced Tibetan orange-eyebrowed deity named Kakasya.

But hey, I'm getting ahead of myself.

I'm Sam. Just your average New Havenite. All about good music, bad television, downbeat lyrics, upbeat poetry, weak lattes, strong liquor. Riley is my actually kooky friend in a college full of fakes, squares and losers. She has pink and green hair done in mahoosive liberty spikes and a tattoo of an anchor and instead of saying 'Be True to Yourself' it says, I shityounot, 'Beetroot to yourself' and if you look closely there's a jar of beetroot resting against the anchor. She's insane! Know where she got that done? Coney Island. Know where else? On her left butt cheek.

We met reaching for the same Hershey bar at the same time in the same downtown store.

'Nuh-uh, dude,' she said and I think, in fact it's likely, she wagged a finger at me. 'That Hershey bar is *my* destiny. Don't get the gods of Hershey karma pissed at you.'

'Or what,' I said, 'they'll boil me alive in fiery chocolate?'

I remember outside the store we halved the Hershey bar and we got on so well outsmartassing each other with riffs on chocolate and fate that it seemed natural to go to a bar and bond over a small tableful of Chivas Regals. How many twenty year olds do you know who drink Chivas Regal?

What we can't remember is who actually bought the Hershey – we have a running joke about that. One of us will say, 'I think I paid for the Hershey of Fate.' Then the other will put on her best comedy-woeful face and say grimly, like referring to our friendship, 'I've been paying for it ever since.'

So we headed up to Montana for spring vacation. We both always had a love of the name Montana and we both had some idea it was a place of, like, air so pure it vacuumed out your lungs, and majestic mountains and friendly animals and green rivers and tumbling waterfalls and all that epic cinematic shit. We had a few rules about our road trip (we called it a road trip even though we flew there).

1. Be spontaneous.
2. Do one thing every day you've never done before.
3. Stick together even if we have one of our minor falling-outs.
4. Read to each other by flashlight every night, even though the cabin is electrificated.

We'd pretty much broken rules one, two and four by day two. Oh yeah, rule four was based around my copy of a book called *And the Hippos Were Boiled in Their Tanks*, which was written by William S. Burroughs and Jack Kerouac. We both have a love-hate relationship with the Beats. Some of them were horrible human beings, and hypocrites, which obvy wasn't good – all that gaybashing while being practising homosexuals or bisexuals. All that misogyny. Let's face it, all that bad writing. Not to say they weren't amazing writers at their superbest.

But this book is interesting because Burroughs and Kerouac wrote it one chapter each and it's about a real-life murder they were kinda implicated in, though they didn't actually commit murder. Well, you could say Burroughs did when he William Telled his wife. Or, as Riley put it, 'William *Told* his wife.' So each night we were going to read two chapters – Riley a Kerouac chapter and I a Burroughs one. Problem was we finished the book on the third night (Riley's verdict: 'Shame the *hippies* weren't boiled in their tanks') on account of the fact that we deliberately did no research about the place where we hired the cabin and turned out it was a teeny-tiny end-of-nowhere shithole with nothing to do. There was a lake and a wood. But no people our age.

We browsed the main street's half-dozen stores, which took about ten seconds, we loaded up on wine and chocolate and stuff and then in some used-goods store we picked up this book for a dime. A dime! What can you buy for a dime these days? As Riley stage whispered, 'Even the prices in this place are backwards'. The guy that sold it to us had one working eye and a permanent dribbling grin.

We took our groceries and stuff back to the cabin and opened a bottle of red to make time move faster and funner. We sat on the porch and raised a scuffed 'Montana: The Last Best Place' mug each.

'Cheers, big ears.'

'In your face, big . . . face.'

We sipped wine for a while.

'Mmm,' I said. 'Tinged with blackcurrant notes and quiet counterpoints of vanilla, and . . .' I smacked my lips fussily a few times. 'Yes, I do believe it kicks like a professional asskicker.' I gave a relenting grimace. 'My tongue feels like it's been dipped in a sewer full of diesel and paint stripper.'

'Worth four and a half bucks of anyone's money. Hey how 'bout this? It's literally impossible to know how many chameleons there are in the world.'

'I wonder what kind of noise chameleons make.'

'Yeah, cos, like, if you can identify the sound, you can at least know there's a chameleon around somewhere,' said Riley. She took a hefty mouthful of wine and nodded. 'That's the moral of that story.'

'They truly are the ninjas of the animal world. To the chameleons.' We clinked mugs. 'Wherever they may be.'

'Ideally, the noise a chameleon makes should be silence.'

'When, actually, *this* is the noise chameleons make.' Riley smiled to herself, cleared her throat and began: 'Sniff-sniff-kaWOOba-kaWOOba-ickySNORE-ickySNORE-doom-doom-doom. Sniff-sniff-kaWOOba-kaWOOba-ickySNORE-icky SNORE-doom-doom-doom.'

We lay back on the porch and goofed around making cartoon versions of animal and bird noises. My diva-wolf howl and her angst-ridden cicada were, we unanimously agreed, the best.

We sipped wine for a while, and then remembered the book we bought for a dime so we went inside the old log cabin and sat on the floor cross-legged and studied it.

I can't tell you what it was called because there is no way you should be Googling that kinda shit and in any case I already Googled it and there's nothing on the interwebz about it, which is to say the book must be rare and to be honest if it was the only copy in the world it would be one too many. Tells you something that Riley and I coulda got seriously stinking rich but eventually burned the book instead.

The book was like two hundred years old and was illustrated with these crazyass black-and-white ink prints that looked like something Ginsberg might've doodled strung out on some especially heavy acid. Swirly creatures with human faces, icky little humanoids with bird faces, weird symbols that looked like melted arrows and planets with mazes inside them. The pictures actually seemed to swim in front of us – we both thought that – and we also both blamed it on the wine. Did I mention we were on our third bottle when we started doing the chants?

The book had a long introduction by the author describing an expedition she made into Tibet. The author claimed she fainted one day through exertion and lack of food while crossing some huge mountain pass on her own. When she regained consciousness she found herself being cared for by a strange monk in a small, dark monastery. The writer claimed that Tibetan medicine and the monk's healing chants cured her within a few days and she spent three years living there, at first doing chores to thank the dude for looking after her, later learning some of his ancient BS – excuse me, I mean mystical lore.

'So far, so far-fetched,' said Riley, as she paused from rolling the cork from the wine bottle around her tongue. 'When do we get to the good stuff?' She spat the cork so it hit the wall opposite, first time she managed with any of the three corks.

'Good shot. Oh, wait, look. She's giving us a warning.'

'Is it, "Do not read, far less fall for, crap like this"?'

I read out the next paragraph, which in its overblown style basically said the author learned some ancient life-or-death secrets from the monk and you must proceed carefully with the book from this point onwards. Then it started droning on about inner god this and inner goddess that.

'Look, the book has a spell!' said Riley.

'No way. Lemme see.'

True enough the current page was headed 'Chant to Manifest Your Personal Inner Goddess'.

Riley spluttered with laughter. 'My goddess would be Courtney Love.' She sat up straight, positioned the book on the floor in front of her, and cleared her throat. 'I'm going to summon her up.'

Riley was grinning but then she started doing the chanting. 'Eed seb tham tub ee sem tul fuu zub . . .' She began trying to do it in earnest but she couldn't hold a straight face and soon I noticed she was missing out lines.

'The words are jumping around on the page,' she said. 'They're drunk. You try.'

So I turned the book and began, just as a joke. I chanted the words as they appeared, with what began to feel like conviction, and the beat and the melody that came through were lovely. Thanks to the wine I could imagine the animals around the cabin listening in and when I finished the chanting I lingered on the final word 'shazeema' and then there was perfect stillness and I looked at Riley.

Who was gazing at me, mouth hanging open. Took a moment before she could speak and when she did it was a whisper. 'Wow, that actually sounded kinda cool. What now? Where's Courtney Love?'

I consulted the book. 'It says, close thine eyes tight, imagine a golden ball of fire appears in front of thee, let it float in front of thee until the heat from the ball fills thine chest with warmth, then open thine eyes.'

Riley and I looked at each other. 'Shall we?'

I shrugged. 'We came this far.'

I closed my eyes and pictured a little beach-ball-sized sun levitating before me. It flickered red at the edges and I did indeed begin to feel warm. Especially in my chest. Probly the wine, I thought. But then it actually began to feel like really hot. I started sweating and my breathing buckled a little. 'It's the devil's own sauna in here. Let's open our eyes.'

'Okay. One – two – *three*.'

I steeled myself and opened my eyes. I was half expecting to find the cabin on fire, but nothing could prepare me for what was going on.

The air shimmered and swirled before us and colours gathered together like paints draining down a sink, but here the colours met up in mid-air and they spun together and formed a person.

Not a person, a thing.

A person-like thing.

'Fuck me,' said Riley.

The thing was four foot tall, skinny, and dressed in odd colourful robes, purple and gold and red, that suggested royalty but which also gave off an atmosphere of foulness.

'Fuck me,' said Riley.

It had orange hair and thick sprouting orange eyebrows – not an easy look for anyone to pull off – but no sooner had you noticed the eyebrows than you realised it had a third eye on its forehead. The third eye didn't have an eyebrow. Yeah, and its face was dominated by its humungous beak.

'Fuck me,' said Riley. 'Courtney Love's in a worse state than I imagined.'

The thing squawked at Riley in what I imagined was a reprimanding manner, then it turned and pointed a bony finger at me.

'You summoned me.' Its voice was crackly and high pitched.

'Um,' I said. 'Uh. Um. I, uh . . .' I mean, where do you start?

Triple-eyed beak-face glanced at the book on the floor, then at the empty wine bottles, then back at me. The way it moved reminded me of a Muppet. I shook my head, screwed my eyes shut, opened them. Same impossible scenario playing out.

'Uh,' I managed. 'Who – what – who are you?'

The creature frowned. 'Holy Mother of Tshangs-pa Dkar-po,'

it said, 'the ignorance of adepts nowadays. I'm your inner goddess, dumbass.'

'O-k-a-a-a-y,' said Riley. 'This isn't weird at all. Do we at least get three wishes?'

'Silence!' squawked beaky. 'I am Kakasya, a great goddess whom you shall address with respect. I have travelled through dimensions of time and space and phenomena you cannot comprehend in order to comply with this summons. You will treat me with reverence and you will admire me and you will obey me. Now bow down in supplication! Or I shall see to it that you are reborn as a pig's testicle.'

Riley turned to me. 'Did she just say—'

I nodded.

'Gross.'

'Kaka – ka,' I started to say.

'Kakasya!'

'Kakasya, can you really do that? How do we know? I mean, this is all new to us.'

'Do not toy with me. I can control your future rebirths in the sphere of non-conditional causation. I can see to it you are reborn as a pig's testicle, a blade of grass that gets constantly pissed on by a herd of cattle, or a plastic freakin' spork. Any rebirth I will for you, it shall be so.' She squawked it like she meant it.

I looked at Riley. 'I feel like I just don't want to take the risk.'

'Same,' said Riley.

So we shrugged and, right before this ridiculous creature, we bowed (clumsily, thanks to the dead grape beverages).

'Humans these days,' muttered Kakasya disparagingly. 'Now sit straight, zip it and listen up.'

Kakasya began pacing back and forth in her odd puppet-like manner, as though her spindly legs were made of wood (they weren't; she looked like she was made of flesh). Her speech was long and boastful and intriguing. The chase to which it cut: Kakasya was a goddess, but had limited powers in what she called 'the world of dust', meaning our universe. She had last visited the world of dust when the author of the book we bought used the chant to summon her.

'Yeah, so what happened then?' asked Riley

'*She* refused my request and I reincarnated her as a doorknob.'

'What happened to her next?'

'Next? She's *still* a doorknob.'

A shiver ran through me.

Riley gave a flyswatty hand gesture I recognised as 'meh' and said, 'Doesn't seem so bad. I mean, how high can cows piss?'

'A *sentient* doorknob, fool. Imagine the boredom. Decade after decade of doing nothing, just being there, with hands, germy bacterial hands, touching you against your will, time and time again, smearing their sweat and filth and bugs on you, wrenching you this way and that, treating you like something to be used and there is nothing you can do about it.'

Something about the pathos of being a doorknob slid in beneath my defences. 'What did you ask her to do?'

'Same thing I'm going to ask you to do. I want you to remove someone from this sphere in order that he is transplanted back into his rightful realm, the god realm.'

'Wait, what?'

'A person on Earth needs to go back to the god realm. He snuck back here, has been doing so for lifetimes, but he doesn't belong here. We're not meant to have the kind of influence – interference is a better word – that this charlatan perpetuates on the human realm of existence. We want to know how he does it.'

I frowned. 'By remove him do you mean . . . kill him?'

'Nothing dies, you stupid creature! You don't kill him. Think of it as bumping him up a level in a computer game. Just a slight promotion of one named Jetsun Jamphel Ngawang Lobsang Yeshe Tenzin Gyatso from the world of dust to the god realm.'

'Holy guaca-freakin-moly,' I said, looking at Riley, who hadn't fully understood. 'She just told us to assassinate the Dalai Lama.'

It took a few moments for the outlandishness of the task to sink in. At last, Riley said, 'No, hang on. I don't know much about Buddhism, but I'm pretty sure that if there's one thing guaranteed to bring bad karma it's assassinating the mother-hugging goddamn freakin' Dalai Lama.'

'Yeah, this ain't right. You're putting us in an impossible position.'

Kakasya nodded very slowly. 'Alright. Sporks it is.'

'Do your worst, Gonzo,' growled Riley. (Ah, I thought, *that's* who Kakasya reminded me of.)

'Don't be hasty, Riles.'

'I won't do anything now! Only when you pass on from this body into the *bardo* can I influence your rebirth.'

'So we have, like, our whole lifetime to decide on this?'

'No. The coupon expires tonight. You decide here and now. Listen, all you have to do is go to a talk he's giving at Yale next month—'

'And kill the Dalai Lama. No probs. Might get, y'know, badmouthed by a few classmates, but whatevs. IT'S NOT LIKE WE'D GO TO JAIL OR ANYTHING AND BE A MONUFUCKINGMENTAL DISAPPOINTMENT TO OUR PARENTS AND ALL HUMANITY.' Riley was yelling now, and thudding her fist off the floor.

'Calm yourself,' said Kakasya. 'I've had a long time to devise a plan. You won't be suspected, far less caught. And one of you will use a fake bullet, so you'll never know which one of you actually did the . . . promoting.'

'I always kinda reckoned on getting through life with committing, like, a minimum of murders, maybe even zero,' I said, trying to buy some time.

Riley fell silent, an unusuality for her, and that's when I began to seriously worry. My anxiety increased multifold when she offered to clear up. I looked at her in blood-drained surprise. It was the biggest shock since, well, since I'd been asked to murder the Dalai Lama.

She began gathering the wine bottles and errant corks and book and mugs and she slouched into the kitchen like someone very defeated and very unlike Riley. A tear swelled up in the corner of my eye, escaped and slid down my cheek.

'Your friend will come round,' rasped Kakasya in what I think was meant to be a warm and supportive tone, but just sounded creepy. 'And if not, you could do a solo job.'

I thought I could hear Riley praying in the kitchen. I got up to go and comfort her.

'No,' said Kakasya. 'Stay.'

The kitchen doorknob caught my eye, and checked my impulse to go to Riley. Kakasya warbled on about the merits of 'upgrading' the Dalai Lama. I sniffed heavily to try and hold myself back from breaking down altogether. Maybe I should just do what Kakasya said? I was being asked to do something by an entity I didn't understand – surely there was a karmic mechanism behind everything to make sure I'd be alright?

But that might be fine if I were offing some paedophile or genocidist or something. This was the Dalai Lama – wasn't he meant to be one of the good guys? Or was it like those conspiracy dorks who can 'prove' that Jesus was a space lizard and Satan is the true benevolent creator?

My head hurt fit to bursting. Tears began to stream down my face and I let out an ugly sob. This was so unfair. I cried some more and through my tears saw Kakasya hobble towards me with an arm outstretched to comfort me and I wept and Kakasya turned into a serpent and began aggressively chewing and munching on her own tail.

Yeah! Before my wet and salty eyes, she transformed into a snake! And began eating herself!

And she vanished!

Gone!

My tears turned to tears of gratitude. 'Riley! Riley! C'mere! Gonzo's gone!'

Riley poked her head round the kitchen door, with an uncertain look, almost a smile, on her face. She put on a squawky voice. 'Did that bitch done snake herself and be gone?'

'Yes,' I cried out. 'How'd you know?'

Riley bounced into the room. 'I did that! I did that!' She raised the book in her hand and shook it up and down like a pom-pom. 'Did you see me? Did you see how natural I took the book and everything into the kitchen? And sobered up enough to find a chant to make a goddess disappear and never return? And I got all the syllables out and I chanted them like a boss and they worked and I freakin' well saved our asses.'

I leapt to my feet and shouted 'I love you, Riley-Ri' and hugged her tight and warm and long. After that, all we knew was that we'd better go outside and gather up wood and build a fire, stat. When the woodpile was pretty darn huge we got some methylated spirits from under the kitchen sink and spilled it all out onto the logs and Riley had the honour of lighting the fire and when it was blazing good and fierce we took a hold of the book, one hand each, and swore at it a few times and on the count of three hurled it onto the pyre and watched it burn.

We felt kinda jubilant, maybe we were still a little drunk.

We were going to watch every last part of the book get eaten by the flames but it got kinda boring standing there so we got some marshmallows and skewered them on sticks and roasted them and hunkered down in the warmth of the fire and chewed the gooey sweetness and had a marshmallow-spitting-fight and joked about what dull hedonistic lives the Beats had. Life was bright and lively and warm and unpredictable and essential, just like a conflagration, as it always is to the newly saved.

And hey. We did go and see the Dalai Lama give his talk at Yale. How the hell we were ever expected to evade security there I'll never know. Dude's bodyguards had bodyguards. His talk was punctuated with giggling and sounded a lot of fun and it was all about non-attachment and how we don't really own things and it was about being non-judgmental but you know we did feel a real sense of ownership towards the Dalai Lama and still do whenever we see him on TV or in the media. We saved his enlightened ass.

And oh boy, it was, I confess to my total shame, *days* after the whole thing at the cabin, and we were back in Connecticut and the book was long burned and cremated utterly before we realised a more sympathetic pair of hot New Havenite chicks would've probly searched through the damn thing first and found a chant and done something marvellous for the doorknob woman. Our bad.

Summer Kelly's piece, despite being long, maybe one of the longest we'd had at a B&F for years, received a rapturous reception from the audience. Everyone listened intently and reacted spontaneously to the story's best qualities. She downed a few bottles of beer while reading and she just looked so very happy as she soaked up the applause and cheers, radiant in beer and acceptance. All the insecurity had vanished and she knew, we all knew, her story could be the winner. Yes, it was a little longer than it needed to be. Yes, it was true she stumbled over a few words during her performance. Yes, it was a ludicrous plot.

But it – and she – seemed so vibrant, youthful and . . . fun.

I confess I felt a poignant, yearning tremble in my heartstrings. I recognised, distantly, the kind of joy and carelessness that charged her story. Everyone had laughed at the right points, loudly and frequently. But I almost wept once or twice. I couldn't be sure if I was inwardly pining for an uninhibitedness I had once possessed, or feeling the sore lack of something I'd never had.

These thoughts occupied my mind while Dalston Moomintroll chatted with Summer. I was less interested in her words, in any case, than I was in what I could discern of her future. So I looked at her with my mind and tried to read her as a person. She'd had a taste of something that could, like poison, be curative if taken in a measured dose, but could so easily be deadly. Not necessarily to her physical person, but to the better parts of her that spirited up her beautiful vitality – the naiveté and unforced charm. Which, like most good things, could be commodified and perverted.

Macy was talking. I snapped out of my dwam. 'Earth calling, hello? She was pretty damned brilliant, wasn't she? Tell the truth, I kinda want to be Riley.'

'She was fantastic,' I said, almost sighing. 'I think winning this could actually be bad for her.'

'Killjoy. What do you say, Archie? Her, me or Ray, so far?'

'I'd say it's between you and Summer,' said Archie. 'But Ray was good, too. Dear god. What the hell's this?'

Hurling itself onto the stage, with a kind of waddling swagger, as if his sneakers had trampoline soles, throwing weird hand signals at the crowd, and nodding as if to say, 'Yeah, it's me, can you believe your luck?' was a massive pair of sunglasses with a skinny guy underneath them, a guy whose trousers were belted loosely a fraction above the knees.

'I think the first thing you oughtta do, if you want to win a literary competition,' said Archie, 'is show the judges your blue boxer shorts.'

Macy rustled through the programme. 'Here it is. J-M-Boy. Pronounced "dshay emm boieee". He's a performance poet.'

'You don't say,' said Archie.

'Got to applaud his confidence,' I said. 'It takes guts to do something like that. I bet the whole thing's a self-knowing piece of performance art, with ten layers of irony going on.'

'This goes out to my homeboy, Borges,' said J-M-Boy. He twirled the microphone round his hand with the fluidity and ease of a sleight-of-hand musician. He nodded repeatedly. 'For giving me belief in stories. We're all stories, motherfuckers.'

I cringed. Perhaps every single person there winced – even, or especially, J-M-Boy's family and friends. A skinny white guy in his late twenties. A rapper. And mispronouncing Borges didn't help.

He looked off stage and flashed a hand signal. 'Kick it, DJ Tigerteeth.'

Out of the PA system a complex beat pattern thudded. J-M-Boy started jumping on the spot. The stage, knocked up two days ago by a carpentry firm well known for its 'joints', shook alarmingly.

'C'mon, Tigerteeth, set the riff free,' said J-M-Boy, leaping as if heading an invisible football.

A sampled Miles Davis riff, energetic, colourful and melodic, kicked in and I found myself nodding along. The notes flashed red and gold and blue through my mind. I realised I was smiling.

'I got plenty of rhymes, ladies and Gs. And a shout-out to the alpaca massive,' said J-M-Boy. The alpacas cheered at that. 'But this ain't about my rhymes. This is my story. This is death. And. The. Book. Shop.'

'Kinda weird,' said Archie. 'I like, don't know if I like this. But I like the fact he's doing it.'

'Maybe it's a jazz thing you just don't get,' I deadpanned.

J-M-Boy took his baggy baseball shirt off and to the beat he swung it around his head a few times before throwing it into the audience.

I warmed to him. He surely must have a well-founded sense of humour. I liked the fact he was doing something almost revolutionary in this context, liked the fact he was siding with alpacas, liked the fact he was throwing his chances away along with his shirt. He just didn't seem to care. The sight of his bony torso and puffy blue boxer shorts – which really did look like a boxer's shorts – provoked good-natured catcalls from some of the women in the audience.

And what's more, it turned out his writing had more depth than anyone expected. 'Rapping' it – really, he just spoke it in his native lilting accent, exaggerating the cadences into a sort of free-form rhythm and melody – was a brave move. He'd set himself up as a loser. Now he was jazzily intoning his story:

Death and the Bookshop

I was browsing upstairs in a bookshop as large as a Borgesian library. An old friend of mine – old in both senses and friend in all senses – had recently cut her throat and bled to death in a public toilet. Somehow I was seeking solace in books. I wonder if I haven't always found more answers in books than in real life.

I scanned the bookshelves. Bukowski. Hoffmann. McCullers. Virgil. This was not so much a collection of inked-on papers as the human potential for imagination solidified.

Death and the bookshop
Death and the bookshop

I remembered a haiku about two flies in a bookshop landing together on the same romantic novel. A genuine haiku must be based on an actual experience; I doubt that really happened.

What kind of peace does death bring about? Perhaps that is the most important question we can ask of the imagination. Perhaps that is the main reason we have an imagination. Perhaps the imagination holds The Answer and only those who find it will earn an afterlife.

Death and the bookshop
Death and the bookshop

The shop's closing. I haven't managed to choose a book. 'Write one instead,' says a voice in my head, goading. I close my eyes, pick a book at random. I flip it over, check the price and take it to the till without looking at its title or author.

Outside, the autumn rain feels cold and relentless. Miserable faces drone past over advertisements on dirty buses. Taxis and cars chase each other, predatory as sharks. Everyone thinks they know where they are going. Not one person in this town looks happy.

I am desperate to find somewhere quiet to sit and read the book. It could be about anything. It could be about nothing.

Death and the bookshop
Death and the bookshop
Death and the bookshop
Death and the bookshop

After the final 'bookshop', there was an instant of what seemed nothing; the beat had cut, J-M-Boy had frozen, and the Castle Green was silent and motionless. But in that moment all kinds of thought processes were surely going on.

What did I just witness?

Do I like it?

What's the general consensus and will I make a fool of myself by cheering?

Is this a glimpse of the future or a strange joke?

Most people played it safe by applauding so politely it was almost an insult. There were some enthusiastic cheers from certain sections of the crowd. It was clear the J-M-Boy fans were mainly young people and alpacas.

Dalston Moomintroll approached J-M-Boy almost warily.

'Very interesting,' he said, aiming his slick smile at the audience. 'Would you mind explaining to an old fogey like me what that, in fact, was? I'm closer to hip op – that's hip operation – than hip hop.'

'That was my piece. That was my performance,' said J-M-

Boy, sassy in voice and stance – legs as wide apart as the trousers would allow, arms crossed over his skinny chest. 'I wanna shout out to all my fans out there and to DJ Tigerteeth and everyone who supported me. You're awesome! Peace!' He flashed a V-sign, the friendly way round.

Cheers rose quickly, but fell quickly too.

'Music was part of your act. How important is music to you?' asked Dalston Moomintroll.

J-M-Boy nodded confidently as he spoke, as though hearing some inner drum encouraging him. 'Music's everything. We built this island on rock and roll. Except the graveyard. We built that on death metal. And the villages, constructed on folk music. The cafés are made of jazz, my favourite. And that stinking landfill site? That's One Direction. Everything else round about is country.' He grinned; everyone laughed.

Except Dalston Moomintroll. 'I believe you made reference to Borges there,' he said, conspicuously pronouncing it the right way. 'Is he indeed one of your, ah, "homeboys"?'

His smarm drew superior chuckles from the front rows.

'I got Miles Davis in there, I got Kafka. And yeah, I got Borges.' He defiantly mispronounced it. 'Because like he said, "Reality is not always probable, or likely."'

'Ain't that the truth,' I said to Archie, who was unconsciously polishing his spittoon, engrossed by what he was witnessing on the stage.

'In which case,' said Dalston Moomintroll with a slightly malicious grin, 'good luck in the B&F. J-M-Boy, ladies and gentlemen. There he goes. Maybe the topless-with-silk-underwear look will catch on among young ladies, too?'

'Oh brother,' said Macy. 'Somebody should just deck that guy. I probly should have.'

'I actually liked J-M-Boy,' said Archie. 'I mean, he hasn't got a hope in hell. But he's got spirit. So, that's two reasons to like him.'

Peter Projector-Head was up next. He had no introduction; we all knew him, all felt for him. Peter was born with a film projector in his head, situated just above his eyes. His head is continually projecting images, ideas, memories, aversions, wishes. He cannot be fully present, hence he is perpetually frustrated. It need only take the smallest thing. If he eats a piece of shortbread, say, he is at once transported back in his mind to every previous New Year's Eve, and to the time he shared a piece of the sweetly Scottish biscuit with a sweetly Scottish girl he crushed on like mad in school; he'll remember the best and the worst piece of shortbread he ever ate, the ideal shortbread he will never eat, the piece that coincided with a bout of dysentery in Birmingham, and the one his ex-wife's lover is probably feeding her on a sunlit balcony in Beverly Hills. Peter Projector-Head enjoys no consolation, he feels no in-the-moment-ness. He lacks the remedy of the actual and, doubling the torture, pines for what is vivid in the here and now, like somebody being intensely homesick for the place where they already are. He can only see where he might be going and where he has been, not where he is. As for his own literature, he writes memoir, or fantasy, or both combined. Many of his writings are lists, tableaux, collages. To know him is to pity him.

'Um,' he said, approaching the microphone gingerly so his projector head didn't bash into it. 'Am I here?' His projector was flashing a series of nervous images too quick to take in, but including what seemed to be memories of singing at a primary school Christmas concert, being lost in a dark wood, and fantasies of flying above Edinburgh in a UFO, with further spacecraft on either side.

'Yes,' bellowed the crowd, trying to focus on Peter, not the projected images.

'I'll just take it that I am here. And that it's appropriate for me to read now, whatever "now" means.' He took a page from his pocket and unfolded it into A4. 'This is all about a time when I . . .' He stopped. Tried again. 'When I . . .' His voice trailed off, quivering. 'You know, I realised that in my stream of consciousness there are no red herrings. I guess that's one good thing. But the stream is, uh, is not free. It's contained. It's not singing, this stream. It's grinding. Toiling. Wrestling.' He cleared his throat and said in a loud, anguished voice, 'You know what Akutagawa said? He said, "Isn't there someone kind enough to strangle me in my sleep?"'

We stared, moved by his plight. We knew him well enough to understand this was not melodrama, this was his truth. It was very hard to interact with Peter, or relate to him, but I think a great many of us resolved there and then to try harder.

'This is about a time I had of it in Edinburgh. It's called "Wasted, Gifted".'

Peter Projector-Head looked up at the sky.

Someone told me once that every year on the first of May, Peter's birthday, a faint cloud the shape of a cinema projector passes slowly, wispily, over his house, then disappears again, only to return the following year, like a recurring thought, a message that must be deciphered. It is also said that when he deciphers the meaning of this, he will be able to live in the present like the rest of us. Many believe in the message, but not the redemption.

Peter spoke quickly but clearly, in a kind of insistent tumble, like a waterfall that transfixes with its constant sparkly restlessness:

Wasted, Gifted

You could find yourself thrilling as you absorb Edinburgh's moonlit skyline, her gothic twilight, her dusky hills, those furtive alleys you darkly explored all wet and tingling and you could wake up thick-tongued and inarticulate and find yourself, for the first time in your life, comfortable in an unknown bed and you could turn a corner and suddenly glimpse a jewel at the end of the street, only to notice, with an equal delight, that the bright jewel is a living and precious and rare and everyday one – the sea glittering under the sun – and you could eat biculturally within a single eating house, Scottish fried breakfast and Chinese buffet lunch, and you would never know which meal did the real damage and you could watch the Balmoral Hotel morph, with its austere head, square shoulders, chunky torso, into an immense, terrifying Transformer and you could lie in the sun pretending to read a work of philosophy only for a stinking friendly hobo to amble up and, coughing into his beer can, ask if he can 'borrow' a cigarette, and he will glimpse your book and launch into a slurred, impassioned discourse on the categorical imperative, making no more and no less sense than the book did and you could stumble around, blind through whisky and fog, making only right-hand turns, and find yourself outside your front door before the fog lifted or the hangover began and you could go jogging by Blackford Hill, beside the leafy stream, with real-life birdsong outdoing your earphones, and everything sparkling and green, and you could believe serenity actually exists and you could stare at beautiful works of priceless contemporary art and still find them ugly and inscrutable, yet feel the afternoon was not wasted but gifted and you could feel as though the maroon night buses swishing past as you swagger from bar to show to bar are full of calm good cheer and whisky and sheer crazy Edinburghness and you could feel as though the fireworks which are blossoming, fleeting and graceful, over the Castle and its ten-mile treasure box are actually diminished by the city's grandeur and history and future and you could feel that any city cool enough to name its central train station after a novel is alright by you and you could feel as though the classical and jazzy and punky architecture is scrutinized by slow-nodding trees and you could feel as though the seven hills are peopled by Hobbit-like creatures who live little fairytale dramas nightly and you could discover the massive resting elephant at the far side of the Meadows is actually an extinct volcano and you could see a heron hunched over the Water of Leith in such an old-man fashion – wizened, silent, staring at nothing in deep meditation – that it makes you believe, really believe, for a split second, in reincarnation and you could wonder at the ineffable, encountered on Blackford Hill, seen once and forever in the natural beauty of a woman's face, and she's smiling at you, with Edinburgh laid out behind her, and you could know this is, and might always be, the single most beautiful moment of your life and you – well, you could see a man falling or jumping down from on high, plummeting off the Forth Road Bridge and realise at once that it's just a bird at play, it's a gull diving, but a tear has so swiftly formed at the death of that unknown man that it is already trickling down your face and now it pools in a smiling dimple as you think, 'I am a writer divided. Between. Moments. And I do not know my life.'

Peter Projector-Head's piece went down very well. But he couldn't take in the applause, he wasn't truly present, wasn't aware of how well he had done.

There was no interview per se with Peter Projector-Head. He, more than any other writer, 'couldn't cope with a live interview' – in his case a literal, not figurative, truth. The festival organisers had therefore emailed him some questions previously.

He bent over a page and spoke, rapid-fire, into the microphone.

'The first question I was sent . . . Uh, you know, I'm just going to read each question then the answer I prepared. Question: what is it like, never being really present? Uh, answer: it means you cannot exist in the pre-symbolic world. You are always distracted. You cannot discern progress, just an ongoing kaleidoscope. You lose the sense of both journey and destination. Your mind is compulsive, never serene. You carry a lifetime's baggage, everywhere. Question: how does not being fully present aid you in your writing? Answer: I'd give up the ability to write for the ability to be present in a racing rabbit's heartbeat. I mean, don't get me wrong, if I'm not writing, I'm not happy.' He paused. 'And if I'm writing, I'm not happy.'

He turned and walked away as if nothing that had just happened had any meaning.

'Damn,' I said, 'I feel so sorry for him.'

'You and the rest of the island,' said Archie. 'How's it going to work if he wins? He won't even register the win for weeks.'

I shrugged. 'The interviews and media stuff would be hard. But that shouldn't matter.'

Archie shook his head, resolute. 'There goes one guy who ain't gonna win. Now I feel worse still for him.'

Even Dalston Moomintroll seemed humbled, for a moment. 'Peter Projector-Head, folks. The one and only. It's very um . . .' He gazed downwards and shook his head, staring for what felt like a full minute. He looked up, semi-bewildered, as though awakening from a daytime nap. He shook his head another couple of times as if that explained everything then straightened his bowler hat and burst back into persona. 'Next we have a lady who has published extensively online, and, if I may say so, is absolutely terrific at self-promotion. Well, you might add, she's got a lot to self-promote. She's only been at this for a year, but I'm sure you all know her. Ladies and gents, Tabitha Tessington.'

Tabitha Tessington was one of those people who's an expert in self-belief and fake modesty. She wore a short dress with a large castle motif and –

'What's that on her dress? The yellow thing?' I said.

The camera feeding to the live screen was not zoomed in enough for my eyes.

'It looks like custard,' I said. 'Is it custard?'

'No way would Tabitha Tessington come on stage with custard on her dress,' said Macy.

'Unless custard on your dress is a thing now?' said Archie. 'Cos then she'd be the first to do it.'

'Ssh. She's talking.'

Tabitha Tessington jumped daintily on the spot twice and clapped her hands. 'What a thrill it is for a mere scribbler like me to be here on stage in front of you, you lovely crowd, and in front of this equally lovely castle. It's appropriate that I read this piece as it concerns a castle. Though not the one, I hasten to add, that is so resplendent behind me.' She gestured towards the castle with diffident grace, as though it were really her own arm she considered resplendent. 'I feel I'm among friends here,' she said. 'So I know you won't be too harsh with me. Looks like this year the trend is to go long or to go very short. Which is what I've done. No!' she tittered. 'Not my skirt.'

'You're not among friends,' an uncharitable voice behind us said, 'unless you mean the judges. Goddamn whitehouser.'

'Shurrup,' said someone.

'Just saying, pays to be connected. I heard she's getting a publishing deal regardless.'

'Whitehouser privilege,' another woman's voice said.

'Let her speak,' said someone in a poncho.

Tabitha Tessington spoke with a high, soft, cooing voice, as if trying to be all kittenish and seductive, but it actually gave her piece an almost sinister edge. She read:

This is a Castle, This is a Kite

Her father gave her a castle. Stephie tried to think of what to say.

'Um. Wow.'

They read the flatness in her voice as shock.

'Look at her,' Stephie heard Fatima whisper. 'She's overwhelmed.'

'My little princess can't believe her luck,' said her father as he put a proprietorial arm around Fatima, his latest.

Stephie thought for a moment. 'I don't deserve it.'

'Make the most of it, princess,' said her father as he led Fatima away, beaming.

Stephie looked at the vast, cold castle and wondered what to do.

Time in a castle works differently. Each day, huge and silent and empty, will not be filled. Filling time in a castle is like trying to fill the sky with kites.

Stephie didn't know what to do. When she bought a bike, it rained. She got a guitar, but her music was just noise. She grew sad. The locals avoided her because she frowned all the time; they believed sadness was a disease. Which it is.

She took up photography, but threw her camera away when she realised not one of her pictures had a person in it, smiling or not.

Stephie began talking to herself. Since people avoided her,

she avoided them. She thought it might be useful to learn how to cook well instead of ordering takeaways all the time, but cookbooks don't account for solitude and in any case her energies were draining away with each eternal day. Many years later, her father returned with a new Fatima. 'It's been six months already,' he said. 'How are you enjoying the castle?'

Stephie pointed at a beautiful yellow kite she had made. Her father's smile faltered as his eyes took on that sad yellow sheen.

She placed a hand on her father's shoulder, looked at him closely and said, 'I didn't deserve it.'

The close-up camera revealed that her dress had a yellow kite over the heart area, which I had mistaken for spilled custard.

Custard that is really a yellow kite. This was one of the main benefits of the B&F, one of the reasons it was so attractive to islanders; it let us see beyond the people we thought we knew and look directly into their mind.

'The B&F gives us all greater empathy,' I announced. It gave me a good surging feeling to realise this truth, to sense understanding as an actual, physical thing, shared here among friends and strangers.

But I immediately tuned out of her interview. When a writer starts showing more interest in her own characters than the real life human beings around her, it's time to engage the mind in other pursuits. Also, I heard her say, 'I do my sun salutations, perform a bowel movement and then the Muse deigns to visit me; she whispers precious visions in my ear.'

'Guys,' I said, 'I'm starving. Let's split for lunch.'

A great many burger vans, pizza trucks and cupcake tractors had set up on the west side of the Castle Green and it was to

Honest Johnmurdo's Authentic Italian Family Restaurant & Mini Marquee we headed. It smelled glorious, like a six-mile-radius pizza.

We sat at a fixed wooden table-and-benches. Macy and I shared an Exploding Heart of the Sun pizza, which had every kind of chilli pepper on it and a fried egg in the middle, while Archie chowed on a grass and grass salad. Occasionally he bent down, picked at some grass from around the bench, and added it to his salad.

'That's like taking a carry-out to the pub,' said Macy. 'Who d'you think's got it so far?'

'Hard to say, but you, I think,' I said. 'Or Summer. No – you.'

'Doubt it. Anyway, don't leave any pizza between your teeth, you're next.'

'Jeez – I'd forgotten,' I said.

Archie spluttered so hard he almost choked on his grass. 'How in the hell could you forget?'

'Because I'm kind of resigned to not winning. And I've learned not to be nervous in front of people who are, after all, only people.'

'And alpacas.'

'And alpacas.' I grinned. 'They don't make me nervous either.'

'Wow,' said Macy, 'I'm impressed by your equilibrium. You get antsy before a party, but before the B&F you're tranquillity itself! What about you, Archie, you anxious?'

He finished chewing and sighed. 'Yes. I'm going to be honest. I had a bad feeling even before the B&F party. I hardly got any Zzzs last night – maybe a solitary Z.'

'My spare room always gives everyone loads of Zzzs. You'll blow them away,' I said.

'It's the People's Decision that's bothering me.'

'Oh you definitely don't need to worry about that,' said

Macy. She looked around, lowered her voice. 'Stella needs to be biting her perfectly manicured nails over that one.'

I shook my head. 'She's eye candy. Too sweet to get the People's. Plus,' I said, 'have you seen how many alpacas there are out there, north and south?'

'It's not like they get a vote,' said Archie. 'All I'm saying is, I've got a bad feeling.'

'I thought you weren't superstitious. Don't make it a foregone conclusion.'

'This isn't superstition. I can't explain it. It's like, if you're hungry or thirsty, your body tells you so, and you don't doubt it. You know it's true. I've got as strong a feeling as hunger or thirst, but it's coming from my mind, and it's saying I'm going to lose the People's.'

'Why didn't you say something earlier?'

'Didn't want to give it credence. Thought I could shake it off.'

Macy and I exchanged glances. I hadn't given any real consideration to any of *us* losing the People's. I didn't want to think about it. An uneasy silence opened up between us. I found myself wishing an unpleasant extremely elderly man who drowned kittens and couldn't write was also in the B&F, then I felt horrible. I pushed my last slice of pizza away, closed my eyes and breathed deeply; just behind the aroma of pizza and burgers and grease and frying fish you could smell the sea. I concentrated on my breath, sending out good wishes to my two best friends. Life, I decided, would not be cruel to such good beings.

Dalston Moomintroll's introduction for me was at best desultory. He said more about the lunch he'd shared with the judges than he did about me or my work. No matter. I knew I wouldn't win, and equally I had convinced myself I wasn't in line for the People's.

The crowd didn't faze me too much. I smiled and approached the mic at a slower saunter than I really wanted to – it made everyone think I was laid-back so they didn't tense up in anticipation of a disaster.

I cleared my throat, and started to read:

The Day Everything Was Grey

A greyish version of the land is sliding past the window by your side. A book you've been looking forward to reading lies with an early broken spine on the pull-down table in front of you. Your small First Class segment, doored off from the rest of the train carriage, has recently been invaded by a party of women. They are inebriated. It is a grey, softly drizzling, very typical, morning.

You had been staring out the window, concentrating on that immersive gloom as the women opened up bottles and mindnumbing conversations. Why are they so interested in minor celebrities, whose personalities are cultivated (or hidden) by image consultants? You declined to look any of the women in the eye. You refused to participate.

So they've started chatting with a man sitting nearby. He's quite the character.

'I did a big murder last year,' he says. 'One of my highest profile cases yet. I'm a lawyer.' He grins, pleased with himself.

The women shriek and pour him a drink. He accepts a plastic cup of wine. They beg him to tell them about it.

'Maybe later. Actually, I'm a bit of a wine snob,' he says. 'But what the heck – give me some more cheap plonk.' They begin to drip feed him plastic cups of a urinous paintstrippy wine.

'This is hardly the standard I expected. After all, this is not the riff-raff carriage,' he declares. The women scream, delighted at his bluntness. They do not have First Class tickets but the train is overcrowded. They feel rebellious and privileged. They have not realised the difference in classes on this train is largely nominal. First Class is no different to Standard except that a beleaguered young rail employee sometimes pops his head in and asks if anyone fancies a cup of tea or coffee and a muffin (and there is no charge). The drunken women make him blush: 'I don't fancy a free muffin right now son, but I do fancy you!'

As the teenager scuttles away, his trolley trembling with miniature glass bottles, the man helps himself to more plastic wine. 'You'd eat him for breakfast,' he says. 'You can gobble me up any time you like. I'm as lush as a tart when it comes to women. I will sing, I will dance . . .' His voice is louder now, his honed vowels are slurring into something more working class, more genuine.

You try and read for a while, but there is too much merriment in the air. You can't settle. You read the same sentence half a dozen times and still don't take it in. The man holds court and the women listen and encourage him to drink. They are drunk and he is getting very drunk and it is only eleven o'clock.

The blur of washed-out countryside to your left suggests weariness and dull hangovers; the villages at which the train calls have an air of inertia and grinding routine. You idly wonder if it is possible for an actual village to have agoraphobia. You want better – much better – for your country.

'Did I say lawyer, I mean liar,' he quips. All these pithy lines sound well practised, like his accent did.

A lawyer, you think. Makes sense.

As you leave another grey village he talks about how he and his wife illegally download books and music. 'Everyone does.'

He has a wife?

The lawyer boasts about the jewellery he buys her. She once refused a ring. 'Made me take it right back to the store. "Stone's too small," she says. "I don't do small, I do bling."'

The drink goes down, the volume goes up. You stare at your book. The land slides north, the train south. His spoken sentences have defeated the written ones. Such, you think, is all too often the way of things.

He says, 'Lawyers would chop their arm off to work for my firm.' Prompted by one of the women, he even names his company. You write it down. Just in case.

'Do you know, I love feet,' he exclaims at one point. The women, coarse and excitable, roar with laughter and clap their hands and encourage him.

Later, one of the women complains that her breasts are too big, they give her a sore back.

'I have to say: women's breasts, if they're properly formed – absolutely beautiful.'

A large woman puffs out her chest, agrees and mentions how hard it is to get a bra that fits.

'Oh wow, look at the nipples.' He says this very loudly. No one speaks for a while. An anonymous grey station arrives at the train. One of the women finds a bottle of gin.

'Okay, hush, everyone,' says the man. 'I've just got a text, I've been told to phone my wife. So could we all be quiet, please.'

After a few moments of drunken pantomime hilarity, the women settle and sip at their drinks, listening in to the lawyer.

He jabs at his phone. 'Hi baby, how you doing? I hope you've got some nice cakes because I've got about seven tarts here . . . No, I'm not in cattle class. No . . . No. Honestly. Don't be daft, woman. I'm a lawyer not a lover, a liar not a lawy– no, a lover, never mind . . . No, I'll be in at the office but I'll be home early. Remember, I'm the man who saw Mud in 1973 when they were at their height . . . Aye. You just wait. You'll get a surprise . . . I know. Love ya. Bye. Bye. Bye.'

At the same moment the women, as if of one mind, burst out laughing. You like their camaraderie, how natural they are with each other. You forgive them their head-nipping noises.

The lawyer, who earlier described a famous someone as 'the most reptilious man I ever met', intrigues you more than the characters did in the book you couldn't read.

You twist and stretch, do a fake yawn that turns into a real yawn and surreptitiously angle your head to look at him. He is a silver-haired man with, frustratingly, a face that is handsome, or was. His eyes are watery and sad.

And right then you see into his mind. You know his life. You know everything about him. You have sympathy for him. He is one of those people whose pillow speaks at night.

Yes, you know it. Know how, at night, his very pillow talks to him.

(You resolve to write one day about the things your pillow says to you.)

But what does *his* pillow say?

Regret, his pillow sadly whispers. *Shame. Pity. More regret.*

You get off the train at a suburban stop even though you meant to continue to the central station. As the train pulls away, you can still hear the women shrieking. You left your book on the train. The gin fumes were getting to you. You feel dismayed, and will experience a deflation, an actual physical ennui, for the rest of the day. You will never again try to read the DeLillo book because it will always remind you of the strange despondent feeling that came over you that day when you got off the train one stop early, at great personal inconvenience, and you suddenly felt you understood what synesthetes mean when they describe the emotional meaning of colours because on this day you understood that grey has a meaning, you knew what greyness really means, and greyness has had that tinge and meaning ever since.

And the man? You might put him in a story. It would end like this:

> 'Later that night the man rolls into bed and the pillow starts up with its talk of regret and pity and insecurity and shame and he slams his hand down on it repeatedly and a babyish tear trickles down his cheek and he vows, finally, to take that fucking bastard pillow to court.'

I guess people tolerated my story, some liked it. Maybe some people truly *got* it. For whatever unconscious reason, I thought, I had possibly not taken my best story to the B&F and for similarly buried motives I felt at peace as the audience clapped their hands and stamped their hooves politely. Maybe I truly didn't want to beat Archie and maybe I genuinely didn't want to beat Macy. I liked the story. It was real. I was fine.

Yes. I smiled and waved. I realised I was happy. I didn't need to win.

Dalston Moomintroll asked me some inane questions about the need or otherwise for fiction to relate to an author's real life. People on this island were apt to be interested in a person's affairs. I answered the questions honestly and walked off stage feeling like a man freed from a prison he hadn't quite realised he'd been in. The only comment I remember making was 'People think I write fiction. The weird truth is that reality in this place corresponds to the outpourings of a fevered imagination – or vice versa. But anyway, here's the thing. Something affirmative has to be made out of it.' I think I even repeated the last line.

I missed Myrtle Budd's introduction as I had to go backstage and take a 'natural break'. The facilities backstage were of a superior class to those out on the Castle Green, so I had to go now, intrigued though I was to see what Myrtle would come up with. None of the B&F staff I saw congratulated me, although they were pleasant enough. I knew my chances of winning were zero. QuickQuidSid's 100–1 odds were, after all, realistic. The thought didn't cut me to the quick. I felt like I was growing as a person.

I found my way back to my place in the crowd as Myrtle took a neutral stance at the microphone. Macy and Archie both commented on how much they liked my story. They knew, and I knew, that I was not going to win the Brilliant & Forever. I trusted they could see my smile was genuine and I harboured no real disappointment in myself. Everything was what it was.

At least I didn't miss any of Myrtle's story. A generously proportioned woman in a black and lime-green dress, she seemed unfazed to be at the B&F. The very ordinariness of her attitude made her stand out; all the other writers I'd seen today had been far more self-aware. I hoped I had achieved something of her insouciance when I read (though I privately doubted it). Her fingers flashed with colourful costume jewellery – she had at least one ring on every finger. Bless her, Myrtle's make-up looked like it had been put on with a paintbrush. Her expression was weirdly empty, giving her the air of one whose life has had so many disappointments she no longer entertains high expectations, yet neither will she release her inner tenacity. I wondered if she had witnessed tragedies that put everything else in perspective; the B&F then would be only of relative importance. What would *her* pillow whisper to her at night? I envisioned her watching as paramedics tried in vain to bring a young daughter back to life. I shook my head. Where did that come from?

Myrtle began reading in an almost impassive tone, but as she continued she began more and more to engage with the work and her whole body began to move with the cadences of her increasingly impassioned sentences:

Fried Chicken

She took a seat beside a window where the light entered glowing and helpful like a good thought. She took out her pen and notebook.

But a man was compelled to squawk out dissonant noises on his accordion. She could now see him, standing there, almost smug, right outside the library. She tried to concentrate, to fix her mind on fresh ideas, but couldn't.

So, she said to herself, that gentleman is busking at the same time as he is teaching himself how to play the instrument.

She glanced round at the other library users – frowning students, intellectuals and creatives – and felt important to be among them, though at fifty she was older than most. She wondered how many pieces of writing the accordion man's racket was ruining.

Or perhaps, she thought, I'm just making excuses. Occasionally someone dropped a coin in the busker's direction. He would nod, give an obsequious smile that almost seemed patronising, and set his box screeching with a redoubled effort.

I shall try, she thought, to write a poem about the difference between sympathy and empathy.

But not today. Today my mind is tearing at itself like a mad widow's hair. She wrote that image down, but writing it made her uncomfortable and it made no sense so she crossed it out.

She realised she hadn't even taken her jacket off. She decided she wouldn't.

Upon leaving the library she noticed, standing there in the street, that her stomach was actually aching with hunger. She frowned and pulled money out of her pocket. The busker looked at her, insincere with eagerness. Hmm. Coins only. Maybe I should start busking. I shall throw him, she thought, not a coin but a disparaging look.

And so she did.

His eyes momentarily hissed in response.

Walking past a fried chicken outlet she halted, squinting, as she realised that its meals, like the sign that told her so, were aggressively cheap. She went in, ordered as much as she could afford and ate ravenously the chicken burger and salted chips, and all but a couple of the chicken nuggets.

As an exercise to get herself going, she imagined she were someone else, a stranger, looking over from another part of the premises and watching her right now. He – the stranger was a he – would notice her rounded black-clothed figure sitting with an irretrievable slouch at the table, notebook open, a three-quarters-filled page of text slashed with crossings out and scribbles. He'd see her paper plates, on one of which the pair of chicken nuggets sat in an America-shaped smudge of grease. He'd see her eyes ping-pong like an intellectual engaged in a deep problem, or like someone who, knowing they're being observed, gets nervous or pretends to be more intelligent than she is.

No, he wouldn't see her like that. He would not fall in love with her. Nor would he cast his eyes once, even frictionlessly, over her. Because, she thought with a downturn of her lips, he doesn't exist, and if he did he'd think me too old, too ugly. My hair is grey and my body looks like a sick man's painting of repulsiveness. Or a sicker man's painting of attractiveness. I don't want a sick, sick man.

She wrote down the image of the America-shaped grease then stroked it out; people only believe in such things in real life, not fiction.

She looked at her notebook, and at her polystyrene cup of weak, already cold coffee. What am I doing? What are my origins? Isn't it something to do with loneliness? She wrote the word down, absently misspelling it:

'Lonelioness.'

That's me, she said to herself. I'm the Lonelioness. Serendipity makes of me the Lone Lioness, gives me random buskers and fried chicken outlets to immortalise in stories.

Her thoughts were useless, like planets forever revolving towards their own horizon.

I am, she thought, crucifyingly lonely.

She imagined she had a friend here right now. Well, an acquaintance. Okay. Try that. He worked here – yes, the guy who'd served her. Here he was now, at the fryer, dipping chicken nuggets into the sizzling fat. His name is Habib, she thought. The badge was hard to read. And so what, she thought, I too am hard to read. Maybe Habib was more of a person she could trade words with than a friend, but that still counted.

She was putting on weight alarmingly. What was in those tasty yet unappetising fried chicken nuggets and burger she just ate? They were gratifyingly, worryingly cheap. She reckoned she had put on half a stone in less than an hour. More of her hairs had turned grey. Maybe she would sell some stories outside the library and make enough money to buy hair dye.

Wait. Why would anyone buy her stories when they could walk a few more yards into the library and get better ones for free? Pity, the thing that prompted them to throw coins at the accordionist? Pity was a shaming thing.

She would sell no stories on the streets. She would sell her book to a publisher. She would be successful.

She liked Habib. His movements were swift and smooth, the sign of a hard worker. His family had probably moved here to escape conflict. Perhaps he considered everyone in this country over-privileged and too over-privileged to see it. Yes. He had skeletons but he buried them under hard work. No, that thought needed rephrasing, refining. Let's see. He was a former soldier – a terrorist-slash-freedom fighter, now reformed. Yes, he had fought on both sides of a civil war. How could such a great contradiction exist? Something, perhaps, to do with death and pity.

Nothing seemed to have meaning any more. Perhaps Habib, like she herself, felt modern times were moving too fast and in the wrong direction, like a train biting into a house. She saw it on TV. In the beginning she had gone to the TV room, thinking the stories there would provide comfort, but all the telly did was blare out atrocities or adverts or inanities that left her confused. Everyone with money or a crass attitude these days was a 'leg', pronounced 'ledge', an abbreviation of 'legend' (which her dictionary defined as 'an unverified story sometimes believed to be historical but often unauthenticated.') People were afforded 'iconic' status if they, for example, pushed a football with their foot into a net some number of times.

But the most abused word nowadays, and likely in all history, was 'love'. She had formerly believed this word terrific with promise. Happiness. Fulfilment. But the word was so debased, its promises so actively degraded, that the word was almost meaningless.

Life, she thought – perhaps not life itself, but my experience of it – feels meaningless.

'I love my life,' she said to herself, to see what it sounded like to put two - no, four - meaningless words together in an impossible sentence. Habib shot her a blank look, then went back to his dead chickens. The chicken corpses wore coats made of breadcrumbs and floated in spattering oil. Habib tailored their tiny breadcrumb coats.

Maybe, she thought, my loneliness is iconic.

As a Lone Lioness.

But, like a mental sob, came the word - no. Her loneliness was real and painful, a stain that spread through her with a flush like internal sunburn. She wrote this down. A breadcrumb-suited fried chicken could be iconic. She could not.

Because she grew up on an island (and to return there would be a confession of failure) she pictured London as an island. This took an act of effortful imagination, but hadn't imagination saved her from solitude countless times?

She sighed and a lump swelled from nothing in her throat. The inevitable tears wobbled up in her eyes. Water balloons. Childhood. She swallowed the throatlump, wiped her eyes. Her skin was saggy and made her feel ancient.

'Cheer up, love,' called Habib from behind the counter. 'Might never happen.' A cliché.

She heard herself asking 'What might?' Her tone was bitter, strange, and Habib's eyelids flicked wide like a puppet's. He hesitated.

'What might never happen, Habib?' she continued. 'Death?'

'Death comes to everyone,' he said, plunging a breaded chicken into the sizzle of oil. 'And my name's not Habib, it's Hamid.'

'And I am the Lone Lioness,' she said, with a hint of triumph in her voice. It gave her a thrill to speak her thoughts aloud. Speaking creatively was very like writing, only it was shared more spontaneously. She ought to talk to people more often, especially when she had imaginative things like this to say.

But Hamid was again absorbed in his work, perhaps deliberately ignoring her. She felt like sighing, thought of roaring, but did nothing. The Lone Lioness played things cool.

She took hold of her pen and wrote:

'Gregorina Samsa awoke from a restless nightmare to find herself transformed into a monstrous fried chicken.'

She paused. Could she imagine herself into that?

Her phone trilled, shook her jacket pocket.

'Hello?' she said and then, with a coy smile, 'You have reached the phone of the Lone Lioness. Please share spontaneously after the roar. Roar.'

'Mum? Mum, where are you?'

'Who is this, please?'

'It's Liza . . . Your daughter. I need to know where you are. Did you go outside?'

'A daughter, imagine! Well, you are funny—'

'Look around you, Mum, please. Please. Just . . . just describe what you see. We'll come and get you. It's all going to be fine.'

'Of course it's fine. Who are you?'

'Oh Mum. It's Liza, your daughter. I'm frantic here. Are you in a shop somewhere? Could you hand the phone to someone?'

'Hamid,' she shouted, holding the phone out. 'There's someone on the phone for you. Someone's daughter.'

Hamid eyed her solemnly. 'Lady, this is a quiet family business. Please, enjoy your chicken.'

She touched the phone back to her ear. 'He's busy putting bread jackets on the chicken corpses.'

'Chicken? Are you in a chicken shop? A fried chicken place, is that where you are? Nearby?'

She picked up a fried chicken nugget and said, 'I am picking a chicken out of the America grease. Now here's the thing, the thing to do with the next story. It would be enough if in a fried chicken outlet the chicken which calls itself chicken tasted of chicken the way chicken is meant to taste. You see, how can even 'meant to taste' be an affront to meaning? You think the Lone Lioness doesn't deserve chicken to mean chicken?'

The voice on the phone was struggling. 'Mum, Denzil and I are on our way, we're coming to get you, stay there. Is it the one near the mobile phone shop or the one opposite the cinema?'

'That's another thing – you would think the cinema would have good stories. But I do. I could tell you about the island.'

'Stay there. Just stay there, okay? Have some more food. We'll come and hear your stories. Ten minutes, just ten minutes. Don't move. Promise me?'

Images floated before her, the kind she gets before a story starts. The sea.

She found it very difficult to believe she had a daughter, far less that the strident voice on the phone belonged to such a person, a slithered-out-of-me creature now walking frantic in the world, frenetic, towards her right now. Really?

Am I to make myself available to other mother-seekers? I, in my vibrating phone jacket, with a pen in my hand and a thousand stories, or at least story beginnings, in my head?

No. The stories struggle, they're looking for a mother. No, not a mother, they have that, they have a mother, and they have an upbringing, they just don't have a final, what would you say, denouement, climax, ending, none of that.

Nothing ever seems to truly end.

How, then, do we know what the conclusion is? The chicken dies and is, we suppose, desecrated, hacked and hurled into the designated factory bin and injected with water – is slurry involved? At any rate something inhumane, inchicken-ane. There is a denaturalising of the chicken, it is rendered into something the pre-deceased, pre-corrupted chicken would never have recognised, then the stuff is packaged and transported and deep fried by Hamid and it is chewed and scoffed by me and sent down my gullet into my digestive system and the chicken's very own denouement climax ending is his or her, we'll never know, being expelled, voided, by my big fat butt, tucked into the egg of my faeces, ultimately skittering out into the toilet bowl, plop, gone.

That's no life.

That's no death.

And yet – that is what was a life and that is what was and will be a death.

Suffer the little chickens.

A vision of the sea came to her. The island. London. The London Island.

The island I inhabit, she thought, and she decided to say it aloud: 'The island I inhabit is an urban island, with a sea made of concrete. All the boats have wheels. And the palm trees are fried chicken outlets.' She realised, saying it aloud, how good it sounded. It was musical, if you made it musical, and it had rhythm, when you believed it and said it right. Yeah! She clicked her fingers, both hands.

'The island I inhabit,' she half spoke, half sang, 'is an urban island. With a sea made of concrete.' She stood up, moved to the side of her table and shimmied. 'All the boats have wheels.' Her voice grew stronger, giving her confidence and best of all a man at a corner table clapped and laughed and said, 'Yeah!'

'And the palm trees are fried chicken outlets!' This got a terrific response. People laughed at her wit and whooped and one person shouted, 'We's eating in a fucking palm tree, innit!'

and she could see how much happiness she was spreading and so, encouraged by the jovial atmosphere she had brought about in the fried chicken shop, now much busier than she'd realised, she started her rap again, louder, with a more complicated beat which involved clicking fingers and clapping her hands. 'The island I inhabit / is an urban island / with a sea made of concrete. / All the boats have wheels. /And the palm trees / are fried chicken outlets.'

She learned, as she repeated the verse, to maximise her volume as she rapped the words 'fried chicken outlets' and she understood in the energy crackling and stomping in the room that what she had created was a mantra. Everyone, or at least some folks, joined in that part each time, anticipating it like a great chant: 'FRIED CHICKEN OUTLETS.'

Someone, now two of them, teenage boys, at a table over there were moved to tears, they shook with the emotion. She too was carried away by the swell of excitement. She felt young and sexy, swung her hips to the beat, pounding from over here to way over there. 'Yeah! Palm trees! Islands! Sea of concrete! Sing it! The boats have, the boats have, the boats have what? Wheels! And the palm trees! And the palm trees! And the palms trees! Sing it with me. Are fried chicken outlets.

'No no no no no. All together, like you mean it – all at once!'

'ARE FRIED CHICKEN OUTLETS.'

That's right, she thought. Now we're together.

'At once now. And the palm trees! And the palm trees! And the palm trees!'

'ARE FRIED CHICKEN OUTLETS.'

But behind the hubbub of the ragged mantra, there arose a need to be somewhere very silent.

Seized now by a terrific wild energy, she hurled her last chicken nugget at Hamid, who ducked skilfully towards the wall-mounted phone, and she dashed across the ugly plastic floor and ripped the door open and bolted out into the street. The wind that washed over her in a swift, heavy tide had a taste of salt, or maybe that was the taste of chicken still on her lips. No, it was the sea.

She marched along the pavement, not calming herself in the slightest, but not regretting it either, even when she realised she'd left her notebook behind. The wind blew in gusts, sending birds flurrying over this riverful of reflected stars. She felt free and wild and crazy with desire for the kind of life she'd never wanted. She stepped into the river, ran towards a bus.

This was a strange one. Myrtle Budd's story felt disquieting – sad and disorientating – but she performed it increasingly in character and when she jiggled about and started doing the fried chicken rap, some audience members joined in heartily, but others felt that the contrast between the mentally ill woman's situation and her launching into a boisterous rap was too disturbing to bear. Thus, in some quarters judgemental looks were exchanged and in others an outbreak of clapping and chanting arose on cue. 'Are fried chicken outlets! Are fried chicken outlets!'

Dalston Moomintroll approached Myrtle Budd with a wary politeness. 'My, now, wasn't that something,' he said. 'Tell us the, uh, genesis of your piece.'

'I needed a change from island life. Sometimes we know a place so well it's not that place we see any more, but ourselves. Every island's a mirror. Anyway, I moved to London,' said Myrtle. 'And – wow. City life is very different to life on the island here.'

Murmurs of recognition and approval rumbled through the audience.

'And, y'know, that city might as well be situated on another planet. It's so alien. There was nothing for it but for me to treat the urban environment as an adversary.'

People and alpacas were listening with respect. In common, I think, with most of the audience, I knew very little about Myrtle Budd beyond her 'garish dress sense'. We have a tendency up here to judge people on what seem to be their surface choices: clothes, hair, tattoos, car, house. If someone dresses in a loud or attention-seeking way we tend to think that is who they are and we thus have no real need to get to know them better. They are defined by how they look. In this manner, we label a person like Myrtle Budd superficial, without realising the irony of doing so.

I had thought Myrtle was a maybe-detached, maybe-self-absorbed person without much of an inner life. I now cursed myself for being so narrow minded and forgetting that every other person in the world is fighting battles of their own.

Almost no one today had read a piece of writing I'd have expected them to write. Certain individuals were far deeper and more unpredictable than I had admitted. I felt a little sick at how patronising my attitude had been, of how unaware I'd been.

Far from being a shallow person driven by her own wants, Myrtle was proving herself a woman of intellectual substance and emotional depth. My body flinched, as if admonishing itself.

'The city,' she was saying, 'claimed to house people of every kind. But where were the people of my kind? Those who live without wants and who open themselves to nature? Opposite the noisy, thin-walled, smoky hostel in which I lived, there was a fried chicken outlet that defied me utterly.'

Humans and alpacas alike were rapt. Who talked liked this? Of being defied by fried chicken joints?

'I wrestled with the strangeness of this fried chicken outlet

143

and tried to overcome its ways, tried to beat it into submission, like a mind scenting its territory. But it defied me.' Myrtle paused. 'In the end I laughed and accepted the fried chicken outlet for whatever the hell it was.'

Which was broadly the same reaction Myrtle Budd and her story received. People laughed, showed their acceptance through applause, yet even as Myrtle was making her way off stage it was as though a huge invisible question mark hung in the air, clinging and goading, like the smell of fried chicken, or perhaps the way fried chicken smells to living breathing chickens.

Macy and I reached out to each other and clasped palms while Dalston Moomintroll introduced Archie. We looked at each other wordlessly and nodded, meaning 'I'm nervous for Archie and you're nervous for Archie but let's try not to be nervous for him and whatever happens we're all three of us in this together.'

Dalston Moomintroll wiped his large forehead with a tissue and bestowed upon the audience a smile that seemed sweetly malicious.

'Ladies, gentlemen . . . alpacas. It is many years – forty, I believe – since the Brilliant & Forever stage was last graced by one of our alpaca brethren.'

A restless stirring manifested in those parts of the crowd that were anti-alpaca. I consciously deepened my breathing, squeezing Macy's hand.

'That all changes today when we sample the literary delights of an alpaca who is . . . a real character. I have it on good authority his writing prowess is superior to his dancing skills.'

An unpleasant scoffing laughter tore through the front rows of the audience. I glanced back towards the shoreline. The alpacas were gazing at the stage with an air of calm intensity, as if they had rehearsed a scene like this in which prejudicial comments had no effect on them. The impression they gave was one of surface equanimity, but with something edgier simmering underneath. It unnerved some of the humans standing nearby, but I found it comforting.

'He's here today not for tokenistic reason but because he deserves to be – Archie the Alpaca!'

Now the alpacas let themselves go, stamping the ground, hollering Archie's name and cheering. Archie's human supporters applauded and shouted and whistled. Those who harboured anti-alpaca sentiments clapped their hands slowly, sarcastically, or stood still, neither gesturing nor vocalising their dissent.

We Archie fans redoubled our support when he appeared on stage. Archie walked with a purposeful stride. He looked great: his stetson sat at a humble, jaunty angle on his head and his cuspidor sparkled in the light.

I felt relieved that he looked so composed, so confident.

As he approached the microphone, he tipped his head at the alpacas along the shoreline. They cheered him as one, southern and northern flocks alike.

Archie smiled. 'Thank you. Thank you, alpacas, ladies, gentlemen. Thank you so much. It is an honour for me to be here.' His voice broke slightly with the emotion. 'I believe in a world in which we all get along, in which we all act mindfully and selflessly, not mindlessly and selfishly. I believe in a world in which we are, all of us, equal. I trust it is in such a spirit that I was invited here to compete at what I consider, as I'm sure many of you do, one of the world's most unique and meaningful literary competitions. And I must believe, therefore, that my offering will be judged on its merits, as all the other entries will be judged, and not because it was written by an alpaca.'

This went down well with a good proportion of the audience. I beamed. 'I'm so proud of him,' I said to Macy.

Macy nodded. 'C'mon, Archie. Give us a winning story.'

Archie spat into his cuspidor, gave a slight bow to the audience at large, then started to read:

Aliens that Weren't and a
Spaceship that Was

They were at it again.

'I'll show him. Prick.' His voice was loud and snarling. 'Piece of shit. I'll kill him.'

I shook my head, frazzled. My wife and I had come to think of them as alien. Not the child, obviously, but them. The couple from hell. The wife, for whom we had initially felt pity and concern, was exactly like him: screaming, selfish, enraged. They smoked and drank. Drug abusers, likely. Our sympathies diminished along with our sleep.

'Arseholes, the lot of them,' he bellowed.

The wall vibrated.

Isabella gave a long, quivering sigh, the kind you might hear from someone emerging alive from a car crash. 'That poor, poor child.'

I knew what was coming next.

'No more putting it off. We have to report them.'

I moved closer on the couch. 'Look, when we come back from Gortahork we'll see if things have quietened down. They can't live like this all the time.'

Isabella nodded but her green eyes were dimmed with scepticism.

'It's as well we *are* going away. Much longer on three or four hours' broken sleep and I'll be clean out of my mind.'

We had moved in ten days ago, bright with the excitement of living in a new part of the city, and bone-weary from carrying boxes. When we fell into bed that first night we hugged and talked about how great it was to be living near the park and how cute the apartment was, with its old-fashioned air-heating system and garish retro wallpaper. Our murmuring voices grew slow and sleepy and our breathing deepened and we spooned and sank into a contented sleep.

But. A scream soon woke us. Adrenalin thrummed in my heart. Isabella clutched at me. 'What was that?' She sat up and froze, her eyes wedged open in the half-light.

Noise. A deep rumbling. A high pitched wail – a child, I thought. 'Fucking kill him!' An explosion. A woman's scream. 'Ya beauty, ya fucking beauty!' Raucous laughter, male and female. Another voice, shrieking over some horribly stirring music. Something about a species from another planet.

'It must be next door,' I said. 'They're watching a film, they sound drunk.'

'For god's sakes. Was that a child? What time is it?'

I brought my watch up to my good eye. 'Five fifty. Unbelievable. Just how thin are these walls?' I raised myself to a sitting position.

'They told us this was a nice area, peaceful. Why are they drunk, watching a film, when there's a child in the house?'

Racket or not, I could hear, just, tears in Isabella's voice. My heart thudded. 'It'll be okay. Must be an occasion, a birthday or something. Try and get back to sleep. We'll go and see the deer in the park tomorrow.'

'Today.'

And that was our introduction to the neighbours from hell.

It was as if they didn't own a clock and had never spent time in civilised society. I started calling them the aliens, trying to make a joke out of it, to soothe Isabella's nerves. 'They've actually only ever had one drink,' I told her. 'When they first came to Earth.' I smiled, warming to it. 'Yeah, they saw how much humans and alpacas enjoy drinking, tried out a beer, and because their bodies aren't designed for it, they've been pissed and regretting it ever since. It's one of the reasons they're angry.'

Isabella giggled. I am never happier in this life than when she laughs.

'Yeah,' I continued, 'they were drunk at first, y'know, for months, on that one beer, but now they're sobering up, the hangover's kicking in.'

'Dear god,' said Isabella, 'how long is that going to last, then?'

Over the next few days, Isabella and I argued about alerting the authorities. We debated it, I'm happy to say, in a calm and reasoned manner. Eventually we reached a compromise. I'd been asked to read at a book festival that was taking place in Gortahork, Ireland, three weeks after we moved house. I'm fond of Gortahork as that's where I first met Isabella. This would be my third visit to the festival. If the aliens were still causing problems when we got back, I promised, we'd contact social services.

I hadn't fully figured out my reluctance, but it had something to do with not wanting to be a snitch. What could I tell the authorities? Please lock up this child's parents because they're noisy and they drink and stay up late? Christ, my own parents did that.

We survived those first days by learning strategies. We timed our work for the mornings, which the aliens and their baby slept through. I said to Isabella, 'The alien suckling's temporal biomechanism has autochronously adapted to primarily nocturnal activity.'

Isabella, however, was laughing at my alien jokes less often and I had to concede the witticisms were losing their sheen, despite my comedy motto, 'Repeat until funny'.

My nickname for the noisy neighbours soon grew more apposite. On our fourth night in the new flat a torrent of prejudice erupted beerily next door.

'Fucking send them home if they don't like it here.'

I turned to Isabella. 'Now there's irony for you.' Her smile was so very cute, a little part of me swooned and melted inside.

Mrs Alien barked, 'Fucking stealing jobs from the locals.'

'I ask you,' I said in mock horror. 'But hey, you gotta admit, they're really picking up on local culture.' This place had treated me to its share of anti-alpaca abuse.

But Isabella was massaging her forehead. 'Dear god, make it stop.'

'I'll put the TV on,' I said, picking up the remote. 'And if it's so loud he has to come and complain, then good. We'll see if the lizard tail is visible when you look closely. Or the circuitry beneath the hairline.'

I paid no attention to what was on TV, it was just an aural shield. But at some point, maybe half an hour later, it was as though the volume suddenly doubled.

'What?' Isabella was frowning.

I picked up the remote and squinted at it. 'Maybe I was sitting on it.' I started pressing the 'volume down' button, glancing at the screen as I did so. A spaceship was taking off from a red planet. The spacecraft looked like a toy, all the more so as I decreased the volume. But when I muted the volume altogether we could still hear booster rockets.

Isabella and I looked at each other as it dawned: they were

watching the same film next door. Very loudly, just as they did everything else.

'Maybe it's a transmission from the home planet,' I said.

'You think the planet they come from was knocked up for a tenner in Pinewood in the 1950s?'

I grinned. 'What it is, they *know* there's alien life out there but they don't know these are movies. To them, these are documentaries.'

That was how we learned they watched the sci-fi channel every night.

Our thoughts were turning more and more to the poor child. We knew he was called Rex. 'Because,' I explained to Isabella, 'his parents, when they first landed on earth, didn't realise Rex is more of a dog than a human name.'

'No', she replied, 'it's because to them he's just a pet that can look after itself. Selfish bloody creatures.'

What did poor Rex's future hold? Lack of discipline, fierce parental anger. Feral behaviour. Skiving off school. Joining a gang. 'Petty' crime and 'casual' violence. Alcohol. Drugs. An up-scaling of antisocial activity, culminating in prison time. Ignorant, child-spawning sex. Dole. More jail time. Entrapment, whether within or outside of prison. Horizons of possibility shrunk down to near negligible size. No creative life, no spiritual development. A brood of hostile, deprived, impoverished children. Stress. Alcohol and/or drug dependency. More stress. Unhappiness. Six foot under in a cheap wooden box. Reborn into the same situation, different body.

'I feel sorry for them,' I said. 'They must always have had unfulfilling lives. Think of what their childhoods were probably like.'

'That,' Isabella replied, 'is why we need to let the authorities know what's going on. Break the cycle.'

'There has to be a better way, a way towards a more lasting positive change.'

'You know, what's worse than living with that,' she said, pausing dramatically and tilting her head towards the thin wall that barely screened the chaos of noise behind it, 'is living with myself knowing I heard all that going on in there and did nothing about it.'

How tiredness impinges on the mind. My rich and colourful dreams were first drained of their colour, then they disappeared completely, as if snatches of restless sleep were not enough to merit a dream.

Rousing groggily, fog-brained and tender-headed after another night of it, I turned to find Isabella awake, staring at the ceiling.

'Morning, my love.' I kissed her but, either because of my morning breath or because of how things were, she didn't respond. 'How are you feeling?'

'Terrible. They do the drinking, we get the hangovers.'

I grimaced. Isabella had past issues with alcohol.

'Listen,' I said. 'This here is suffering. As the Buddha said, all of life is suffering. This is a . . . a sore reminder of that. It could be good for us. There is no I. Just as there's no self in the dreaming, there's no self in the waking.'

She turned her back on me as she sat up and searched for her slippers, 'But this is heartless and wrong.' Her tone was cold.

'Baby, we'll meditate this through, I promise.'

'Will we.'

I spent the rest of that morning sitting in a meditative position in front of a blank wall. Isabella did not offer me lunch, nor did she come and ask if I was going to make myself something. So it was midday and my stomach was growling but instead of going to the kitchen, I went and sat beside her on the couch and gave her a big hug, which she received but did not particularly return.

'We'll get through this,' I whispered in her ear.

She stiffened. 'That's a fallacy,' she said sarcastically. 'There is no "we".'

In the afternoon I sat in a local café that had nothing local about it, sipping a wheatgrass smoothie. A tired jumble of mental images kaleidoscoped around my head: pictures of a grizzled man and a sourfaced woman hurling cigarettes and beer cans at each other with their tentacles while a baby in a filthy cot screamed and writhed; my wife sobbing her rage into a damp pillow; a spaceship descending ominously to earth from a cold and suddenly alien sky.

I remembered my mindfulness practice and silently counted my out-breaths for a few minutes and thus gathered myself back into the moment.

The café was quiet and even had something of a relaxed atmosphere. People talked in gentle voices and listened to each other. They smiled easily and sipped at steaming drinks. At a nearby table a woman with a superior facelift was saying to a well-turned-out, glossy-haired boy of about four, 'There's strawberry tarts and cinnamon buns and vanilla slices. Which one is your favourite?'

And the little boy gave a small radiant smile and clapped his hands and said, 'Any.'

Just so, he broke my heart and made up my mind.

'The sun shines constantly,' I remarked to Isabella that evening. 'If there are clouds that prevent us from seeing it, that makes no difference to the sun, which shines on. It is in its nature to do so. Does the sun vanish out of existence at night? No. In the act of being a sun, the sun expresses and fulfils its true nature.'

Isabella stared at me in shocked disbelief.

'What's wrong?' I asked.

Her tone was controlled and venomous. 'Does this sermon have a purpose?' She had never spoken to me quite like this.

'Baby, think about it with me. We're the obstacles here. The family next door are just expressing their nature their way. He doesn't know better than to yell and shout, just as the baby can't help crying.'

She folded her arms across her chest, pressed her lips together. 'That's it? That's the best you can come up with?'

'I promise you, I could go and sit down and talk to him, to both of them, for hours. And they might listen and they might even quieten down for a few days. But soon enough, the yelling and arguing and all the rest of it would start up again, that's for sure.'

'Your big idea is just to do nothing? Let them win, trample all over our sleep? Cos we're special. We don't need sleep.' Her voice was rising.

'This bitter attitude really doesn't suit you.'

'Waking up tireder than when I went to bed doesn't suit me. Being a doormat doesn't suit me. Moving to a home worse than the last one doesn't suit me. Why can't you be assertive about this? I've given you days to come up with what's obvious to anyone else. And you have the audacity to solve it with "Let's do nothing. The problem will go away." No, you've done better than that; we're the fucking problem!' Isabella was shouting now.

'We prove by example.' My own voice was rising in conviction and volume. 'We redouble our own efforts at meditation and being mindful. They'll see our way of life is better. They'll want what we have. This is real. Grassroots. Buddhism. We'll show them the Way.'

She screamed: it was a wild sound, pure frustration, and it went on for ten or fifteen seconds.

And there was a moment of grace, of silence, actual silence, before it was broken by the sound of the baby next door letting out a piercing wail and in a second there was a deliberate hammering sound as if a fist were – in fact, a fist was – beating on the wall. Thump. Thump. Thump.

A harsh, familiar voice thundered, 'Quiet in there, we've a fucking baby trying to sleep here.'

And that's when it happened. Rage – utter rage – seized hold of me and shook me bodily. My legs were trembling, all of me was, and just as I couldn't stop my body shaking neither could I control what I did next. The powerful fury marched me out our front door and across the brief corridor to the aliens' flat and I was striking at the old wooden door again and again and again with a strength I didn't recognise. Each blow that landed on the door set it vibrating in its frame, but I felt nothing. I believed I could tear the door out of its hinges, if that's what it took.

Isabella was pulling at me from behind. 'What are you doing? Stop it. Come inside.' Her voice was a pained whisper. I turned to her and growled. 'Get inside. I'm sorting this. You wanted it sorted. GO!' As I shouted the last word, she cowered back into our doorway, though I could see from her eyes that what scared her was not me, but – I turned to see what.

He was a squat man with tattoos on his neck, old faded blue-ish tattoos that were smudgy yet spoke clearly of violence, contempt, prison. He wore a dirty vest and either the flat emanated a bitter, smoky smell or he brought it with him. I idly wondered what crack smells like when he spoke out, rough and loud, from a place of deep malevolence.

'The fuck d'you want, camelface?'

My fury withered.

He took a step closer, reeking of beer and vodka. 'I said, who are you and what the fuck d'you want, camelface?'

Focus on the breath. I let out a long, slow exhalation and said, 'I'm here for you. I'll explain—'

'You what?' As he spoke, a strange little yelp of laughter seemed simultaneously to burst from him. Behind me, I heard Isabella's voice – illegible, but it was her telephone voice.

'Yes. With compassion and wisdom, we can get you out of the animalistic realm,' I heard myself saying, 'and back into the human.'

He shook his head as though I were some manner of creature he had never seen before.

'See,' I said, 'I shouldn't have allowed myself to succumb to the anger. I'm not going to do that. I got angry. But I've now gathered my metta, my loving-kindness, and I'll show you how to do that, too. It means that, as I'm breathing, I'm thinking, "May you" – about you – "May you be well, may you be happy, may you be free from suffering, may you progress". The progress I mention is advancement through the wheel of life—'

A connection, swift and sure: his fist launching into my face like a boxing glove.

My reading went badly. I mean, I'm my own toughest critic, but still. My swollen face and weepy half-shut eye (thank goodness it was my bad eye) elicited sympathetic winces from the scattered Gortahork audience when I first took to the stage, but the reading, as became increasingly clear to me and to the politely grimacing book lovers, was haphazard at best. As if my mind were elsewhere – which it was. My thoughts were at my in-laws', where Isabella was spending a few days mulling things over.

In the hospital I'd begged and pleaded with her. There were tears, outbursts. I tried to fix things, but Isabella felt she had seen a version of me that changed her whole conception of who I am.

'I don't know who you are anymore.'

'I'm no one. There is no I. And I love you so very, very much,' I told her. 'Do you still love me?'

She didn't answer and later that day she phoned social services to report suspected maltreatment of an infant and she moved back to her parents' upper middle-class home 'for some well-deserved thinking space'.

I travelled to Ireland on my own. And there I was sitting on a slab of rock by the shore in the evening chill. In a field behind me some sheep bleated their version of chit-chat at each other. To my right a rowing boat tugged at its mooring, sending ripples through the reflected stars. Overhead, I saw a star winking and, it seemed, moving. A shooting star!

No. Too slow. It was large and bright and twinkling and had definitely moved. Of course; I recalled a news item on the hotel TV. The International Space Station was visible for a few nights. And there it was, amazing, tinily winking and flashing in the vast shimmering sky. There were human beings up there inside that flickering light right now, living and working.

I sat back on the slab of stone. The evening seemed to blacken, the bright glittering lights in the sky intensified. A seagull wheeled overhead, cold-eyed, hungry, and swooped enormously below the space station. It gave a mewling, yearning call.

A thought struck me: if all is one or if we have a creator, then all that is earthly is first of all unearthly.

The sea gestured and sighed, steadily churning its fishes and corpses alike. I leaned forward and cradled my face. My cheeks were wet with brine. As if sick of how things are, the sea repeatedly pushed itself away from itself and lunged forward in ever more desperate waves that swam up and fizzed and dribbled and hissed and fizzled out on the black wet shingle, dying flatly in gone bubbles.

I have never been myself.

A moment's silence filled the air, then the applause started. It was a mixture of the awed, the strident, the begrudged.

'Least he wrote from the point of view of a person,' called a fat man in a baseball cap.

'No he didn't,' said someone else.

'Remember that's the alpaca who ruined the B&F party,' someone said, to a chorus of like-minded disapproval.

Macy and I turned to each other, speechless for a moment.

'Wow,' I said. 'He's never written anything like that before. All the other stories he's done are, well, nothing like that.'

'There was so much in it. He's obviously going in a new direction.' Macy shook her head in wonder. Then a shocked look came over her face. 'Oh my god. I think he's going to win.'

'He . . . he really could.' I beamed.

We turned to look at the alpacas. Both groups, northern and southern, had come together and were chattering excitedly, moving their legs in restless excitement. I caught the eye of one, raised my fist in triumph. He tipped his stetson and grinned.

'Can you imagine what this could mean?' I said to Macy. Someone turned to me and said, 'Yeah. Camelfaces'll be demanding to become an even bigger drain on civilised society.'

At once a cold fury sizzled in my blood. I breathed evenly, counted backwards from ten in my native language. The best revenge here was to be civil, and then go insane with joy and pride when Archie won.

On stage, Dalston Moomintroll said, 'Uh, how, uh, I mean, that was something. Where did it come from?' He sounded confused, as though unexpectedly impressed, but his tone also seemed vaguely, but I thought noticeably, loaded.

Archie blinked and looked down, as if the answer were on the floor. 'Well . . .'

Don't screw this up, Archie, I thought. Please. Remember what you said. Do it for all alpacas. Don't throw it away after reading that terrific story. You could actually win the B&F.

'I guess it came from . . . Just an idea.'

'An idea you had?'

There it was again. A hint, an undertone. An implication.

'Yes. I wanted to say something about life and understanding. Identity. About sharing the space we have. And finding ourselves in it. We all, human and alpaca alike, have the same fears and drives and questions. We all have to face who and what we are.'

'This all sounds very profound,' said Dalston Moomintroll. He controlled his voice so well you couldn't tell if he was being serious or sardonic. 'What is your writing saying to us?'

'The alpaca mind, just like the human mind, is extraordinary. Despite – or more likely because of – our using it every day, we think of the mind, if we think of it at all, as an ordinary, humdrum thing, a living wallpaper, a moss, an entitlement. We don't appreciate how truly extraordinary the mind is. I believe it's important to . . . to stay true to the values that make truth worth staying true to.'

'Ah,' said Dalston Moomintroll, 'so yours is a true story?'

'In a way,' said Archie. 'Realism begins with the author casting doubt on reality. I write of real qualities in an unreal world. Anyway, it's . . . it's essential to create art out of a deep and honest concern.'

'Concern for what? The uh – fandango?'

There was an uproar of sharp, delighted laughter from some people in the crowd. To his enormous credit, Archie didn't so much as blink, but continued in a professional manner. I don't know if I was ever as proud of him.

'Concern for justice. Equality. For positive ways of living.

And this has much to do with overriding the ego, and much to do with living wisely, having a real understanding of implication.' He smiled, opened his eyes wide and shrugged. 'Imperfection at the fandango is part of it.' People and alpacas laughed. 'Fiction doesn't dictate flawless solutions, but it can lead to understanding.'

Archie was in his stride now. He picked up his spittoon and gob-spat into it and the phlegmy gunk was thick so that a string of it stretched visibly from the spittoon to his mouth and even when he pulled the spittoon away, the little bridge of liquid held, shining in the light, amplified on the large screens. People laughed; the alpacas shuffled their hooves and looked around.

Archie didn't panic, quite. But he didn't keep his cool, either. He tried to; he dropped the spittoon to the stage floor and kicked it 'nonchalantly' away, but the adrenaline or nerves or fear or anger gave him unexpected strength and he ended up hoofing the spittoon right off the stage and into the front row of the audience, where the invited dignitaries and industry bigshots sat. A camera swivelled around and showed everything. The spittoon flew into the lap of a shrieking woman whom I, and the whole island, recognised as the head of Inevitable & Essential Books. The audience reacted with gasps of shocked laughter. A potbellied man in a smelly jacket near us said, 'I know who won't be publishing him.'

The distraught woman got up, blushing with fury, and stormed to the side of the stage where some B&F staff gathered her up and whisked her away.

Archie's perma-grin was never so incongruous.

A piercing voice rang out: 'And he doesn't even have the gumption to look ashamed.'

I could see him mouthing an apology, knew from the way he hung his head that he was upset. The video screen showed he was close to tears. Maybe if you didn't know him, you would just think his eyes had a wet sheen. But I had seen him cry, and I recognised Archie pre-tears. My heart panged for him, sank, panged again. I swore.

Dalston Moomintroll was hesitant; he looked to the audience a couple of times as if to take his cue from them, but it's fair to say that while the audience was predominantly either hostile to Archie now, or indifferent, a proportion of us were on his side. I started chanting 'Ar-chie! Ar-chie! Ar-chie!' Macy, the alpacas and the ardent alpacaphiles joined in. Others, while privately supportive, were not of a mind to make public their sympathies. An old story.

'Ladies and gentlemen, esteemed audience,' said Dalston Moomintroll, motioning for us to be quiet. 'An unfortunate mishap. May I express our gratitude to you for your forbearance. I think, uh, all else being equal, we might draw the, ah, discussion segment of this particular author to an end, don't you think?' He addressed this last question to a mortified, deflated Archie. It was all he could do to nod his head and shuffle off stage while the audience gave a mixed reaction of enthusiasm for his story and enthusiasm for his leaving, pity for his public shaming and pity for his audacity.

I started threading my way through the crowd, as politely and swiftly as I could, but there was an inevitable amount of jostling. Macy trailed in my wake. I had to see Archie and comfort him. In this state, there was no telling what he might do. I knew he'd see this as a disaster both personally and more so for alpacakind.

While I was dashing and contorting my way through the crowd, I missed Tan the Ageist reading his story 'Please Be Upstanding', which I append here. I was hardly aware of him performing.

Please Be Upstanding

The Best Man closes the curtains again, glad the stag night took place last weekend. And in Prague, too, a city he rather fancifully thinks of as being achingly delicate. He's also grateful that no one in Prague has connections with the island. The humiliation of a night in those Czech cells obscurely convinces him that a massively watered down whisky is acceptable on this nervous day. Doesn't count. Even a couple of them won't count.

The Groom's heart is palpitating with something that feels more like cardiac arrest than love. He fills a hip flask with Lagavulin, tucks it into his sporran. Takes it out, samples it. Nice. Tastes it again. Again. Gently upends it. Nothing more until the reception. Flask's empty anyhow.

The girls – knowing that happiness is a great hangover cure – have organized a champagne breakfast for the Bride. They enter into the spirit of it merrily and giggle because the Big Day is here at last and because of the way it fizzles in your nose.

The ushers – two twins who wear T-shirts that say 'Dare to Be Different' – have met the Groom, their cousin, twice. They are skinning up and cracking into a litre of stolen vodka, confident it will mask their cluelessness over what their purpose really is.

The Bride's mother is sitting on her hotel room floor, shaking, photos of the Bride at various ages scattered about her on the flecked green carpet. Sighing, she reaches for her Valium and swallows two 10mg tablets dry.

The Groom's parents are no longer with us, but will receive an emotive, skewed, incomprehensible toast from the Best Man.

The Day draws to a close and the night kicks up its heels, but that is not what it is about; the whole nuptial shebang is not about chaotic dancing, nor awkward accusations, nor loose-tongued admissions, the whole god-blessed thing is about looking into each other's eyes, the trembling of ring fingers, the vowing to love one another, to care for one another, to look after one another in sickness and, as it were, in health.

I also missed Tan the Ageist's interview. Dalston Moomintroll asked if the story was about dependence or what and Tan the Ageist apparently just looked at Dalston Moomintroll for about half a minute then said, softly but clearly, 'Within a year,' before walking off stage while the audience assimilated, with a muted gasp, the implications of what he had said. Dalston Moomintroll eyed daggers at the departing Tan and said something disparaging about the Lucky Golden Eel and its misfortune cookies and 'weird, unsettling, unpleasant' staff.

Macy and I found Archie, weeping, behind the castle. I told him how proud I was of him, how proud the alpacas all seemed of him, how proud his departed parents would have been to know their only son was a competitor in the B&F. I don't know how much of this Archie genuinely believed but he wiped his eyes and nodded and said, 'Thank you.'

He seemed strangely calm, as if reconciled to defeat the same way I had been when I read. But Archie was doing this for bigger reasons, for equality and social cohesion and a better life for future generations of alpacas.

'I still think you can win,' I said. 'I mean it.'

'Sure.'

'No, really. It's no big deal if you inadvertently kicked your cuspidor.'

'Yeah,' said Macy, 'there's plenty other publishers. And if the Inevitable & Essential woman can't get over a stupid silly accident like that, she's not professional enough to be your publisher anyway.'

Archie surprised us both by saying, 'Listen, let's get back to the event.' His words were brave, in the context, but his eyes looked sad.

'Are you alright?' I said.

'I'm fine. Let's go back. I'm going to hold my head high.'

'Good for you, Archie,' said Macy.

I couldn't let go of the thought that Archie knew more than he was saying.

We walked back to the crowd and found as discreet a place as we could in the audience. Calvin O Blythe, luckily, was about to start reading so he had pretty much everyone's attention. He was a tall, bearded man with a soothing voice. He was dressed in casual, pastel-coloured clothing, like a politician on vacation or a grown-up whose mother still dresses him. He spoke in a long soft drawl that was, pretty much everyone agreed, enjoyable to listen to. I don't know him very well. He grew up in a blackhouse but now lives in a whitehouse. He took a strong, relaxed stance by the microphone and read:

Chase

When the other guys in the office killed their computers, whipped their ties off and assumed their weekend personas, Chase would sit back and stare at his screen.

At first, the guys (not including Jamesie of course) had chummily expected he would go to the Half and a Half pub round the corner.

'No, thanks, I have to be somewhere else,' was Chase's excuse.

They cajoled him and he finally confessed, 'I don't drink.'

They found this suspect, bullied him with passive-aggressive tactics. 'I'm hurt,' said one of them. 'You obviously don't like our company. You can still come, you don't have to drink.'

'I'm beginning to think,' said another, 'he does drink. And he only said that because he doesn't like us.'

Chase gave a thin smile. 'My father lived and died a horrible alcoholic. The hell I'm going to turn out anything like that.'

They glanced at each other as if looking for confirmation – of truth or a lie, it was hard to say. They shrugged, set off for the pub, and were whooping and spouting inanities before they had reached the lift.

They stopped asking him.

Besides, thought Chase, you're my colleagues, not my friends. Friends would understand.

The air was icy and refreshing. You could smell the promise of snow in the air. He loved the purity – or, rather, the illusion of purity – this crispness brought to the evening. All around him, men exactly like his colleagues swarmed past. On non-Fridays they grimly shouldered their way through, with cancelled faces. But today they babbled and swaggered with an animated purpose. They poured into featureless pubs, slalomed barwards and ordered pitchers of lager.

What did they talk about? Chase wondered as he twisted and ducked his way through the crowd. Work, gossip, football – sure. But every week? Weren't they bored? Of each other? Of themselves?

Once inside the park, Chase followed his usual route, enjoying the crunch of his shoes on the path. It seemed to him the lovely *crmmf crmmf* sound his shoes made was clearer this evening – a happy portent, perhaps, even if it was a mere side effect of the chill in the air.

He branched off to the narrower path that ran beside the old canal. Here the track was overgrown, lesser used. Your feet were not so happy here; they became alert, wary. Broken glass. Dog turds – massive ones (Chase had seen the Staffie dogs, like 'roid-rage bouncers). Once or twice a hoodrat on a BMX had come whipping along the path – no lights – almost swiping Chase into the cold rancid water. By mentally rehearsing and sometimes enacting it, Chase taught himself to lean or fall towards the non-canal side, whichever direction he was going.

Chase thought that while his colleagues had come to resent him for being, as they saw it, antisocial, some of them would respect his walking here. For he had come to the end of the lamp-lit line. The path was now a grassy track, slippery with the cold and damp, and dangerous for other reasons.

What would they think if they saw me now? Chase thought.

Even Jamesie would struggle to understand. Chase's charcoal suit and black shoes were invisible in this darkness. He had mussed his hair and removed his tie and watch, just in case. His wallet was cleverly concealed in a belted travel purse, worn round the waist and tucked into his boxer shorts.

He didn't care what his co-workers would think. Except for Jamesie – he felt he had some obligation towards thinking Jamesie's opinion important. Jamesie had got him the job with such good intentions that Chase found it impossible to refuse, though he didn't like office work of any kind. Hated it.

'Your Dad and I,' Jamesie had said to him in the café that day, 'we were a right pair. The things we got up to . . .' He looked away and shook his head, not with the twinkly nostalgia-mischief that often comes over people when rose-tinting the past, but with a frowning solemnity. He turned his grey-blue eyes on Chase. 'I sometimes think I should have tried harder, to keep your Dad in the programme.' He was referring to the twelve-step programme that had taught Jamesie to eat food, listen to the other person in a conversation, walk upright, wake up bruise-free, and live like a regular human. The programme that had given Jamesie Jamesie back.

'I know,' said Chase.

He remembered one time Jamesie – who had looked like a corpse at the time – had rolled Chase's dad up the garden path like a carpet. It was six in the afternoon, a fragrant summer's evening, and many of the neighbours witnessed the scene, dumbstruck or tittering with embarrassment. At the top of the path you had to climb four steps to get into the house and Jamesie, eyes blazing and drifting out of focus, had no energy left. Chase had dragged his father into the house, deliberately allowing his dad's knees to thud against the concrete steps.

Inside, Jamesie had helped himself to the secret stash of whisky in the toilet cistern. Chase's dad, when he eventually came to, eyed the bottle, clambered unsteadily to his feet, called Jamesie a thieving cunt, and collapsed onto Chase's lap, puking.

'If your dad had only stuck with the programme,' Jamesie said, stirring another sugar into his coffee. 'I hold myself responsible—'

'He didn't even last one month,' Chase said. 'And I think we both know he was still drinking when he was going to those meetings.'

'I was every bit as bad an alcoholic as your father was. Worse, if anything. Did you know I put Katie in hospital twice?'

Chase's eyes flared. 'No?'

'All that and more, Chase. It's poison. There's those who can take it and those who can't. Your dad and I were - in my case still am - someone who can't.'

Chase nodded, a little embarrassed, wondering where this was leading.

'I got my life back. But I was this close—' He held his thumb and forefinger out, almost touching. '—to joining your dad. There's three exits. The madhouse, the prison, or the wooden box.'

'Or just quit drinking,' said Chase.

'There's three exits if you carry on with the poison. If you break the habit, the whole world opens up to you. Look at me. I got a flat, a job, I'm paying my debts - the money ones and the other kind. Making amends.'

Chase made a noncommittal sound, unsure what making amends meant - really meant.

'I've got a lot to be grateful for. And a lot to make up for. This job I have, at William Paine Services - Billy Paine himself, well, let's say he understands my story. And I've been there long enough now he trusts me.'

'Cool,' said Chase, losing interest a little.

'I got promoted last month.'

'Congratulations.'

'So I got my own team. My own group of hardworking young men, men like yourself. Couple of years older, maybe. Decent guys, reliable guys who turn up on time and get the job done.'

'Uh-huh.'

'So what do you think?'

Chase frowned.

'Yes or no?' said Jamesie.

'I don't understand.'

'Jeez, you're no as quick on the uptake as your ol' man was. A job. Cushy job, working indoors on computers. I'm offering you a job. Data entry to begin with.'

Chase blanched. He was holding out for something in the Harley Davidson garage up the road.

But Jamesie had laid a hand on Chase's; his eyes looked worryingly watery. Chase squirmed inside. He'd never learned to be comfortable with visible signs of emotion.

'It would make me feel like I was doing something for your ol' man. It's what he would want. Once you're at Paine's, you've as good as got a job for life. Computers are the future.'

Chase felt hounded, trapped. A silent foetal howl spasmed in his mind.

Jamesie patted the hand he'd been touching and said, 'You start Monday. Here's money for a suit. Pay it back when you can.'

Chase wished he could articulate something about the nasty way life seems to have of depriving you of joy and freedom, even if these are actually small, small things in the scheme of things. What did it mean to the universe if he got a job at the

Harley Davidson place? It only meant something important to him.

Jamesie stood up but then stopped and stared, bulge-eyed, frightened as though heart-attacking. 'Chase,' he said, anguished, 'you don't – you don't touch the poison yourself.' It was more a demand than a question.

'No, I hate it,' Chase said reflexively and afterwards he was to regret taking the path of truth, which led to his current misery, rather than the path of lies, which would some months or years later have surely led to a Harley Davidson and a little fleet of pride-and-joy motorbikes he had built with his own hands.

Coming here on a Friday night gave him something akin to solace. It felt like the thing to do. The path was familiar, even in the dark. He pushed on, walking quietly and purposefully.

Chase had decided he would work at Paine's long enough to save up for a brand new Harley Davidson. And then he would just hit the road. He'd rent out his house, which in any case harboured many bad memories, and do unskilled or low-skilled jobs as he toured the country, seeing the land, meeting people, having adventures. He'd take a GoPro camera and mount it on his handlebars. Make a road movie. Have a life.

But now Chase wasn't so sure. His heart was set on the Harley, he'd saved up four grand already – it was just that leaving town seemed an impossible wrench. He wasn't fully convinced he had the courage to break loose.

There they were. Must've managed to collect some combustibles, for a fire flickered orange and yellow, lighting their faces. From a further distance it might look cosy. But the three faces that seemed to writhe, anaemic and pinched, in the changing light and flaming shadows looked weathered and haunted. You could hardly tell the grimy face in the middle was that of a woman. The man to her left wore a dirty maroonish beanie, the one to her right a battered trilby.

Chase crouched and found his usual seat on the slab of rock beside the overgrown bush; his butt cheeks instinctively sought their semi-comfy spot and the initial roughness and coldness of the stone yielded to a bearable numbness.

He watched, as was his custom, half hidden in shadows. The trio stared, milky-eyed, into the fire, periodically raising a can of superstrength beer.

'Oh-ho!' one of them, Trilby, shouted. 'There he is. Look!'

The other two gave a sound like a slurred cheer. 'Are you no' coming over for a wee visit, loverboy?' said the woman.

'She's ready and waiting for you,' said Beanie, laughing roughly, his lungs rattling.

'Give us a fiver and she's yours,' called Trilby and his laugh, too, gurgled with decades of fags.

'Or three quid and you can keep her,' said Beanie. 'Come over, you daft bastard.'

'No point freezing your bollocks over there,' said the woman.

Chase watched, impassive, silent.

'Suit yourself,' said Trilby. 'Bring sausages next time.'

'Beer!' said Beanie.

'Beer!' said the woman.

They all rattled with laughter.

The men drank their cans faster than was their custom. Or maybe they'd begged more money than usual due to the cold snap. And maybe the woman, who was often the first to pass out, had had a bad night the night before. At any rate, the men, after innumerable beers and a fair few roll-your-own cigarettes, gave up on their increasingly senseless chat and slumped down into sleep or unconsciousness.

Chase seized his chance. He got up, nervously shook the stiffness out of his limbs and walked the dozen or so yards over to the woman, who was poking a stick, with stray coordination, into and around the dying fire.

'Um,' he said.

She looked at him with drifting, scornful eyes, and made a grumbling sound.

Someone somewhere – or was it in a book? – had once said a fire is just like a raging drunkard, glowing red, possessed by sudden evil, thirsting to consume everything, to spoil things forever, leave nothing but ashes where there had been a home, a human being. Chase daydreamed this for a second, then checked himself. This was real, vital.

'Look at me,' he said. 'Look at me properly.' His heart was battering his chest.

'Sit down,' she said, but her eyes showed no recognition.

'It's me. Chase.'

She paused, looked at him, eyes sliding in and out of focus. She scowled. 'Chase?'

'I want to help you.'

She gave a bitter, spluttering laugh.

'I want you to come home.'

She cackled.

Unfazed, Chase said, 'I have . . . well, I have the old place. Dad's gone, you knew that. But I . . .' Chase hesitated, wondered if he was really going to say this and if he really meant it. He breathed deeply and spoke slowly. 'I have some money. I'll get you a flat and I'll pay the rent on it, until you've got yourself cleaned up and got a job.'

She stared at him, slackjawed, bewildered.

'I mean it,' said Chase. 'I've been working hard. Jamesie got me a job. I've saved up. Four grand.'

She gave a sound like a low growl.

'It's not too late. I can help you to save yourself from all this. Be happy again. Have a life. This could really work out. I promise.' He put a hand on her shoulder, and mentally chastised himself as he winced at the dirty feeling that prickled his fingers. He withdrew his hand. 'Please. I'm begging you. Don't end up like Dad. You can't end up killing yourself, drinking on the streets with these, these tramps. Say you'll agree at least to come to the house. Stay the night?'

She sighed, burbled a few words to herself.

'Okay,' said Chase. 'You don't have to decide tonight. But it's going to be freezing tomorrow night, I mean properly freezing. Just come to the house. You can even bring some cans of beer. I'll run a hot bath for you. We'll talk. I'll show you how easy it is. I figured it out, how to get you a flat of your own. Please. I'm begging. Please, Mum.'

She looked at the embers, made that low growling sound again.

'Listen to me closely. I'm promising you I know how to make things better. I got the money and the means. You'll get your life, your self, back.'

She said something that sounded like 'hot bath'.

'Yes! A hot bath. Bliss, Mum! You'll feel so relaxed. It'll make you a new woman. I'll get some new clothes for you. It'll be amazing. You'll hardly believe how much your life will change for the better.'

'Hmm.'

'Just be here tomorrow night. I'll sort everything out. I'll meet you here. Just – just take it easy with the cans tomorrow, I mean just a little easier?'

'Hmm.'

'I'll make up the bed in the spare room. I'll get a hot water bottle. Imagine. It's going to be great – you'll be all warm and toasty and, you know, you'll remember what it's like to have a decent night's sleep, warm and comfortable. Safe. It's going to snow tomorrow night. This'll be one of the best choices you ever made.'

'Bath and a bed,' she said.

'Yes. Yes!'

Trilby stirred in his sleep and started cursing a blue, methylated streak under his breath.

'I have to go, Mum. But I'll be here tomorrow night. So you look after yourself. Okay?' Chase stood up. He felt a warm glow inside, knew he was doing the right thing. He wanted to do something crazy, something spontaneous like hug or kiss his mother.

'Well, till tomorrow,' he said.

'Aye.'

Chase was grateful to have so many chores to keep him busy on Saturday. He was brimming over with energy, thrilled at how excited he felt about doing something meaningful – something noble. He wasn't sure what size his mother was (12? 14? 10? He had a feeling she'd been all of these) so he decided the best course of action was to go to a charity shop and buy up a wide variety of clothes as a temporary measure. As her drinking diminished, her appetite would come back, so she'd probably put on weight. Then he'd buy her some properly nice clothes.

He bought a hot water bottle and did a large grocery shop at the local Aldi. He cleaned the house, except the bath, which he would need to scour thoroughly tomorrow. He thought about putting a throw on the couch, but then had a better idea: he'd convince his mum to have a bath as soon as she arrived.

He bought tea lights and placed them around the tub. Bad idea? He'd wait and see how drunk she was. He put a portable TV and an old-fashioned radio and some trashy novels in the spare bedroom. He hid away the photograph albums, for the time being. Tomorrow he'd casually ask Jamesie round and see if he could persuade Mum to go to those meetings. Jamesie insisted worse cases than anyone could imagine had found the cure in those meetings.

Chase surveyed the living room. Clean, friendly, calm. A good job well done. He hesitated as an unfamiliar feeling washed over him.

Bloody hell, he thought. I'm actually happy. Happy! Feels weird.

Then he thought, wow. It had been so long since he'd felt happy, he hadn't recognised the feeling.

He resolved to make a better effort at being happier. Helping others seemed to be the way to go about it.

He walked along the path with a bounce in his step. The brittle ice underfoot didn't worry him, he knew he wouldn't fall. He couldn't say how he knew this, he just knew that it was true.

As he turned the corner he heard voices – slurred and good humoured. Hell, he might even take it upon himself to help Trilby and Beanie if it worked out with his mum.

He halted. There they were.

Except.

'Where's my mum?'

Trilby turned slowly, eyed Chase from an alien distance. 'Where did you leave her?'

Beanie laughed. 'Aye,' he added, 'Careless to lose a mammy in this day and age.'

'My mum,' Chase said, angry. 'My mum, you pricks. The woman who's always here with you.'

'Gail? Gail doesn't have a son.'

'Aye, Gail doesn't have kids. Told us herself.'

The strength went from Chase's legs. He hunkered down.

'Sure, it's as cheap to sit as it is to stand,' said Trilby. 'Here. Have a swig.'

'The woman – Gail – she never recognised me until I told her. I'm her son, Chase. She walked out on my dad and me when I was twelve.'

'I'm sorry for your troubles, son,' said Trilby. 'And I hope you find your mum. But Gail has no kids.'

'You don't understand. She does have kids – she has one kid. Me. Where is she?'

Trilby shrugged. 'Was gone when we woke up.'

Beanie nodded. 'Haven't seen her all day.'

'Don't worry,' said Trilby. 'She'll come staggering around that corner any minute now.'

But as Trilby said this, Chase knew that he would never see her again.

'Have a can,' said Beanie.

'She's gone,' said Chase, talking to himself. 'I left it too late. I tracked her down and then I . . . I couldn't talk to her at first when I found her. I had to readjust my idea of who she was.'

'We thought you had a crush on her,' said Beanie and he laughed but Trilby and Chase didn't.

'I blew it,' said Chase. He felt a tear swell in his eye.

'Seriously, pal. Take the edge off it,' said Beanie, handing Chase a can of beer.

Dazed, self-pitying, hurt, Chase found himself raising the can to his lips. He sipped, sipped again, tilted his head back so the tears wouldn't fall, and gulped hard.

Calvin O Blythe's story drew a great deal of sympathy from the audience. The kind of narrative this was, the kind of island we were, there was no way a tale like that wouldn't resonate.

Dalston Moomintroll strolled back on stage, his grin smarming from ear to ear.

'Calvin O Blythe, that was a most interesting story. Does it, do you think, hold a mirror up to society?'

Calvin O Blythe pointed at a camera hovering a few metres in front, filming him. He ducked to the left, the camera panned and tilted correspondingly. He jumped to the right and again the camera copied his move. He then stood straight, self-composed, and spoke in his easy, measured tones. 'People nowadays are obsessed with "selfies". Photographs of themselves. People have always been obsessed with screens. First of all it was probably a dew drop. A puddle. Ice. Then a mirror. A camera. A television. A computer. They're fixated on these screens because deep down they want to see themselves, really see themselves and, increasingly, at a deeper, and yet more superficial level, to see themselves as having been seen.'

'Unlike that camera there I'm not sure I follow you. Who are we as a society in that story? Are we Chase? His mother, if that's what she is?'

'How can we know ourselves? The most Brilliant & Forever book this island could create is if one chapter were written by Macy Starfield, one chapter by Summer Kelly, one chapter by me and so on . . .'

'So, all you need to write a book is lots of friends who will do most of it for you?' Dalston Moomintroll was now enjoying himself, grinning dementedly at the audience as he attempted to barb his guest.

Calvin O Blythe paused. His eyes laserbeamed through Dalston Moomintroll. 'The writer sees a connection between the city lights spread below the descending plane and the stars reflected in a puddle he saw a puppy splashing in a short while and a continent ago, pawing and shattering the moon and the Milky Way into liquid shards. To write you need to have the concentration of a writer.' With a graceful move, and with no acknowledgement whatsoever to Dalston Moomintroll, Calvin turned, waved farewell to the audience and walked off stage to considerable applause. It was as if he had very politely slapped Dalston Moomintroll in the face with a damp fish. The crowd loved it.

Dalston Moomintroll smiled insincerely. 'Calvin O Blythe. The future of literature, ladies and gentlemen.' Before people had a chance to react, or Dalston Moomintroll could introduce him, Seth Macnamara strutted across the stage and grabbed the microphone.

'Hello, you wonderful people.' Seth lapped up the attention he automatically received as an incomer who was in the B&F, and handsome at that, with cheekbones that could split a coconut. 'You're the best. I came a long way to read here today and you people, let me tell you, you people are alright.' Applause – a lot of it. Minority cultures are always eager to lap up external validation, and if it's coming from a guy in sky-blue jeans and a fresh white T-shirt and aviator shades, all the better. 'This is called "Good Grief, Death".' He read in a slow, confident drawl:

Good Grief, Death

Is there anything more intriguing than death? Why more people don't indulge in the proactive exploration of death through the justifiable medium of murder is a conundrum I may never, for the life of me, fathom. Murder is a great intensifier of life; death is wasabi to life's fresh sushi.

Watch a mindnumbing game show on TV, sure. Purchase the songs the music companies tell you to buy, sure. Wear a tie and/or fishnets because your boss likes it that way, sure. But to interrogate the boundary that separates the living from the Great Unanswered, even by a simple accidental nudge as you picnic with a certain parent at that clifftop beauty spot – the thought hardly crosses people's minds. And those whose brains are occasionally lit up with sweet morbid temptation will almost always suppress the beautiful glimpsed instinct and revert to dim routine.

Imagine living such a banal existence. You're better off out of it.

Yet I'm sometimes almost a little – just a little – jealous of Candy. How simple it must be to drift through life vacant, unworried, content. Fulfilled by society's very emptiness. Weird.

When I shot Sparks in his stupid windowless garage he'd looked at me quizzically. That's the word. I'd like to think the questions he was – sorrycan'thelpit – *dying* to ask were,

'Will such a thing as I, Colin "Sparks" Gray, continue to exist in any meaningful form?'

'Where will I go?'

'Do I get to come back?'

'If not, why not?'

But it's more plausible his questions were usual, boring:

'Did you just shoot me?'

'Is this some kind of elaborate joke?'

'What. The. Fuck?'

'Am I going to die?'

And, immortal question of the imminently mortal, 'Why?'

Maybe his brain was already swirling into darkness and his last thought was, 'What's the word for that thing, the whatchamacallit, the thing that, uh . . .'

If so, his death was banal and that, any way you slice it, is a shame.

As a red stain spread over his Fleetwood Mac T-shirt I said, 'Answering one of them, yes you are going to die.'

To emphasise the point I was making I squeezed the trigger and shot him again, this time an inch or so higher. He plummeted to his knees. I winced. The garage floor was concrete, so there was no way that fall didn't smack hard pain into his knees right there. I wondered, where does that pain go, when someone dies?

A pumping red puddle spilled across the band logo on his chest. I must say, I never liked Fleetwood Mac. His face now registered more fear and self-pity than confusion. I thought of lullabying him off with a Fleetwood Mac song, but I couldn't think of any. They had that one, 'Albatross', but I couldn't quite get the tune and in any case it had no words. Now I think of it, that's one of those superslow dreamy tunes they use on exotic holiday programmes or overpriced-dessert adverts and I was too hyped up to have performed it anyway. I'd have rushed it and surely just ruined the song for him.

'You're probably wondering why this is happening.' I knelt down so he could hear me better. 'I mean, Sparks, these are your last fucking moments of life. Isn't that, when you think about it, incredible?'

I gentled my voice. 'Ssh. Don't say anything. Let's just take a moment.'

His breathing was offbeat. As if the air was jumping in a very amateurish fashion in and out of his body, the in-breath and the out-breath at loggerheads. He slumped forward a little, tried to hold himself up, but the angle was sharp and he was weak so he just went ahead and faceplanted. Again, I winced. His arms embraced himself, cute, but all awry – so, not cute, but creepy, really. Arms don't look natural, sticking out like that. Blood was spilling around him. Spilled liquid always looks like it has a life of its own. Ever notice that? How blood often seems so ridiculously desperate to escape? I have to say, it's hard not to find that kind of disloyalty offensive.

'No disrespect, Sparks, you look grotesque.'

A dark rattling sound snaked out of his throat, like – no, with – blood.

'And I hope you're not expecting me to clean up.'

His body juddered. Twice. His breathing was more uncoordinated than ever.

'Jeez,' I said, shaking my head. 'Oh hey, I just realised what it made me think of. See if you can understand this. Your breathing reminds me of two kids, and one of them's fat, jumping up and down on a trampoline. It's all messy and out of sync and someone's liable to get hurt.'

181

I was about to make some important remarks about metempsychosis but, wouldn't you know it, he'd lost consciousness, so the last thing he heard in life was my trampoline image. He left me standing there to the side of an advancing pool of blood, not quite knowing if he had got, far less appreciated, my analogy. Frustrating as all hell. Murder can be like that, but this is where perseverance, discipline and sheer stubborn dedication must be applied. What I'm really talking about is diligence, whether you're using a gun, a knife, a rope or poison. Faint heart never won decimated corpse.

Meanwhile, Sparks lay there with the 'that's that' look which dead men do so well.

Candy was sitting in the car applying lipstick.

'Goddamn it, Candy, will you quit always moving that mirror? It's for safety, to see cars behind.' I put on a girly voice to make Candy laugh. 'No, officer, I didn't see that busful of schoolchildren barrelling up behind me but don't you think "Cherries in the Snow" looks divine on my lips this season?'

Candy didn't laugh. She smacked her lips together. I love that sound. She looked beautiful. Like, photoshopped beautiful. I'm a lucky guy.

I was just about to strap my seatbelt on – can't be too careful – when I froze.

'Fuck, where're my manners? D'you wanna have a look at him? It's a really good opportunity.'

'Seth, I can't even go to the dentist without pills.'

True, that time she needed a filling she had to get spangled on diazepam first.

'But what the hell's a dentist got to do with it?'

'Does he look bad?'

I guffawed. 'Sorry.' I tried to straighten my expression.

'Apart from one monumentally bad hangover that time he drank three half bottles of vodka, he's definitely looked better. You know, aliver. Movementier.'

'Oh, you're a funny one, you.' She grimaced because she didn't mean ha-ha.

I lifted my feet off the pedals, checked the soles of my shoes for blood. Clean. Goes without saying, a murder performed neat is one of life's rarest pleasures, probably even the rarest.

'His last words were, "What's the name for when the ending of a book or film leaves you unsure, like did she die or not?"'

She sat up straight. 'Oh! I know this, I know it. Ambivalent!' She beamed, proud. A little lipstick was smudged pinkly – CherriesintheSnowly – on her top right incisor.

Who had the heart to correct her?

'Who's my clever baby?' I pulled her in, kissed her, licked the lipstick off her tooth.

'Candy-can, you could tell him.'

'What?'

'The word. Put him out of his misery.'

'You mean – is he still – alive?'

'Alive? Like you and me? Breathing and unharmed and tinkering with that motorbike engine the way he does every single other day of his life? Like Sparks always is?'

She brightened a smidgen. 'Yes.'

'Hell no, he's dead as daddy-o.'

She darkened a smidgen or three.

'But Candy-can. What you could do, you could write "ambivalent" on a piece of paper and put it in his pocket so when he goes to the afterlife he'll see it and know the word and be satisfied. Then he didn't die unhappy and incomplete.'

'Really?' She shook her head, scowling. 'No. No way.'

'No, seriously. If you want to. People who die all riled up

and antsy are the ones who're sure to come back as ghosts and haunt us poor innocent humans. That's why only some people come back as ghosts.'

'Don't mention ghosts.' She shuddered. 'Ooh, someone just walked over my grave.'

'Someone usually pisses on mine.'

'Do you have some paper then?'

She was really considering doing this.

I heard the distant siren of a cop car.

I thrust the key into the ignition. 'Fuck it, sweetcheeks. They'll have dictionaries in heaven.'

Seth looked up. The audience started applauding. Hell, they were laughing and cheering.

'Crime pays,' Archie murmured.

On stage, Seth shook his head, gestured for everyone to be quiet – there's a modest side to him, then, I thought.

As a quietness descended and spread, he said, 'A born storyteller's first story is "waaaaaaaaah" and some of them have been wailing and whining ever since. I'm here to change all that. Now, I know this is unusual, but I figured, since I came all this way and since I'm new here, and since y'all are so nice, you wouldn't mind if I read a little bit more. You can think of them as companion pieces to the first story as they're about the same character – in my book, the autobiography of a serial murderer.'

Many people and alpacas shuffled uneasily. You were only supposed to read one piece of work, submitted many months in advance. Breaking the rules was a serious issue, resulting in disqualification and, if it impacted on the People's Decision, much worse. This departure from the rules was, even by the B&F's crooked yardstick, troubling.

I glanced at Dalston Moomintroll, who was studiously

ignoring the crowd's misgivings and the fact that Seth was breaching convention. He picked at a fingernail as though that necessitated all his concentration. I realised: they're in cahoots.

Cahoots. Funny word. I said it aloud, to taste it. 'Cahoots.'

'Cahoots,' said Macy. 'Strange word. Yet it's exactly what they're in.'

'Cahoots, cahoots, cahoots,' said Archie. 'The fuckers. And he's one hundred percent anti-alpaca.'

But Seth was already reading:

Swagger, Bump

If there are any problems in the world that can't be solved by a hot black espresso, a cinnamon Danish and a loaded shotgun I don't want to know what they are. So I guess I never expected to have an altercation with someone who may at some point have served me my lava java and sweet treat.

One of the things that ruins my day is when some young buck on the sidewalk with a distorted sense of self-importance bumps my shoulder as he's swaggering past. Most bumpees feel murderous towards the bumper in this circumstance. It's where we get the phrase 'to bump someone off'. So, see, you're duty-bound to do it when you get bumped.

I'd loosened my belt one notch, enough to keep the gun snug. I was wearing a sharp black suit; it had a cool purple lining – silk. The suit didn't cost much, but it cost more than it should have. Two bullets.

I looked good in it, especially teamed with my aviator shades in which, it pleased me to think, the man sitting before me in the dust could see his own face looking back at him, wearing an expression it had likely never worn before: confusion-anxiety-fear, that whole am-I-going-to-die thing.

I asked him. 'What do you do? For a living?' The last word echoed silently between us. Talk about awkward.

'A ba-ba—'

He'd saved the moment by providing comedy potential.

'A ba-ba? What kind of baby talk's that?'

'Ba—'

'A ba-ba-bam, bam-bam-bam-bam,' I sang, Joey Ramone style. No reaction. 'Tough audience.'

'Ba-ba—'

'Baa baa black sheep?'

'Ba-barista.'

'Barista!' I exclaimed. 'You mean coffee monkey?'

'Uh.'

'You know, barista, that's Italian for coffee-pouring monkey. You wiseass motherfucker who looks with disdain at people like me who just ask for a coffee.'

'N-no . . .'

'And who stares daggers at me if I ask for a medium instead of a fucking venti-medio-supernonextreme or whatever the fuck lingo your overpaid corporate fat-ass bosses dictate.' I paused.

'Course, it's them I should be shooting.'

'Yes.' He nodded vigorously. 'Yes.'

'But they didn't treat me with contempt by barging into my shoulder while I walked down the street.'

'I, I was just walking past. I swear. I've al-al-always had bad coordination.'

'I fear it's about to get worse.'

'No, my – my brother always said I couldn't th-throw a—'

'You have a brother?'

His eyes looked into my shades with a deep pleading look. 'Yes.'

I gave an exaggerated sigh, raising and drooping my shoulders, said, 'Well. Now he doesn't have one,' whipped the gun out and shot him in the face. His head gave a kind of very fast sigh, exploding in blood and gore and mush. Think of the ugliest person you've ever seen. That person is not as ugly as anyone –

anyone, no matter how pretty – whose face just got stoved in point-blank by a bullet. Poor young Pulpface down there, his head looked like a half-carved turkey that'd been left out all morning in the rain. He'd actually been quite handsome, a touch of the young Johnny Depp about him. Well, such is the way of things and we should be grateful at this moment that our face, however unpleasant to look at, is not smashed-in and wet-turkeyed. Amen.

People laughed and applauded, despite themselves.

'Goddamn it,' said Archie. 'He's actually getting away with this.'

'Writers, eh?' I said. 'Can read books, can't read the rules, can't read audiences. Quit already, Seth, you narcissist.'

'The nerve of the man,' said Macy. 'He's carrying on.'

Now, strangely, as Seth spoke this next bit it was hard to know if he were reading this as fiction or speaking directly and honestly. He didn't look down at his pages once. Was he acting, or . . .

The audience seemed bemused. I heard someone behind me say, 'And people call us islanders eccentric.'

If Seth felt bad about violating the B&F code, he didn't show it. He pulled the microphone closer and said, 'Maybe Chad, who features in this next extract, was a good person and maybe even those who knew him said so before he died. If you think that's a spoiler, it's nothing compared to this, the mother of all spoilers. You. Are. Going. To. Die. You probably don't know when or how, but you will die. And we're not getting any younger, even the young ones.'

An unexpected chill feathered up my spine, goosebumping the skin on my arms. I pulled Archie close for warmth. 'He'll get his,' I said.

Seth spoke, slow and earnest:

Black Sludge and a
Model Rail Enthusiast

When you start bumping people off, life becomes more vivid, more fascinating. More alive. And that's got to tell you something, right?

The true murderer's mind is not that of the bloodthirsty maniac, the berserker. No, indeed. The professional is cool and unharried. Even in the frenetic midst of business, his mind ticks on consistently, clear and detached, like a clock during a thunderstorm.

Such demeanour separates the professional from the amateur who will find himself (they're almost always men) dead or injured, or jailed, which is as good as dead. One must always take pride.

Gosh. I simply love a good murdering.

In the interests of fairness, I'll mention one guy, a tattooed musclehead, who said that the moment he despatched his first victim into non-life a sludge began creeping into his world. He really saw it. This black sludge oozed into his bedroom at night. It came splodging under his door and advanced gloopily towards his bed and it even made its way into his dreams.

I know the name of that sludge: guilt.

The pussy-ass sludge-haunted murderer forced himself to bop a few other folk to see if it would make the sludge go away.

Nope. Instead it got so he could smell the sludge before it appeared. (The sludge did not smell good.) And sure enough, given time and a few more boppings, the sludge worsened. It grew so thick he believed it would choke him in his sleep.

In the end, he ran bawling to the cops and confessed to everything. I don't know much more about him. Except that if he did what I told him, he also admitted to one or two of mine. C'est la vie, c'est la mort.

I met someone once, a model railway enthusiast, who told me unequivocally, 'A man needs a hobby.'

'Why?'

'Something to enjoy, something to fully understand and appreciate in life. Bit by bit, you become more involved – more imp-li-ca-ted.' (That's the word he used, 'implicated'. I enjoyed it, like the burst from a semi-automatic.) 'Something you gradually, almost without realising, become expert in. Then one day you turn around and you realise you have all this knowledge about this one thing, all this wisdom, and you are really, really good at it. At that moment–' And here he leaned in, his green teeth shining, and for a split second I wondered if he were from another planet and if a green cloud would accompany the stench that gassed out of his cakehole. '–you have become at one with a metaphor for life.'

He sat back, proud, though his green stench remained.

I thought, yes.

And, just in case he was an alien, I invited him – poor friendless model rail enthusiast Walter – to my home to look at my invisible train set and I bopped him over the head with a hammer until he fell to his knees, dead and gone back to his home planet or heaven or hell or nowhere.

Contentment is when you give your whole self to doing something, so you are that very doing. Such is the pure joy that arises when I commit myself to a murdering. Murder, Walter taught me, is my metaphor for life.

Also, I need to tell you 'The Achingly Beautiful Tale of Me and Chad and Superman'. When I was eleven years old my neighbour Chad asked me to check if Superman was still alive. Chad was stupid, being only nine. I guess he was a plaything. It amused me to have a younger kid around.

'Superman?' I said.

'My pet lizard.'

Chad was blowing his jets because Superman hadn't moved for several hours.

'Don't worry,' I said. 'Superman will be fine. You're a douchebag, anyone called Superman is not going to die anytime soon. Those are the rules.'

'But how d'you know? You haven't even looked at him yet.'

'Why did you call him Superman if you think he's just going to die?'

'Please, Seth.' Chad grasped my hand and began tugging repeatedly.

'Alright.' I put down the stone I'd been sharpening. 'Quit pulling my arm or I'll goddamn flatten you.'

We ran into his house, avoiding the kitchen. (Chad grew up as an appendage to his mother. He slept in her bed until he was, like, seven.) Upstairs, his bedroom made my nose scrunch – it smelled of something I could neither name nor like. 'What's that smell? Lizard shit? Or just Chad bedroom stench?'

Beside the TV stood this lizard, Superman, staring out at the room, observing things intensely like some chess genius. He was pretty cool. Not just because he was figuring something out but because he looked like a tiny dinosaur. For a moment I pretended he was a dinosaur and I was an enormous giant or God or some such.

'See?' said Chad. 'He's a goner.' He sniffed and wiped his nose on a snottery sleeve and his eyes grew glassy and I knew what this meant.

'Don't cry. Don't you dare cry. If you cry I'll tear Superman's legs off right now.'

'You mean – he's alive?'

'Alive? Of course he is. That's just what lizards do. They stare at nothing for days on end. It's how they get the sun. Like how I thought my dad was dead once but he was just asleep in his chair, drunk.'

Chad looked down at Superman, a foolish grin spreading on his face. 'I knew it, Superman!'

'Careful. The worst thing you can do is wake them. My dad beat me black and blue with a hammer.'

Chad's eyes widened. 'He did?'

The lizard was motionless, like a tiny statue.

Very motionless.

The room suddenly seemed to change dimensions.

'Wait,' I said. 'How long have you had Superman?'

Chad hesitated. 'Not long. Why?'

I spoke slowly to get some menace in my voice. 'How. Long. Exactly?'

'N-not long.' Chad looked like he was going to bubble up again.

'Days, weeks? Answer or I'll–'

'Since eleven o' clock.'

'What?'

'Maybe eleven thirty.'

'You little dicksplash!'

I lashed out and grabbed Superman and threw him with all my might against the bedroom wall. He smashed against a Star Trek poster, piercing it just as any plastic toy would, then fell inert to the carpet.

Chad did a double take. The plastic lizard on the floor. Me. The plastic lizard on the floor. Me. I was wondering who was smart enough to sell it to him but also wondering just how sure I'd been that the lizard was a toy.

Twenty years later I'd take pleasure in organising a bit of a hurling-over-the-side-of-a-bridge for poor depressed Chad. He was something of a chess prodigy himself, and a palaeontologist, and he was wearing a blue T-shirt with the Superman logo when gravity and water did him in. They say these things are written in the stars. Go figure.

The audience applauded Seth in a loud and prolonged manner. Largely, I think, because they admired people who did things they couldn't, writers who went to places where islanders like us were usually too polite to tread. Still, it all felt wrong to me. And to Archie, who was seething. 'That guy.' He shook his head. 'He can't get away with all this.'

'Take it easy, Arch,' I said. 'He's not going to win.'

Dalston Moomintroll made a show of shaking Seth's hand. He was sweating. I even detected a nervousness in his voice. 'Seth Macnamara, ladies and gentlemen. That was quite a performance – or two! Most vivid and entertaining. I hope no one from Fleetwood Mac is listening.'

I realised, and said it aloud, 'Dalston Moomintroll is scared of Seth!'

Macy nodded. 'True enough. Look how he's sucking up to him.'

'It is always a joy to introduce to the B&F a visiting writer to the island. Tell me, where do you get those extraordinary ideas from?'

Seth smiled into the microphone. He was very cool – too cool by half, I thought. 'French guy named Zola said, "Art is a corner of nature seen through a temperament."' Seth paused, sniffed, nodded a couple of times. 'I guess it just happens mine is a murderous temperament.'

Many people guffawed at that, thrilling to his audacity.

Seth loves an audience, I thought.

'No thug as dangerous as an intelligent thug,' said Macy.

'If a sadistic, alpaca-hating, misogynist wins the B&F,' I said, 'it will be disaster for the competition, for the island.'

'For alpacas,' Archie added.

'That's what I meant,' I said.

'Dear god,' said Macy. 'Will you take a look at that.'

A surge of interest swelled through the audience. I realised we'd missed Seth's exit and now, catwalking across the stage, very slowly and very carefully, was the elongated, polished, seventy percent real body that belonged to a woman nowadays known only by her first name: Stella.

Stella, though you wouldn't know it from her accent, was originally from the island. A blackhouser, she left here with no qualifications, harbouring an enormous hunger to make her way in life as a successful model. She headed south. She succeeded, more or less. She made money and became something of a celebrity. But the fickle tabloid newspapers had turned against her and when she made a habit of falling over on red carpets and catwalks they destroyed her reputation by alluding to drugs and vacuous naïveté and an inability to walk without falling over.

A number of people in the audience were making snide remarks about how well she was doing in that she hadn't stumbled yet. Many were ogling her. She's what's considered beautiful.

Leering, Dalston Moomintroll said, 'Yes, ladies and gentlemen. It was not a misprint in the programme. We have the honour of hearing from the legendary Stella tonight!'

A jagged, piercing earful of wolfwhistling splintered the air. I winced.

'Welcome, welcome, Stella,' said Dalston Moomintroll and he bent down ostentatiously to kiss the back of Stella's hand.

She tittered. 'It's nice to be here.'

'It sure is,' said Dalston Moomintroll to her hand, which he slobberingly kissed once more. He stood up straight, looked deep into Stella's eyes and smiled.

Half a minute passed, or so it seemed. Dalston Moomintroll jolted out of his daydream, looked surprised to find an audience of twenty thousand people and alpacas staring at him, and mumbled, 'Please welcome the only person from our island ever to only need one name – Stella!'

As Dalston Moomintroll departed the stage, Stella curtsied at the microphone a few times until the shouts and whistles and cheering died down. Then she spoke and I was surprised to note she wasn't addressing us in the breathy, Marilyn-wannabe voice she had adopted for TV and radio appearances. Instead she reverted to her native accent and bellowed in what seemed an unguarded, brash manner:

Stella

My name is Stella. S for Sexy. T for, um . . . T for That's a hell of a sexy body. E for Everyone wants to be me. L for Loveable. L for . . . Loveable even more. And A for A-lister. S-t-e-l-l-a. Stella! Woohoo!

I'm only telling you my name is Stella – which you already knew – because they asked me to. Like, duh.

So my name is Stella and I'm famous. Which is the reason I'm even here.

Y'know, my story's awesome. Go books, woohoo!

I'm probably famous for being famous, but you know, that only increases how famous I am. You can see that – 'famous for being famous', that's twice as much 'famous'. Haters meanwhile can go to hell, I've worked hard for my fame and one day I will likely be the most famous person on the planet. Being famous is the whole point of life.

I feel sorry for all the people out there who just don't get it. But then, like, if everyone was famous, nobody would be famous. That's philosophy.

My mum probably isn't here. Did I ask her to bring me into the world? Is it too much to say she probably only exists because of me, so that I could come into this world? She should stop getting it the other way round. I'm part of a bigger plan. Other mothers would be proud of having a beautiful, famous daughter.

I can understand the rest of the world being jealous of me – but my own family?

I was born in a blackhouse here, but that's not the point. I suppose the good thing about it is my agent says it gives me background colour. That's why I wore tartan in my first topless shoot. Tartan is one of my things.

My agent says people just don't understand that being famous is all about creating your own reality. One that other people can aspire to through, for example, imitation, yearning and jealousy.

By making people feel their lives are empty, you are giving them a chance to fill their lives, to hero-worship you, and that gives you – well, them – well, you – them – a sense of fulfilment. So everybody wins. If people didn't need me, I wouldn't be such a star.

Just across the harbour there is the newsagent's where I first worked. Stacking the magazines, I used to look at the celebrities on the covers and say to myself, 'That's what I'm going to do. People can put my face on the shelves.'

And to any girls out there who are like I was, stuck in dead-end jobs, tired of the daily grind, desperate to have fame and money and success, I send you this message from the heart: get lost. You can't be me. Only someone like me can be me. And there's already too many other girls out there. So stick to what you know, darling. I'm only kidding.

I mean that in a loving way.

Yeah, I'm addicted to fame. I've done photo shoots, I've gone to film and restaurant and gallery openings, I've been on magazine covers, I had my artistically nude image projected onto the premises of the Liechtensteinian government on their day of National Peace Through Nakedness.

I hope in the future to have my own fashion label, a recording career and my own fragrance.

Fame is the greatest high I've ever had.

Guys want me, girls want to be me. All those eyes staring at me in magazines, on TV or, if they're lucky, in real life, like you are right now – this gives me such a rush I have to pinch myself.

I mean, think about it. Can I really be me? Am I that lucky?

Well, I say to myself. I am me. So, the answer is yes. I am lucky enough to be me. And, I mean, how many people are able to say that?

You're looking at my dress. The way I see it, designer dresses and beautiful bodies go together like colours on flowers. And nobody charges anyone for painting sunflowers, do they?

If you look like a million dollars then, sooner or later, someone will give you a million dollars. Beauty doesn't die, it just evolves into a new and, what is it Max says, a new and more characterful grace. Meantime, there's Botox, that's why God invented it.

'Stella takes a fall'. You saw that front page headline?

Well, yeah. Some idiots said that it was because I don't eat enough.

And some other idiots said I fell cos I fainted with nerves. The nerve of *them*! All that really happened was that I was wearing inappropriate shoes.

You see, it's hard for famous people to keep their feet on the ground.

I'm glad the tabloids bitched about me. That shows I'm important enough to be talked about. The only thing worse than being talked about, said Oscar Mild, also a writer, is when the tabloids ignore you altogether.

I used to practise walking in front of the mirror, so you see it's really impossible that nerves would make me trip up.

The world needs to know this: I am really good at walking.

You have to earn self-respect and you begin that by making others respect you.

I love London. After I met Max and got my first glamour-modelling job, men were always interested and I was loving every minute of it. Who doesn't crave attention? It's a natural human feeling. I mean, even God wants to be worshipped. That's theology.

I soon got myself the whole lifestyle. Max, photos in the press and the magazines, some TV roles. It's like, I attracted fame. Beauty itself is a fame magnet. So it's like fate.

Hey, that was good, you can quote me on that.

My friend Jenny, she decided to become a damsel of the night. I couldn't do that.

She is a street-side sexual distribution facilitator.

Then again, I mean, who wouldn't do anything for a pair of shoes like this? They're like works of art. And my job is to be a living work of art. It's actually a noble and glorious thing.

We – Max and I – decided it would be worthwhile to put my name to some charitable causes. I thought back to my own unhappy childhood – no offence – and started volunteering at a local children's nursery. Of course the best ones, with the best looking kids, were taken by other famous models, but we found a suitable one in the inner city. I mean the kids weren't what you would call decorative, but I really enjoyed it.

Oh, the feeling I got being around those children. I was so happy playing with them, kissing them better if they grazed their knees, teaching them to colour in or showing them how to do their hair properly or just showing them how to get along with each other. They needed me. They loved me.

I would have loved to have kids of my own but, as Max said, they weren't compatible with that stage of my career development. Made sense, because why not wait until I was super-super-rich, then I could give the kids everything they would need and more.

And meantime, I had twenty kids two mornings a week.

Max invited some photographers along to an open day at the nursery. They took photos and they . . . they printed ones that made me look spotty and pale. I mean, they photoshopped the pictures to make me look bad. Like with inferior models, they touch up the photos, airbrush them to make them look good. Now here they were doing the opposite to me. I think some other models got together in a vendetta against me and started the whole thing.

The nursery had to let me go. You should have seen those poor kids' faces. And I was as heartbroken as they were. I mean, they really, really needed me. Everyone could see that.

Of course, all this made me want to teach the ugly paparazzi and journalists and the jealous models all a lesson. I would become more famous than every one of them put together. They would end up needing me just as much as those children had needed me.

My mum publicly disowned me – very publicly, as you know, via a tabloid newspaper, which I never would have thought she'd be media-savvy enough to do. Then I learned that she had been duped by a mild-mannered stranger who she invited in when he spun her some yarn about his car breaking down. The lowest of the low. Too trusting, I suppose; that's the island way.

Well anyway, London was getting so expensive.

My brother got a job as an air traffic controller. I guess I was so out of his life I hadn't even known he'd trained for it. But he was earning a fortune, and yeah, he did help me out with the rent once in a while. I always loved my brother, he knows that.

I had a vicious letter from my mother one day, telling me to stay away from my brother too. My mother always had a strange relationship with me. When I was a kid, one of her threats was, 'Don't make me put you back in the womb.' I mean, double-yoo tee eff?

I wrote to my brother and tried calling him, but he never responded.

Eventually I said, fine, good. All the family I need is me, myself and I. Now I have more time to spend on my career.

My plan was to get so rich that giving a million pounds to my brother would be like losing twenty pence.

I still will. I'm getting there.

This whole fame game has taken such a toll on me – inside and outside, physically and mentally and you-name-it-ly. Sometimes I think, I can't really imagine what it's done to my brother and maybe even my mum.

Sometimes it's like a part of me is already dead.

Anyway, this is what happened. Watch, I'm dramatising it.

It's the opening night of London Fashion Week. Okay, here we are. It'll be easy, a walk in the park. Red carpet. Deep breath. Positive thoughts. I am beautiful, I am here for me, I am worth it. I am beautiful, I am here for me, I am worth it. Living legend, living legend, living legend. Let's go!

Oh, god a walk in the park, but it's Central Park at four o'clock in morning after a jailbreak.

No, I'm cool. I'm cool.

Easy as putting one foot in front of the other, one foot in front of the – aaaaahhhh!

Shit! Wh-what the hell?

I fell. And it was in all the papers.

They wanted me to fall in the other sense: mephatorically.

My message today is wake up to reality. The world is bigger than the island. That advice is for free.

Because what else? Loving yourself is wrong? Well, screw that, because I am adorable.

But more than that. Listen. Because I don't think the stories people tell on this stage at the B&F always have a clear message. Which is a great shame. I am taking this opportunity to speak to you, especially, the kids of tomorrow, with a clear message. Follow my example. Love yourself.

I love myself. I love my lipstick, my eyelashes, my extensions. I love my image. I love being in control of my own hot self. I like people to look up to me not for who I'm not, but for who they think I am.

And that, ladies and gentlemen, is true heroism right here and now.

I thank you.

She bent forward from the waist and blew kisses left, right, centre, to the audience. Her mirror rehearsals were reflected in every pose, every pout and smile.

Dalston Moomintroll sleazed his way over and asked about her love interest and she replied, 'My bed is half full, not half empty,' which even made me smile.

'Goddamn it,' said Macy. 'Narcissism and entitlement.'

Maybe there was more to Stella. She glided unobtrusively from Dalston Moomintroll's orbit and now made her way off stage, bowing elegantly and blowing more well-practised kisses. She slipped away into the backstage area and into the minds of folk with certain yearnings.

'Well, ladies and gentlemen,' said Dalston Moomintroll, 'that brings us – and alpacas, of course – to the end of the readings. And what a Brilliant & Forever it's been. As ever, your patience and close listening will be the envy of the non-island world, your loving endurance of literature a credit to

202

yourselves and ancestors and descendants alike. In cities all over the world there are grown adults who can't sit still through a cartoon. But you, my island brethren, are the very stuff of stamina. And what use is stamina without a passion for literature?

'We've had a very diverse day of readings. Long, short, very long, very short. With a strange, eccentric host of characters, and that's just the authors ha ha ha.

'Okay. Well now, ladies and gentlemen, as is customary, and alpacas too, of course, the esteemed judges shall take their time, such time as they adjudge necessary, and as judges it is their right to do so, and the time they take is, is the necessary amount to judge the winner. So naturally, do not stray from the Castle Green.

'When they have made up their, if I may say, their exceptional minds, we shall hear from His Eminence, the Chair of the Judges, Cedric Peregrine, about the, ah, identity of the winner and why.

'And then. Then we shall have the People's Decision.'

Dalston Moomintroll gave a podgy bow and took his leave of the stage.

After a mixed reaction of heartfelt and obligatory applause, the mood changed. The crowd broke chattering into little groups which began making their way to the beer kegs that traditionally appear at this point. Some saw the beer as a reward for their patience, others as Dutch courage.

The more beer that people drank, the more it awoke within them a savage thirst.

A dark, sweet, faintly poisonous aroma filled the air. Children clasped their parents' hands more tightly.

The Judges' Decision

Macy, Archie and I brought bacon rolls and grass sandwiches and coffee up to and past the treeline and sauntered towards a clearing a few feet into the woods behind the Castle. We came here for privacy. I had known this place in childhood, when one of the trees had been famously difficult to climb and I had fallen from it, showing off to someone I fancied, someone whose laughter hurt more than the broken wrist.

'Every single other alpaca and person here is having 110/-,' Archie grumbled, glaring at his wheatgrass smoothie. 'I've earned a proper drink.'

'Patience,' I said, 'will only make it taste better.'

Macy bit hungrily into a bacon roll, talked with mush going about her mouth like a washing machine. 'Yeah, you can drink as much as you like when you win. I'm starving. Good bacon roll.'

'After my pathetic performance, I'll be lucky I don't get the People's,' said Archie.

'Nonsense,' I said. 'Your story was brilliant. I mean—' I shook my head. 'I never read anything like that by you before.'

'Don't you start.'

'What?'

'Well, don't you think Dalston Moomintroll was implying it wasn't original or something? That's what threw me.'

'I didn't get that.'

'Who cares about Dalston Moomintroll. Lousy overprivileged whitehouser,' said Macy.

'Honestly,' I said, 'I loved your story. I think you may well have clinched it. Who cares if you mismanaged your spittoon. You had a cuspidor malfunction, could happen to anyone.'

Archie brightened. 'You mean it? I might have even won? After the fandango . . . and the cuspidor. . .'

'Yep.' I nodded. But an awkwardness descended. 'Well, I mean, yours and Macy's, both. They were the standout stories for me.'

'Hmm. Good save,' said Macy in an I'm-not-fully-convinced-but-that's-okay tone.

'Actually,' I said. 'Maybe you'll share it.'

'Hey,' said Archie. 'Imagine. Because, I mean, it's possible.' He paused, nodded. 'It's not impossible.'

'Maybe,' said Macy, with a sceptical shrug. 'But I think you got it.'

I smiled. 'Either way, I'm quids in.'

'How?' said Macy.

'I put a week's wages on both of you.'

Macy's hand, lifting a fresh bacon roll to her mouth, stalled. She stared at me. 'You what?'

Archie, too, stopped chewing. 'He's kidding,' he said uncertainly.

'Ask QuickQuidSid.'

'Goddamn it. Goddamn it. That is a lot of dishes. One hell of a lot of hard work to risk.'

'A hell of a lot,' agreed Archie. 'I can hardly believe you would have that amount of faith.'

'You're my friends. And what's more, my highly talented friends. Of *course* I put money on you.'

'Yeah,' said Macy, 'but that much? I only put, like, the equivalent of two hours' work on both of you guys.'

'Likewise,' said Archie.

'You're fools for putting any money on me,' I said. 'But then again at a hundred to one I guess you'd be fools not to.'

'A week's wages, though. On each of us?' Archie looked a little stunned. 'A week – no, that's a *fortnight's* dishwashing wages.'

'Well,' said Macy, leaning over, 'it's the fucking noblest thing anyone ever did for me.' She gave me a tight, lingering thank-you-and-I-mean-it hug. 'Love ya,' she whispered in my ear and pecked a quick kiss against my ear lobe.

'Thanks for slobbering bacon grease on my ear, Starfield,' I said, grinning as I pushed her away.

'Get over here,' said Archie and he pulled me in and hugged me good and tight and meaningful.

He held me for so long it kind of got embarrassing.

(Later I realised my shoulder was wet where Archie must have shed a few actual tears.)

'Now excuse me,' he said, and he turned away and began gobbing into his spittoon.

'The famous cuspidor,' said Macy and we laughed, happy and secure in our friendship and in the moment, forgetful, just for those giggling instants, of the competition.

'I need to say something to the alpacas about embarrassing myself and all alpacahood on the stage. I'm going to go over and apologise to my brother and sister alpacas. Might grab myself a cheeky wee half pint on the way – be rude not to,' said Archie, getting up.

'I'm sure there's no need to apologise to any alpacas. Just go to socialise and bask in their adoration of your story,' I said.

'Ah, my old frenemy. You sure did embarrass yourself,' a

voice crashed in. It belonged to Seth, who strode into the clearing and stood with arms folded across his chest, a vision of arrogance.

'S-sorry?' said Archie, thrown by his rudeness.

'Ignore him,' I said. 'Interesting story, Seth. Now, get the hell out of here.'

'And I don't mean the grotty spit bowl, camelface. I was referring to the piece of dross you read. Still, brave of you to put in that line, "My reading went badly".'

Almost unnoticeably, with fight-or-flight swiftness, Archie glanced reflexively around. I stood up. It's alright, I thought. I got your back.

'Seth,' I said. 'We don't use terms like that here. And literature is like food, it would be a lesser world in which everyone loved the same stories.'

He turned his superior, spiteful eyes on me. 'Oh and as for you,' he said. 'What the hell was that immature bullshit? You get in on a sympathy vote or are you blowing one of the judges?'

'Sympathy vote,' I deadpanned, killing his sarcasm's momentum.

'What is your problem, anyway, jerkface?' said Macy.

'My problem, little lady, is time-wasting "literature" like yours. And his. And his.' He punctuated his sneering words by jabbing a finger into Archie's chest and then into mine. 'As for this creature, God had to put a clothes peg on his nose because camelface's story stinks to high heaven.' Archie took a powerful step towards him but I put a tensed arm between them. Archie's nostrils were flared and his eyes smouldered with unblinking aversion.

'I could eat alphabet soup and shit a better story than yours,' said Seth. He pouted and put on a baby-ish voice. 'Aw, little camelface got riled. What's little camelface going to do? Cwy?'

'Wise up, Seth,' I said. 'Round here we have manners.'

'I don't give a shit about you,' said Seth.

'I should hope not,' I said.

'Yeah, and – wait, what?'

'I'd be more worried if you did give a shit about me. I'd have you sectioned if even once you took a crap and dedicated that crap to me.' I smiled at him in sarcastic sweetness. 'When I was a kid, the girl in the playground who pulled my hair hardest was always the one who liked me the most.' I forced myself to grin; it probably came across as a crazed leer.

'You criticise *our* work, Macnamara' said Macy. 'But your story impressed me the way other worm-penised overcompensators do, with sports cars or steroid-bulked neck muscles. Kinda desperate.'

'Oh, she's got spunk,' said Seth. 'The rumours can't be true.'

'Enough,' I said.

'That's enough alright,' said Archie to me. 'Don't try to win over the haters. You are not the asshole whisperer.' He eyed Seth steadily and addressed him with a solemn tone. 'We'll settle this the old-fashioned way.'

I looked at Archie. 'What the hell's got into you? You can't beat the ignorance out of an ignorant man.'

'Camelfaces can't fight humans,' said Seth. He sneered, shook his head. 'You won't make old bones, alpaca features. Hey, isn't it weird, that corpse you're soon going to be is the very body you now wear.'

'We'll see about that, Macnamara,' said Archie, readying to fight.

'No, no,' I started to say, but was interrupted by the triple tolling of a bell that signified the judges had made their decision.

For a split second we paused, not sure what to do, as different impulses coursed through our veins. We couldn't miss the

Judges' Decision. But Seth and Archie looked serious about having a physical fight.

After a moment, Seth gave a mirthless smile. 'I'll see you later,' he said to Archie. 'Unless, of course, you lose the People's.'

'I'm not scared of that,' said Archie. 'Or of you.'

'Alright, camelface. Alright.' He gave a dry laugh and turned away without waiting for a response.

We watched him swagger towards the Castle Green.

Archie was trembling.

'I got a bad feeling about this,' I said.

'What the hell have I been telling you?' said Archie.

'You're wrong. Both of you,' said Macy. 'Somehow, despite it all, everything will be okay.'

Archie shook his head. 'Somehow, despite it all, *something* will be okay. That's the best anyone can ever hope for.'

Incongruously, it had turned into one of those light and breezy summer evenings, when the air itself is eager to run through your hair with fresh excitable fingers, and you remember with a biting kiss of loss those brief eternal teenage summers you spent yearning for the happy cry of human skin moving in innocent harmony with human skin. Strange that life is so brief and easy to waste.

Worldessly, Archie, Macy and I walked over to the area where the other writers were already standing: Ray Genovese (solemn, but with a twinkle in his eye), Summer Kelly (grinning uninhibitedly, drunk), J-M-Boy (confident, unfazed), Peter Projector-Head (semi-oblivious), Tabitha Tessington (smiling self-consciously, unconvincingly), Myrtle Budd (fairly self-assured but distantly anxious), Tan the Ageist (expressionless expression, staring at the ground), Calvin O Blythe (calm, as if nothing were happening), Seth (simmering with a smiling malevolence), Stella (assuming a model's facial expressions, no outward sincerity).

As was the custom, we, the author-competitors, gathered in a group in the centre of the Castle Green. A circle, three deep, of large bouncers formed an impregnable ring around us. They were all tall, broad-shouldered and heavily muscled. I was coming to think of them as human bollards. Beyond them stood the first layers of people, comprising those who had a special connection with a certain writer – through blood, affection or even just a liking for their fiction – and those who had an aversion, for whatever reason, to a writer and/or their work. Usually at this point alpacas were allowed to mingle with humans and they would generally drift away from the shore and circulate among the crowds, perhaps enjoying a beer or two. But today I noticed the alpacas stayed together at the back.

Now, with the exception of the security bollards, everyone turned towards the stage and screens.

Cedric Peregrine, the Chair of the Judges for the last decade or so, ambled towards the microphone to begin his speech. He was one long streak of self-importance. Every year, the oration offered by eminent windbag Cedric Peregrine was dependably dry and notoriously lengthy. Some people said it was like this to heighten the tension, others said it was because the Chairs were always sick-minded whitehousers who liked to prolong the torture of waiting to see who won and who got the People's.

Cedric Peregrine talked about the illustrious history of the B&F; the achievements of each of his fellow judges; the book, radio, stage and movie successes of previous B&F winners; the generosity and company history of each of the B&F's sponsors; the visual grace and musical voice projection of some of the writers (did he mean Tabitha Tessington?); the maverick appeal of some of our contestants (Seth? Summer?); the zaniness of some (J-M-Boy, Myrtle Budd?); the existential pieties some of them invoked in 'us'; and the gratitude we should feel for what we have (did he mean Peter Projector-Head? Alpacas? Both? Was he talking to whitehousers about blackhousers?). He reminded us that the winner would be signed up to a prestigious agency and would be offered, on completion of a manuscript, a very sizeable advance on a book deal, with an option for a second book. He also reminded everyone that the winner would not, naturally, be eligible for the People's.

For the first time, I began to feel nervous of my own place in all this. Standing in the circle, you couldn't help but feel powerless. Hemmed in. And because I knew I had no hope of winning the Judges' Decision, my chances of being on the receiving end of the People's Decision were greater. My heart boom-boomboomed-boomboomboomed into a pounding sprint and sweat broke out on my forehead. I wished I'd thought of going for another bike ride earlier. But there wasn't enough time and Archie and Macy had needed me and I needed them.

I linked arms with Macy and put my other arm around Archie's shoulder. Writers were not allowed to speak or communicate in any way with each other or with anyone in the audience. Jib-mounted cameras hovered over us, watching, recording, broadcasting, watching, watching.

How you behave from here on in determines how the island – how, perhaps, history – will define you. I felt a little faint. The heat from all the people was beginning to cancel out the comforting freshness of the breeze. My breath buckled a few times. I had to concentrate just to breathe evenly. Macy's hand tightened on mine, writhed. Her skin was clammy. I'd never known Macy to be properly nervous.

No one had forced us to be here. I repeated this thought to

calm myself, but it had the opposite effect so I tried to expel it from my mind. I tried instead to focus on Cedric Peregrine's speech, but it was too tedious to hold the attention. I glanced round to see if I could see any familiar faces beyond the security guards, but all I could see were people I recognised but didn't know.

There was one face that did distract me. Standing calmly, as if immovable, one man had an expression of serenity on his face that contrasted profoundly with the nervous smiles and anxious scowls of the masses, those invested with hopes and regrets and bets and schadenfreude and blood obligations and everything in between. He looked at me steadily, as if in recognition – not only of me, but of the truth of the situation I was in. I gave him a slight nod and he blinked slowly back at me as if communicating, and I believed he was, a message along the lines of, 'If you have no fear, there is nothing to fear.' I think I even heard a voice saying this.

Cedric Peregrine was finishing his speech, so I looked back towards the stage. I remembered how this was, quite plausibly, all about Archie and the implications for alpaca rights and I felt mean and selfish for indulging in self-pity, self-absorption, self-self-self.

'We have deliberated at length,' said Cedric Peregrine, 'with very little but Kumlauf's caviar and champagne to sustain us. That and the fresh memories of what has been, I may confidently say, a vintage Brilliant & Forever.

'Choosing a winner was an enjoyable problem. "Enjoyable" because of the quality of the best writings, not to say that of the equally fine champagne. "Problem" because a finite number – two, in fact – of the writers struck us as perfectly worthy winners.' He paused, enjoying the stir he created – gasps, murmurs, people flashing glances at each other.

Had they gone for a joint Overall Winner?

And if so, I thought excitedly, is it Archie and Macy?

'To whom, then, should we award the Overall Prize? Both these fine writers?' He shook his head emphatically. 'No. No, that wouldn't do. A winner, we agreed, must be a winner. A joint first place, we knew, would make the winners but half-winners.

'An outright winner can feel outright satisfaction. Partial satisfaction is a contradiction, we surmised. Plus, the esteemed CEO Jonathan Market-Forbes, of Inevitable & Essential Books, felt, as all of us did, that a single magnificent book deal would be more worthwhile than two book deals.'

Ah, that was it. I'd forgotten – a few years ago, the committee introduced a clause decreeing that the money was not halved if the prize were shared among two, but each winner would receive the full amount, meaning the judges would be less likely to announce joint overall winners.

'We cogitated. We contemplated. We contradicted. We found solace in rereading hard copies of the texts and refilling hard copies of our champagne flutes.'

Get on with it, come on. Come on.

'A confession, ladies and gentlemen, and alpacas, will always win over more people than a sermon. We, the Judges, have unanimously concluded that the fairest and best and most exemplary winner of this year's Brilliant & Forever must surely be, and in fact certainly is . . .

'Stella.'

I sneaked glimpses through little gaps between the guards. A wave of surprise, disappointment and swearing barrelled through the crowd. The injustice was staggering, the corruption complete. I knew at once and with certainty, there is no word in any language that has not been used for a lie.

Stella herself squealed with shocked pleasure and was

immediately hoisted onto the shoulders of two burly security guards, who marched her, flanked by two dozen other security guys, towards the stage. It was traditional for people to reach out and touch the winner, as if fleeting physical contact with the new god or goddess of literature would endow them with special powers; but this was Stella and a sudden swarm of men pushed hard towards her, many of them not just reaching up to touch her lightly on the elbow, but groping and squeezing at her. My face squirmed. The scene was horrible to watch. Lecherous men lunged towards her not because she was good-looking and well known but because they were disgusting specimens, indifferent even to the cameras that were filming everything.

We writers in our circle weren't allowed to speak, but Macy, Archie and I were able via our facial expressions to share wide-eyed disbelief, wouldn't-you-believe-it cynicism and alarmed what-the-hell's-going-to-happen-next fear. Because if the Judges' Decision was that unpredictable . . . what would happen in the People's Decision?

I tuned in to the voices around us, to gauge the prevailing mood.

'Least it went to a blackhouser,' said a checked shirt.

'Yeah, a blackhouser who disses her own island background, blackhousers and all,' said a shiny red dress.

'She's got the right to speak her mind. It's constructive criticism,' said a yellow blouse. 'What's the matter, truth hurt? Can't stand a strong-willed woman?'

'With legs like that she can speak any mind she wants to,' said a beer belly.

'Legs don't speak, sexist pig,' said a woman and people laughed at the beer-bellied man.

'Another rigged B&F,' said a disgruntled Brawth T-shirt.

'Shoulda known it and put a bundle on her with QuickQuickSid.'

'That Stella, she's no bigger then a minute,' said a woman with a silver helmet of hair and an embossed smile, 'but she's a scrapper.'

'What were her odds anyway?' asked checked shirt.

'What are her odds of getting to the stage with clothes intact?' said red dress.

I hunched and caught sight of one of the huge video screens. The security guards were jostling against the heave and swell of testosterone-addled men. One skinny dimwit, boosted up by a mate, was propelled into the air like a basketball player, and clumsily he splayed himself in Stella's direction, reached a matchstick arm out and pawed one of her breasts.

I watched a security guard seize him, pull him down and smash his face with a truncheon. And again. And on the third pounding, the man's face erupted in blood and his face went pulpy. Unconscious, rather than dead, I thought.

The security guard dropped him to the ground; he knew what he was doing. Either the poor idiot's friends would drag his helpless body to safety, or he would get crushed to death in the powerful flow of the masses.

I couldn't see what happened to him, distracted as I was by a strange gurgling sound. I turned to see it was Seth laughing dryly, contentedly, to himself.

Now all of the security guards near Stella had their truncheons out and were swiping and slashing at anyone – man or woman – in their vicinity. They hit many people.

A visibly shaken Stella was delivered to the stage. She took a moment to smooth out her dress and dab at her hair. She closed her eyes, took a deep breath and when she opened them again she looked perfectly composed, and stood beaming her overly white smile as though nothing had happened, her body angled perfectly towards the photographers' scrum that had gathered in front of the stage.

But Cedric Peregrine was motioning for her to come to the microphone. Stella wrenched herself away from the magnetism of the cameras' attention and tottered over to join him. There was a more sensual, knowing confidence about her now, as if Stella had been rebooted. She had found what she might consider redemption from her people, and she knew her stock was about to increase thousandfold. Never mind that her book would be ghostwritten – something elements of the crowd were muttering about darkly.

Cedric Peregrine leaned in to kiss her multiple times on each cheek. 'Stella, you know the reasons we chose your work—'

Stella misinterpreted the beginning of his statement as a question unto itself. She leaned in to the microphone, smiling, looking out at the audience. Her face clouded, though, and she looked perplexed. 'No?' she said, to some laughter.

Cedric Peregrine's lips were struggling to maintain solemnity, so he opted for a smug sneer. 'Ah now, Stella, a woman of your achievements and ambition needn't be modest. We chose your writing for its candour, for the naked – well, perhaps not naked – honesty, a refreshing transparency with which you dress your thoughts.' He paused, looked into the middle distance. 'We are attracted by the manner in which you so effortlessly seem to capture the zeitgeist in your spirited prose. It has been observed that only great literature grows in the mind, and yours certainly grew in mine. This is not the age of communism or fascism but the age of materialism. Where would we be without materials?'

Stella looked to the audience and gave a shrug one could charitably describe as self-deprecating.

'In hearing your impassioned oration, we judges felt moved,

rubbed raw by life. You immersed us in your thoughts, in your world, and you gently showed us that your plight is the world's plight. Your dreams and frustrations, Stella, are ours. When you took your tumble on the red carpet, you had your fall from grace. And which of us has not? Individually, we are fallible. Collectively, we subscribe to the "Local Man Ruins Everything" school of thought – our cultural inferiority is ingrained. Long years of oppression and injustice have rooted this inferiority within us so deeply it is difficult indeed to uproot it. But there is, ladies and gentlemen and yes, you, the alpaca fraternity, there is a way out. And Stella's understated and subtle and subversive story has shown us that there is a better way, should we just have the strength to pick ourselves up again.

'And furthermore, we should overcome our propensity towards stereotyping. Yes. I see it. Those of you who judge Stella on account of her modelling career or because of her shimmering and, and radiant good looks, pause. Pause, I say, pause and ask yourselves, whenceforth this discrimination? We do not like to see stereotyping in our literary characters, why should we stereotype our fellow human beings? I venture to suggest it is no more acceptable than the prejudice, a despicable one, an abominable one, among certain quarters to consider our alpaca brethren as less than first class citizens or indeed our blackhousers likewise.'

The gall! I think few people in the audience could quite believe what they were hearing.

'Let us, therefore, celebrate celebrity. Let us not smother the voices of our time as they did to, for example, Vassily Grossman, who, let us not forget, said, "They strangled me in a dark corner." Let us not suffer Stella to experience such a thing. Let us instead brighten the spotlight that shines on her like a heaven-sent star. Let us smother her, if smother her we must, in love and affection. Let us embrace her: her mind, her ideas, her vitality in every sense, for she is the vital spokesperson for our times. For all these reasons, she is our Overall Winner at the Brilliant & Forever. Her book, *Stella: A Star Shining Brilliant & Forever*, will be available shortly from Inevitable & Essential books, in a lavish coffee table edition. Ladies, gentlemen, blackhousers, whitehousers, alpacas of the north and south, let us congratulate, as one people, the extraordinary talent that is . . . Stella.'

One of the other judges came forward and made a show of presenting Stella with a bunch of flowers and then a judge's young daughter strode on stage and offered her the trophy – an enormous pen-shaped artpiece crafted from crystal. Publishing CEO Jonathan Market-Forbes handed her the scroll that symbolised the publishing contract Stella would be signing within the next few days.

The applause throughout was a mixture of the polite, the sympathetic and the sarcastic.

Stella basked in it, smiling, adopting one well-practised model stance after another as she accepted prizes and applause alike, wiping away the occasional non-existent tear. A youngster emerged from the wings to take the flowers and crystal pen away for safekeeping while Stella gazed, with photogenic emotion, at the scroll that represented a book deal, a new lease of life for her career, and a redemptive appreciation from the island community that made her and, indeed, made her leave in the first place. Finally she spoke.

'Everybody, your acceptance of me today . . . Wow. I promise you I did not expect to win this. This is as much a shock and surprise and thrill to me as it is to you. I hereby pledge to make sure the book looks fabulous and I will be back to do a book signing very soon. I love you all. I feel like crying. But instead

I'm going to whoop.' She whooped a number of times. It was embarrassing. She bounced off stage, screaming with a shrill and naive happiness. A part of me died inside.

I was desperate to get together with Macy and Archie and tear this whole thing apart with shared jokes and silliness.

But.

The People's Decision

But there was the issue of the People's Decision. And the People were in a state of uncertainty. A complex matrix of feelings simmered in the darkening air. Alpacas stood near the shore, restlessly moving, chattering in staccato bursts, spitting, glowering. Some of the humans were fizzing with physical energy, an adrenalised reaction to the violence that had erupted earlier. The beer kegs were emptying. Many people were blazing mad at the lies and hypocrisy that Cedric Peregrine had spouted on stage.

This was more serious than I'd realised. I suddenly wanted more than anything to be at home, preparing some haiku-kery for Archie and Macy, with a John Wayne movie lined up, some jazz music deliciously splintering the air into invisible refractions of multicoloured sound waves, with the peat fire burning, sending a smoked-earth fragrance about the house.

That might never happen again.

Dalston Moomintroll made his way onto the stage for his final appearance of the night. Everyone hushed. An uneasy silence settled over the audience like a heavy shroud. Nowhere was the disquiet more palpable than in the area where we remaining writers stood. The security guards about us stood closer, visibly tense, gripping their truncheons.

'And now,' said Dalston Moomintroll, solemnly, 'we come

to you, the People. Every year, foreign media make an inane hullabaloo about this crucial element, as though you, the People, should have no role in your own proud heritage. It is said that this is the most brilliant and forever part of the Brilliant & Forever, and the most essential.

'Certainly, it is the most traditional. The origins of the ritual are so old they are lost in the fug of time. And I say essential because what is life without sacrifice? Joy is only possible because we have something – sorrow – with which to contrast it. Both must exist. Without one, the other would have no meaning. And so, you see, those people who criticise the People's Decision have a deficient understanding of what it means to be alive.'

I swallowed hard. My forehead was clammy with sweat. I sensed a change in Seth's mood and sneaked a look at him; he had a half-smile on his lips and a keen anticipation in his eyes, like a starving man waiting to be fed.

Dalston Moomintroll had stopped speaking and a stillness thickened the air. A little boy somewhere said, 'It better not be–' but someone must have put their hand over his mouth before he could say a name.

'It is a writer's prerogative to explore the depths, the darknesses we harbour, all of us. Within the limitless brilliance of the imagination, there are dangers. Nowadays, many writers in other cultures see those risks as nihilistic and glamorous – the junky, the alcoholic, the suicide.

'But there is an ancient and noble risk and we know this as the original one, and it is the one we now honour, as we have done for countless years, in the People's Decision.'

He took a breath so deep his chest puffed up, then he breathed out very slowly. I caught the eye of someone in the crowd – it was the serene eye of someone wholly at peace with himself. The same man I'd seen earlier. He looked at me steadily. His expression did not change.

I had decided a few days ago that I would exercise some control over my own mind and body here and shut my eyes tight.

Dalston Moomintroll said, 'Gentlemen of the Guard, blindfold the writers.'

So swiftly did the guards execute their manoeuvre (it's rumoured they practise it for months) that Macy and Archie and I barely had time to give a supportive hand/hoof squeeze before the thick black blindfolds were slipped over our foreheads and tightened at the back so that they would not move. I felt vulnerable in a way that set a loneliness swooning in my stomach. My head pulsed, each heartbeat throbbing rapidly where the blindfold compressed my head. My balance felt less certain now that I couldn't see, and the smells grew sharp – body odour, beer, sea salt, the hot sour breath of the guards. I wanted to be at home, cooking. Or even at work, scrubbing dishes. Anywhere.

'Now,' said Dalston Moomintroll. 'The vote, as ever, takes place in silence. Anyone breaching the silence will be punished.'

No one spoke.

I could hear tension in Dalston Moomintroll's voice. 'I will name each writer in order. When I do so, you must give a clear thumbs up or a clear thumbs down. Anyone not voting runs the risk of being punished. If that is clear and you understand it, give the thumbs up gesture.'

I used to wonder why the crowd didn't give everyone a thumbs up; I suppose that was before I learned about human nature. A sign hangs in the toilet of The Golden Eel restaurant: 'To make the best meal in the world is actually possible. To make everyone enjoy it, impossible.'

With a massively magnified rustling, everyone, I presumed, gave a thumbs up to show they understood Dalston Moomintroll's warning. Alpacas had no vote.

Last year a fireman called Danny Anorak, sunk in beer, was slow to raise his thumb at this point and he was dragged away and beaten so badly he was in a coma for three days and even now remains deaf in one ear.

'Very good,' said Dalston Moomintroll. 'Thank you for your participation in, and your respect of, the ancient way that was handed down to us by our very ancestors.

'Now. We come to our first writer. Remember to keep your hand sign very clear indeed. It should be very obviously a thumbs up or very obviously a thumbs down. You must also ignore what those around you are voting. You must not react in any way to the voting. Any person doing so, whether audibly or by any other method, will be severely punished. The ways of the ancestors are right and must be rightly observed.

'Wonderful. Now. Our first author was Macy Starfield. Vote now. Thumbs up or thumbs down. Macy Starfield.'

I sent the strongest mental goodwill I could muster towards Macy. There was no way of knowing how the voting was going. Lore had it that you could see through the blindfold if you squinted at just the right angle, or that you could tell how the majority were voting because thumbs up and thumbs down have different sounds. The truth is, those blindfolds are black as complete blindness and the rustle of many thousands of hands moving to thumbs up or thumbs down just sounds like the rustle of many hands moving.

'Thank you,' said Dalston Moomintroll. 'Our second writer was Ray Genovese. Vote now. Thumbs up or thumbs down. Ray Genovese.'

I felt fairly confident about Macy and I was certain that Ray

Genovese was popular, perhaps a little unexpectedly, with the audience. Generally the People's Decision was hard to predict, and bets on it were forbidden. Shady though he was, QuickQuidSid knew better than to breach that law.

Dalston Moomintroll spoke in a monotone throughout, always using the same phrasing, with only the writer's name changing. Summer Kelly. J-M-Boy. A litany of names. When my name was spoken I tried to react with equanimity. But I couldn't pretend I had nothing vested in this. My heart pummelled my chest cage and I felt as though I could fall to the ground. I counted my breaths, reminded myself anxiety is a delusion. At last Dalston Moomintroll said, 'Our final writer, other than Stella of course, who as winner is not eligible for the People's, was Seth Macnamara. Vote now. Thumbs up or thumbs down. Seth Macnamara.'

And like that, it was over.

'Thank you for your patience and your commitment to the traditional ways. Not a single breach of etiquette, that is a remarkable achievement. Exceptional, just how it should be. I trust it shall stay that way. Now, the thumbs-up and thumbs-down votes have been analysed in real time by the computers provided thanks to W Look Systems and we shall presently have the results of you, the people, with the People's Decision.'

The atmosphere was thick with anticipation. I realised I was trembling slightly and hoped no one could see it. In a moment the name of the People's Decision would be announced and . . .

And yet some inner part of me was calm. I quietly marvelled at that. Somewhere in the heart of my being there was a tranquillity, a feeling that someone, somewhere, was looking out for me.

A pair of massive hands yanked the blindfold off me. I blinked, dazed, though it had got noticeably darker since I'd been blindfolded. The stage was now lit up, with the B&F sponsorship logos glowing in neon; a spotlight blazed whitely on Dalston Moomintroll. I felt something on my neck and I had started turning round before I realised it was the hot quick breath of a guard. He had a hand on my shoulder in less time than it takes to blink. The hand was strong and seemed to say, 'Keep looking ahead, I am being persuasive, don't make me be forceful.' I obeyed.

I tried to glimpse Macy and Archie out of the corner of my eye but I must have moved my head minutely because again that huge hand was encouraging me to focus straight ahead at the stage.

Suddenly Dalston Moomintroll looked to his right. Here she was: Stella, striding onto the stage. It was the duty of the Overall Winner to hand the compere the name of the People's Decision.

She stumbled slightly. No one laughed. She righted herself quickly and kept walking. She looked serious.

Dalston Moomintroll accepted the piece of paper from her, then watched her walk off without incident before he opened the piece of paper and said, simultaneously turning it to the audience and the cameras, 'Archie the Alpaca.'

My heart stopped beating. There was a collective gasp.

'No!' I screamed. I heard someone shout 'Good!' and that made my heart burn with greater fury. 'No!'

I turned to face Archie, who looked almost calm with fear and disbelief and I said, 'No,' and he looked at me and said, 'It's me,' in what may have been a question as much as a statement.

Macy was weeping, looking at Archie then to me. I leaped towards Archie but the guard behind brought me heavily down to the ground with such brutality I bit into the grass and tasted mud. I tried to stand up and he punched me hard on the back of the head; it felt like being hit by a steel bar but adrenaline was pumping through me and I wriggled free and jumped on Archie and hugged him tight. 'It's not fair. It's not right. Yours was the best story.'

'The *people* have spoken,' he said. His voice was calmer than I could ever have expected. I think implicit in his words was a knowledge that he had, indeed, written a story of which he and alpacahood could be proud.

'I love you,' I said. 'We won't let them do this.'

He shrugged and said, 'It's a jazz thing they just don't get.'

A swift heavy punch smashed into the side of my face and a deep, sour voice whispered in my ear, 'Any more talk, any movements, and you and the girl will get it as well as the loser.'

'You don't understand—' I started, but this earned me another, harder punch in the face. My cheek and upper lip were already swelling and I tasted the tin biology of blood. I realised I was now standing up, or, rather, being held up by two or more sets of arms. Archie was getting dragged away in front of me. He craned his long neck round and gave me a look I have been trying to fully decipher ever since.

He turned away and walked on, with his back straight and his legs steady. The guards stood six men thick on every side. When he had reached a position seven rows from the front of the stage, he was turned to face the audience and the cameras.

'Archie the Alpaca, you are,' said Dalston Moomintroll, 'allowed a few words.' A cramp of terror squeezed my heart.

A microphone was placed in front of Archie, too low. He was forced to bend. 'It's like a jazz . . . No. No. This is my message. Equality for alpacahood. It's coming. Equality for alpacahood. Equality for alpacahood.'

'This. Is. Not. Fair,' I screamed. 'Equality for alpacahood!'

It was the loudest thing I have ever yelled in my life. Just before I was hit on the head with a truncheon from behind, I saw the crowd fall upon Archie, upon his beloved incongruous smile.

Before I came to, they had torn him apart.

When I came to, the night was crackling with menace. I struggled to my feet. 'Macy,' I said weakly, looking about. The crowd of humans had sheered off into small violent groups which were pulling at what was left of Archie, or bearing a limb up with an air of triumph; large groups of homeward-bound people – those with children or those who had seen enough; and disbelieving tourists who had heard of such things happening but never witnessed them for themselves, standing about with bloodless faces, traumatised. The alpacas were still congregated – northern and southern alike – a short distance from the shoreline and were intensely debating something. I decided to make my way towards them. But I was so woozy that when I raised a foot I immediately slipped back down to the ground.

In any case, when I'd slumped down into this seated position, a guard loomed over me and called me an alpaca fucker and punched me so hard in the face that intense tingling stars fireworked in front of me and blackness pulled me into an embrace and as I grew aware of a heavy, sweet taste in my mouth the blackness opened a trapdoor beneath me and I fell down into it.

Fishing with a Straight Hook

I opened my eyes. There was a thin monotonous high-pitched whine of pain in my ear and, behind that tone, a silence that confused me. I hazily wondered why everyone wasn't fighting. My heartbeats sounded distant and heavy, like the moaning of a lost, far-off whale circling under tons of water and I pictured the whale and it had Archie's grin.

I sat up and turned my head slowly. I was lying on an unfamiliar bed in a plain room. 'Drink,' said a voice. Somebody sat on a little bench by the side of the bed. It took a few moments to register that the voice came from this person and that he was not Macy, whom I'd somehow expected it to be.

'Soup,' he said. 'It will do you good.'

Did I know him?

He brought a spoon up to my mouth and encouraged me to drink. I hadn't been fed like this since I was an infant. Half the spoonful dribbled down my chest.

So weak was I that even the little soup that entered me, coursing slowly down my throat, spread warmth and tangible strength throughout my body.

'Here,' he said. He held up a fresh spoonful. Broccoli, I thought. And cheese. Behind it I could still taste blood and mud.

With serene patience he fed me the bowl of soup and only

then, an age later when the bowl was finished and I was beginning to feel human again, only then did I recognise him.

'You're the guy in the audience,' I said. And at once I heard myself saying, quicker than thought, 'You're the statue. You were sitting on Hill Fuji. You're the statue.'

He didn't answer me. 'How do you feel?'

'They didn't break me,' I said. 'My head's bursting. Bones like twigs. Eyes pulsing. Every heartbeat hurts – wait. What about Archie? Was that . . . Did that happen?'

'Archie is gone.'

I fell back on the pillow. A wave of emptiness washed through me. 'Then they *did* break me.'

He shook his head, leaned forward and looked into me (not at me).

For a moment nothing happened. 'Breathe. Just breathe,' he said at last.

'Where's Macy?'

'Your friend? You will see her later.'

'Where am I? Why are you doing this?'

'You are in my room.'

I put a hand up to my head. My skin felt weird, rough and numb, as if my forehead's nerve endings had lost their function. I realised it was a bandage I was feeling – the man had bandaged my head.

'Thank you. I, uh . . .What's your name, again?'

'No need to thank me. My name is Hibiki.'

'How can you be so calm? Archie's gone.'

'Archie's gone.'

'I think I liked your soup more than your reassurance.'

'I will not lie.'

'How did I end up here?'

'I carried you.'

'The guards let you do that? Didn't they threaten you?'

'I do not fear them.'

'Archie. Poor Archie.' I shook my head. 'Ow. Ow. My head is getting sorer. I could have an aneurysm or something, couldn't I? I've heard of that – a bad concussion can kill you hours afterwards . . . Ah, who cares.'

'Your head will hurt. Pain arises, remains for a time, then passes away.'

'I could die. I could literally die from this.' I looked at his big earnest eyes. 'Tell me. Honestly. Am I going to die?'

'Yes,' he said, reaching to throw peat on the fire. 'You will die and I will die and everyone who was at the Brilliant & Forever will die, sooner or later. Now get some rest.'

Later, after I had slept some more, I was able to sit at the low table and eat with him. He had prepared a subtly spiced curry that reminded me just how hungry I was. The pain in my head had downshifted to a slower, duller beat. He didn't seem to want to speak as we ate, but I felt socially awkward and I had a great many questions.

'Why did they let their hatred take control of them? And kill one of the most decent beings I ever had the privilege . . .' My voice trailed away, my eyes bubbled hot with tears.

'Aversion. You've read books, surely. Sometimes tragedy is the king being run through with his son's sword. Yes. But I have seen also how very humdrum tragedy can be. It is also the stabbing of a long-time friend for a second helping of potatoes.'

I wept a little.

He tutted. 'Stop it. This is self-pity.'

'It hurts,' I said.

'Did you know there was a chance your friend could die?'

'Yes, but—'

'And did you know there was a chance you could die?'

'Yes, but—'

'And would you have felt pity if, say, Seth Macnamara or Tabitha Tessington or anyone else had been the People's Decision?'

'Yes, but . . .'

We fell silent for a while. His expression softened. 'Your friend's story – learn from it.'

'The whole thing's messed up,' I said.

Hibiki didn't speak for a few moments, then he said, 'Death would only be a tragedy if some people died and some did not.'

What time I spent with Hibiki that day was lived intensely, despite and because of the circumstances. He was a very unusual person. It was difficult to determine his age – somewhere between fifty and seventy.

We sat drinking green tea by the fire.

'You were the statue, weren't you?'

He grunted.

'That *was* you, up Hill Fuji?'

He placed his cup on a little oak table beside him. He always put his cup down before he spoke, I noticed. 'Hill Fuji! It's nothing like Mount Fuji!'

'It *was* you, then. Sitting there, doing nothing.'

'Sitting in meditation.'

'For how long?'

'Ten days.'

'Impossible.'

He grunted. 'An ant can lift something fifty times its weight, which is impossible.'

I frowned. 'What do you do? Why are you here?'

'So many questions,' he said. He thought for a while. 'Everyone in this part of the world has nice clothes, nice homes, nice cars, nice bikes . . . but your minds are as weak and restless as feathers in a storm. The mind must be strengthened.'

'We're not all well off. My house isn't all that nice,' I said, frowning. 'Wait, how do I strengthen my mind?'

'You look into it.'

'How?'

'You enquire of your own mind what it is.'

'How?'

'You learn to stop your mind movement and watch it flow.'

'How, though?' I didn't really understand what he was saying, which bothered and fascinated me.

'Years of practice. It is immensely difficult.'

I contemplated possible futures. At length I asked, 'Will you teach me?'

Hibiki paused. 'Hmm.' He studied me closely. 'Hmm.' He stared at me for a long time. The expression on his face was difficult to read, but I saw in it the face of a father without a son. I felt a lump form in my throat. It was hard to swallow.

I heard myself telling a story I had last shared many years ago. 'Once there was a fisherman who used to fish the sea lochs around these parts with a straight hook. Always a straight hook. One day a man came to him and said, "Why don't you use a proper, bent hook? Then you'll catch some fish." And the fisherman replied, "You can catch ordinary fish with a bent hook. But I will catch an extraordinary fish with my straight hook." Word of this exchange spread and eventually the story reached the ear of the clan chief. He went to see the fisherman for himself. "You there," he said. "The one fishing with a straight hook – what are you fishing for?" And the fisherman said, "Ah, clan chief. I was fishing for you."'

Hibiki put his cup down. His eyes bored into me. 'I have seen an ant lift an impossible rock.'

Sympathy for Ghosts Trapped in Coffins

The next day, after a nourishing sleep at Hibiki's, I hobbled up the main street. It looked how I felt - broken, maltreated, partially annihilated. Windows were smashed, leaving gaping spiky holes in the buildings, many of which were smouldering, burned out. Weirdly, brilliantly, nothing had been looted. It was as if the premises had been torched with no regard for the value of their contents: TVs, food, clothes, computers. Most of the shops and offices in town had been destroyed. The smell of burning was seared onto the air. (For days afterwards I felt as though my nose-hairs were singed.)

Macy and I arranged to meet up in the Nightingale with Toothache café. I sat by the window, from where I could see a charred clothes shop, the remains of a bakery and, further up the street, a car park full of blackened cars and motorbikes.

The café had survived the riots intact. Although the actual owner of the Nightingale with Toothache was fairly unpopular, grassuccinos and other alpaca favourites had been available there for many years and Ray had long since endeared himself to alpacas, who were always treated with the same respect there as humans, a rarity on the island.

As is always the case with social unrest, the riots were a

retrospective inevitability. The alpacas had gone on a non-murderous rampage. It was a kind of beautiful anarchy. They believed Archie was the finest writer at the B&F and while most of them knew that expecting him to win was probably too big a step forward in human-alpaca relations, none of them had anticipated that he would be the People's Decision.

The door opened and a heavily tear-streaked version of Macy stepped through.

Macy and I hugged repeatedly. Neither of us knew where to begin.

We sat.

Macy shook her head, looked down.

I shook my head, looked down.

Without a word, we reached out and held each other's hands, possessive of, and possessed by, grief.

Ray Genovese shuffled over with some coffees. 'You won't believe it,' he said. 'These are on the house. Owner's orders. I don't think he lets his own mother get free coffee.'

We smiled, relieved not to begin with something bigger than we knew how to say. We reclaimed our hands for the coffee mugs.

'Cheers, Ray. Looks like the café wasn't affected by the riots.'

He shook his head. 'Nope. We were lucky.'

'It's not luck, Ray,' said Macy. 'Nothing to do with luck.'

Ray swatted the compliment away with a coffee-stained dishcloth.

'Your piece was terrific, by the way,' I said, 'and you read it so well.'

'I'm sorry about your pal. I know how close you were with Archie. He was a real character. Came in here often. I liked him.'

'Thanks. Yeah. I don't know what to say.'

'I can't believe it, to tell you the truth. His piece was really,

really good. One thing I've learned. Life is hard . . . be harder.'
Ray's face seemed to toughen as he said it.

'I don't know if I'll ever get over it,' said Macy. 'I for one am bloody glad the alpacas rioted. If they go out rioting again tonight, I'm going with them.'

'They're not. I heard the whitehousers are having emergency meetings already. There's rumours they're addressing better equality for alpacas,' said Ray.

I snorted. 'One thing Archie taught me is that the difference between those politicians and us writers is that a writer tells lies to reveal greater truths and a politician tells half-truths to reveal greater lies.'

'Listen. Working in here, you hear all kinds of things. And let's just say, I really did hear that, about better conditions for alpacas.'

Macy looked incredulous. 'You think whitehousers'll actually start to allow alpacas to be treated with respect? Equality? Like they deserve?'

'I heard, true as I'm standing here, better equality in public places like this joint, better education, better funding for alpaca homes.'

'Believe it when I see it,' I said, shaking my head, and wincing as a pain-blossom flared deep within it.

'They had a contingency of senior alpacas in talks with the highest-up whitehousers at seven thirty this morning. Seven thirty. You mark my words. They're striking deals. There will be no rioting tonight. The whitehousers can't afford it. It would ruin the island's reputation. Things are changing already.'

'If there's no rioting it's because the authorities lied to make the alpacas believe they'll get equal rights,' Macy said.

'Never had you down as the cynical type,' said Ray.

'Life never gave me such a persuasive reason to be cynical before.'

'It could be,' I said, 'that this was the sort of catalyst that was needed for social change.'

We thought for a moment.

'Guess Archie would really be a folk hero,' I said.

Macy smiled. 'He'd have loved that. They'll compose ballads about him.'

I started to weep a little. I picked up a napkin and wiped my eyes. 'Sorry. Think of all the writing he didn't have time to do. I can't believe we won't see him again. I miss him like hell. I haven't even been home yet.'

Macy put her arm round my shoulder.

I told her and Ray about Hibiki.

Something occurred to me. 'Archie has things at my place,' I said. 'He stayed with me the night before . . .'

'I'll help you with everything,' said Macy.

'The thing is, we knew. It's like Hibiki said. We knew there was a risk.' I looked at Macy. 'But I knew for a fact that you wouldn't be in the running for the People's. I thought you and he both had a serious chance of winning outright.'

Macy shrugged. 'You lost that money, you numpty.' She ruffled my hair.

I looked at Ray. 'And I knew you'd come up with something special, and it was even more, you know, powerful than I'd expected. And Archie. I had a feeling he was harbouring a really special piece of writing. He was determined to win this for the alpacas. But for him to lose the People's? That's insane.'

'They were talking about it on the radio,' said Ray. 'The news programmes are all about the rioting, obviously. And they were saying forty years ago was the last time an alpaca got into the B&F, and clearly he had no chance of winning, but even then they had the good grace to let the *worst* writer, you know, get the People's.'

'So we're going backwards as a society?' I said.

'No,' said Ray forcefully. 'I told you. Believe me, changes are coming. For the better. Oh hey, I almost forgot. Be right back.'

Ray walked away, through the door to the back where only staff were allowed.

Macy and I looked hard into each other's eyes.

'You gonna be okay?'

'We'll both make sure we're both okay.'

'True words.' I paused. 'I didn't see everything – did you? What I did see just keeps coming back to me.'

'I saw enough. Don't torture yourself. D'you think that's how he'd want to be remembered? Or for all the great times and the writing?'

'I know. But . . .'

Ray had returned. He lay a plastic bag on the table. 'Friend of mine was near the . . . where it happened. He picked up this. Reckoned you should have it.'

I reached, then hesitated. 'When you say your friend was near when it happened, Ray. Was he . . . involved?'

'No.' Ray shook his head vigorously. 'No. Alex is a good guy. Proof being he got this for you.'

I picked up the bag, put a cautious hand in.

Cold. Sticky. None too fragrant.

I smiled. 'I don't believe it.' I lifted out Archie's spittoon. 'His cuspidor.'

'James Joyce's favourite word in the English language,' said Macy.

The light glinted off the spittoon, stained with the last spit that the living Archie had deposited there.

My nose scrunched. I gave an involuntary splutter of laughter. 'It's kinda vile. It's beautiful.'

The Value of the Blank Page

It's now two years since the B&F that changed everything. Hibiki, Macy and cycling sustain me.

In a warm cocoon of loneliness I take my bike out on long, solitary rides into remote areas, out past the new whitehouses where mostly alpacas live. They always acknowledge me and sometimes I stop off and exchange a word or two. But I have never been good at small talk and increasingly I am coming to doubt my dexterity with meaningful talk.

There's a curious somnambulism to the early stages of grief and love and loneliness. You become possessed by them, then defined by them. In time, even grief becomes an indulgence, a kind of egotism. But really, when someone you love dies, you feel like the world should wake up. When someone you love dies, you feel as though life has failed us all, the living and the dead.

'Isn't there someone,' Macy has often said to me, usually late at night when we are lying on our backs, looking at the moon and the stars, 'who will feel unique in her capacity to understand me?'

When cycling I like to mindfully inhale the fresh air, scented with sea salt and animal smells and peat. In the days shortly after the B&F, over the course of a few bike rides I gathered together as many of the gold ingots as I could remember burying and I took them to an expert and discovered they were, against all odds, real gold. Actual gold! I confess part of me would like to think they were fake until Archie's death catalysed some phenomenal alchemy, but the reality is probably something to do with somebody scamming someone else, believing them to be fake hence selling them on the internet at a cheap price.

I secretly took the gold ingots one night to Andrea, one of the most influential alpacas in the community. I asked her to take them and either melt them down and cast them or sell them on to make the necessary money. She was overjoyed. I told her my one condition was that I was to receive no acknowledgement for my contribution.

And so it came to be that a statue was commissioned. Eighteen months after his death, a gold statue was placed on Archie's burial site, which is on top of Hill Fuji – a great honour, in Archie's native southern end of the island.

The statue is solid gold, three quarters life-size, and depicts Archie reading from an untitled novel with only his name visible on the cover and some words engraved on the pages: 'It's a jazz thing you don't get.' Which has now, of course, become a catchphrase.

At his foot rests a spittoon which already has its own tradition; people and alpacas alike spit in it for luck, which is wonderful. Gross, but wonderful. The expression on Archie's face is, depending on how the light accentuates it, proud or defiant or sublime. Many alpacas and people make a pilgrimage to the statue and leave gifts of cards, flowers, wine bottles, poems, stories . . . so many stories.

Tonight I cycled up Hill Fuji again, and sat at golden Archie's feet. How he would have loved to know he would be turned to gold, would become a symbol for social change and better rights for alpacas. The world is full of things Archie would have liked.

Seth is in prison on multiple murder charges (the Sparks and Candy characters were both real – Candy blabbed to the cops. I told them about the piece of paper he'd dropped in the Nightingale with Toothache and it turned out those it mentioned, too, were real victims and furthermore all of Seth's stories had been true. Seth will never again know freedom in this life).

I settled by the plinth, resting my back against one of Archie-statue's legs and I looked up into the gloominous sky.

Statues have the ageless tranquillity of the dead, suggestive of a tiny, deliberate hole in eternity's one-way mirror. Sort of makes me think I'll see Archie again, one way or another.

There was a full moon, huge and smooth and craggy, hanging brightly in the sky like belief and some magical suspension thereof. It was hard to tell at first which were stars and which were satellites loitering around our planet. I wondered if one of them might be the International Space Station. I remembered Archie's idea that everything earthly was first of all unearthly.

We're all changed, changing. Maybe it's weird that people tend to regard the present as a watershed moment in their lives, the point at which they have finally assumed the person that they will be for the rest of their lives. One huge illusion. But still, sometimes you really feel you can discern patterns beneath life's contingency.

Hibiki and I are about to open a modest Japanese restaurant. Japanese food is the epitome of refinement; sashimi is not eaten, but experienced. It kisses your tongue, clean and filthy at once, like a public kiss that hints at something more private. Sashimi is salt and silk. It melts on your taste buds like a thrill, releasing its oily sweetness; its oceanic vastness is concentrated into little tidal chewing motions the size of your mouth. The sea devours itself forever. You taste its entirety for a few briefly lasting moments. Sometimes the memory of sashimi – salmon, mackerel, tuna – is enough to make your mouth water in communion with all the fish-happy rivers of the world.

Hibiki has been teaching me ancient meditation techniques to strengthen my mind. He also reminds me, quoting Thoreau, 'How vain it is to sit down and write when you have not stood up to live.' That one sentence strikes me like a humiliation.

I will wash dishes in the restaurant; he will be the head chef. Hibiki says that when I have truly mastered dishwashing he will let me start chopping vegetables. That might take a couple of years, he says. I am learning everything again. I trust Hibiki. Don't ask me how, but his ways work, even though (or because) they are very, very hard.

Macy's fishing career has been a steady success; the *Born Surreal, Think Like a Boat* is now one of the most reliable fishing boats in the area, so she will provide us with our seafood.

I sat resting against Archie's statue for a long time, gazing at the sky. The stars turned misty overhead, the moon's glow fell soft and gauzy. A breeze passed through me with a sigh.

Islands, like a sense of self, can either strengthen or weaken a person. But they're all illusory; what we really need is to reach the bedrock that connects everything, and this is hard to find because it is invisible and formless, like awareness itself.

There was a period of about half a year, beginning the December after Archie's death, when I wrote more intently than ever. I therapeutically composed an account of my friendship with Archie. But I deleted steadily, as night deletes day. I didn't keep one word I wrote. Neither, of course, did I enter the B&F the following year, nor this year. I'm not sure I will enter it again. I tried to find within myself a tender feeling for my fellow human beings, so many of whom seemed determined to destroy everything that has significance in a world of well-hidden answers and nuance and imagination. I wanted only sincerity. Why did I need to delete everything I wrote?

In this transient life, immortality haunts us.

Macy and I have campaigned, along with many other humans and all the alpacas, for better alpaca rights. Thanks to a jointly organised Western-themed film festival, alpacas healed the rift between their northern and southern packs.

Public buildings and forms of transport are no longer allowed to segregate humans from alpacas. Progress. Issues still arise, but relationships between the two species are better than they have ever been. We – alpacas and friends of alpacas – are waging war by peaceful means. We use words and ideas to forge and regenerate civilised society. And we are winning.

The dishwashing I do makes the world a tangibly, if marginally, better place. I wash dishes eight to twelve hours a day. I convert dirty, greasy, food-clogged pans into gleaming objects ready for use. I shine plates. In my hands, cutlery is reborn. I increase the universe's store of purity.

'Those who are happy not to strive to be special are the noble ones,' said Archie. I remember that summer with a sad smile and a tear rolls down my cheek. There are places where alpacas cannot yet have their voices heard and people are not enriched by the ways of reading, of writing. Life is changeable and strange and brief.

So many writers seem to want fame, money, adulation. But I've learned that craving these things results in jealousy, desperation, egotism, and the partial removal of the gift that is the present moment. Nowadays I'm simply unburdened. My life is an empty page, glowing. I have stood up to live.

The night-mist lifted, the huge moon brightened and swooned. Our island tonight was wrapped in a deep and tranquil slumber. From the top of Hill Fuji, it looked gentle and lovely. In the broad expanse below – the mellow moorland and the flat, mirrored lakes and the muted sea and the sleeping villages – there was neither movement nor sound, as if time held its breath.

My heart quickened with warm feelings.

The night's silent blankness reminded me of something; I opened my notebook to a fresh page. The scratching of my pen on the white sheet was the only sound in the empty night as I wrote:

'I think the blank page terrifies us, being the visual counterpart to silence. The blank page is an iced-over graveyard, the absolute zero of all contact and warmth. The blank page denies us the comfort of meaning. The blank page is the unknown, hinting that it's unknown because it's unknowable. The blank page makes that which we do seem to know petty and inconsequential. The blank page renders us painfully vulnerable. The blank page is the rejection of every story ever told, thus it is a glowing invitation, a challenge offered to the depths of who we think we are, a provocation to that part of us where creativity meets experience. The blank page says to us, "Show me the essence, show me what matters and why it matters." The blank page is a beginningless void. The blank page compels us to explore our imagination, those diverse unique places we might share with others. The blank page entreats us to prove we have been alive.'

It had begun snowing. Thick flakes of twinkling, silvery-white snow were drifting down from the night sky, falling softly through the moonlight. Snowflakes settled, cool and moist, on my hair, my eyelashes, my shoulders, my whole self. I folded my legs the way Hibiki has taught me, deepened my breathing, emptied my thoughts, made my blank mind blanker. I sat like this for a long time. Bright snowflakes flowed from the sky with a gentle, patient will.

I watched snowflakes absorb the words I'd written. The page itself dissolved. More and more snowflakes came tumbling intricate and unique from the stars, some of them tinily kissing my face. My mind glowed, to be alive in this mad, unreal universe. They say no snowflake ever fell in the wrong place.

Let others believe tonight's moon isn't lit from within.

Acknowledgements

Some parts of this novel first appeared in the following books, magazines, newspapers: *Gutter, The Herald, New Writing Dundee, New Writing Scotland, Northwords Now, The Scotsman*

'Sir cuideachd ghliocairean, gus am bidh thu mar a' ghealach a' gluasad am-measg nan reultan'. Thank you Charlotte, Katsu, Francis, Dad, my late Mum, Paul, Val, Jo, Sherry, Calum, Willie, Young Flossy, Mathy, Innes, Julie, Alison, Vikki, Neville, Jim, Akutagawa, Moniack Mhor, Alex and An Lanntair, my fellow sportivistes, the train that broke down at a crucial writing stage, the plane that didn't, everyone who has supported me in my writing and cycling endeavours, the lovely people of Stornoway, Lewis and Kandy, Sri Lanka.